SHOES YOUR WEAPON

STAN KENT

BOOKS

Published by
Blue Moon Books
841 Broadway, Fourth Floor
New York, NY 10003

ISBN 1-56201-127-8

Manufactured in the United States of America

This book is dedicated to two brothers, Crispinus and Crispinianus, who were shoe repairers around 285 A.D. They donated their skills to the poor. Unfortunately they were also zealous Christian missionaries, which wasn't too popular with the Romans, who, after trying unsuccessfully to drown the brothers with weighted millstones, gave up on subtlety and beheaded them. For this sacrifice they were rewarded centuries later by the Catholic Church with the honor of being the patron saints of shoes.

ACKNOWLEDGMENTS

This book would not exist if it weren't for the advice of Blue Moon publishers Neil Ortenberg and Barney Rosset, and the encouragements of agents Claudia Menza and Richard Derus.

Skin Two magazine (www.skintwo.uk.co) and Pierre Silber shoes (www.pierresilber.com) provided much inspiration and information. Sisters of Mercy provided the soundtrack to countless hours of writing, rewriting and re-rewriting.

Which brings me to my red-pen slasher, Jill Kent. Working under extreme pressure she took my raw words, my plot entanglements and my nonlinear structure and refined them into a fucking good story. I offer her the highest compliment an author can make to an editor—Jill, I can't find the words to thank you enough for your editing patience and persistence, but if I could, I'm sure you'd find something in them to redline.

S.K.

PLATFORMS

ONE

IT'S JUST AFTER Thanksgiving 1990—a month since I'd killed the Dildo Killer—and I have a lot to be thankful for. I am free. The DK is dead. I still have my shoesex power, and the daily news specials about Chief Detective Ellen Stewart's arrest for slaying the Dildo Killer have slowed to a routine mention on the evening news.

I've been a good girl. I stay hidden. Despite the guilt that prods me to come forward I heed Ellen's advice and have not once ventured out of my shoe repair shop. Unfortunately I've exhausted my supply of cereal, frozen pizzas and various pastas in sundry sauces. I'm out of wine, beer and Tampax—that's the killer. Ragtime blues.

So I go to the grocery store. I sneak out of Shoe Leather using the back alley. On the return I can't negotiate the dumpster with three bulging bags, so I chance the front door. After the way the DK surprised me on my doorstep you'd think I'd learn, but I don't. Shit, I'm of Italian descent. What do you expect?

"Ms. Cutrero, can I help you?"

I turn. One of the Safeway bags tumbles. He catches it. It's M. Donovan. Officer Michael Donovan, who gave me a ride back from police headquarters on Halloween day once the shit-for-brains cops realized I wasn't the DK. They let me go because my best friend had been killed by the DK while they held me in a cell for knowing too fucking much about the murders. I can't think about that day without getting steamed. If the cops had listened to me Marsha would still be alive. The DK would be in jail. Ellen would still be the top cop.

Yeah, but Ellen and I wouldn't be a thing. At least I think we're a thing. We've only known each other for a month, of which I've spent two days with her, some of which was not too pleasant, but that last day, wow, what a thing. It was love at almost first sight. I killed the DK and she took the blame. Yeah, we're a thing. A very big thing. The kind of love thing that dudes like Shakespeare wrote about.

So all this love and death happened for a reason. Fate, what a double-edged bitch. Marsha's life was too high of a price to pay for my happiness.

Maybe it's payback time.

Officer M. Donovan at my doorstep is not a good sign. He wears a suit, not a blue uniform, but a rather stylish brown number that looks vaguely designer. But he is still a cop. I can tell. He isn't here for a social call. He holds a plastic shopping bag in his hand. What the fuck is in it?

I try to stifle the oh-shit-I've-been-caught look on my face. He takes two of the bags from my arms and holds them tight to him, his own plastic bag dangling in front.

"Thanks," I say as I open the door. He nods in the direction of my hand-scrawled sign saying Shoe Leather was closed because I was out of town.

"Been gone?"

If that question came from anyone else's lips it would be

perfectly innocent, but coming from a cop's mouth it is loaded with suspicion. From my brief encounter with the San Francisco Police Department I know it is best to keep my answers short and offer no extra info.

"Yeah."

"Probably a good idea. To get away."

Get away! Getaway. Fucking H. Christ, what does he know? When he dropped me off after they'd discovered Marsha's body he'd said that Ellen was a great boss to work for, that he really respected her. I got the impression they were friendly. Has she confided in him? I play it as innocent as my guilty conscience will allow.

"Get away?"

He places the shopping bags on the counter. He holds onto his plastic bag. I hold onto my bag of groceries. It is my shield.

"After your friend's death. Getting away from all the cameras and publicity was a good idea. I know her death hit you hard. When I dropped you off you looked so sad."

"Yeah, Marsha was my best friend."

I decide to be aggressive. Hearing a cop, even one as nice as M. Donovan, mention Marsha makes me angry. I put my groceries down and face him square between the eyes.

"At least you were right. When you dropped me off you said Ellen Stewart would get the Dildo Killer."

I can tell from the frustration emanating from his tall, slender frame that he doesn't know about my involvement. Ellen hasn't told him.

"I wish she'd called me that night. I just don't understand it. She was almost killed. I don't mind what she did to that sicko—I don't think anyone really does—but she is too good of a cop to make that kind of mistake. I could have backed her up. I should have backed her up. She wouldn't be in this mess now."

"Will she get off?"

"There's an official investigation just getting started next week. There will be some sort of disciplinary action, but it's anyone's guess how it will go. Some of the older types in the department don't like homosexual cops, especially women cops. I don't think she'll face criminal charges, but they can't just pat her on the back."

"Why not? She did everyone a favor."

"Yeah, you know that. I know that. But there is the law and police procedure to think of."

"Ah, the law and your precious procedure. Where was that when Marsha was being killed?"

"Look, Ms. Cutrero, I'm sorry we made mistakes and your friend died, but there's nothing I can do about that now, and I didn't come here to fight with you."

"I know. Sorry for being the mega-bitch." I wave my box of freshly procured Tampax at him. He smiles and nods. I feel bad. M. Donovan was nice to me on Halloween.

"How's Chief Detective Stewart taking all this?" I say, pretending to show more interest in the stowing of my tampons back in my Safeway bag than on the question.

"Remarkably well. She's still sore from the beating she took. She's on administrative leave. It's no vacation. She's a prisoner in her apartment. Even though the story isn't front page fodder any more, the press is camped outside her front door in case anything breaks. I saw her this morning. I had to push my way through a forest of microphones to get to her front door. I'm so sick of saying 'No Comment.' "

I laugh. He does too. I feel more comfortable in M. Donovan's presence. Probably because I'm convinced he isn't here to arrest me. As our laughter subsides he hands me the plastic bag he's been clutching.

"Ellen asked me to give you these. She'd like them fixed for next week, when the hearings begin."

I look inside at the pair of scuffed, medium height pumps. Black. Well-worn. The lining has imprints of Ellen's feet. I almost come just from looking at the outline of her heel. Ellen, you sly dog. This is a heck of a lot better than a message in a bottle or an anonymous personal in the *Chronicle*.

"What does she want done?"

"I don't know. She said you'd know what to do with them."

"No problem."

I smile. I can't help it. I know exactly what to do. These shoes are going on my feet as soon as Michael Donovan leaves Shoe Leather.

"When can I pick them up?"

"Is Tuesday okay? I have to get caught up."

Good shoesex takes days. Tuesday would give me all weekend and Monday to play. Fixing them would take ten minutes.

"Tuesday's fine. The hearings start on Thursday, and now that I'm a detective I'm pretty busy. They have us working overtime cleaning up all the Dildo Killer loose ends."

On Halloween he'd said Ellen had put him up for a promotion. The designer suit—it all made sense.

"Detective! Congratulations."

"Yeah, thanks. I'm pretty jazzed. It came through last week. At least they didn't lose me in the shuffle. I was worried that because Ellen recommended me I'd be in limbo, but we're so shorthanded, and there's so much to do."

"Isn't the Dildo Killer case all over with?"

"On the surface, yes. But there's a lot of unanswered questions. Who was he? How many other murders had he committed? Stuff like that. We're getting calls from PDs all over the country who want to clear up old homicides."

"Well, you'd better get busy."

So had I. I've had enough chitchat. Ellen's shoes burn in my hand. On my feet they will be hot. Radiofuckingactive.

"You got that right. Nice to see that you're okay, Ms. Cutrero. I'll be back on Tuesday for Ellen's shoes. If you need anything don't hesitate to call. Here's my card."

He proudly hands me his brand-new business card and turns to leave. I call after him.

"If you talk to Detective Stewart tell her that I think she did the right thing. And thanks."

He smiles.

"Sure."

And he's gone. And so am I, up to my bedroom after I close Shoe Leather again. I'll reopen on Tuesday, but until then I have a date with Ellen's feet.

I tear off my clothes and bounce onto my bed, holding the pumps close to me. I sniff the worn soles.

I love the smell of shoe leather.

It's been so long. I haven't had the nerve to slip on a pair of fuckshoes since Halloween. Having the power in my feet to see and feel the sex people have in shoes isn't always pleasurable. Yeah, being inside someone when they come can be sweet, sexy fun. Being inside my best friend when she dies while being fucked to death by a dildo was enough to make me want to chop off my gifted feet. I just know being inside Ellen is going to renew my faith in shoesex. It's her way of sending me a message, a message no one else can understand but me. Dead romantic. Just thinking about Ellen diddling herself for me makes me wet, and the shoes are still in my hands.

Enough foreplay.

My feet slide easy into the conservative heels.

My soles make contact. Our souls make contact.

Two people, one body, that old familiar lusty feeling. . . .

"VIOLETTA, VIOLETTA, I hope you can hear this. I hope I'm doing this thing with the shoes right. I feel so silly. I've never done this before—I mean, with shoes on.

– 8 –

This is so weird. I didn't think our first time together would be like this."

My clitoris aches. My face throbs. The bruises hurt. The cuts itch. Forget it, Ellen, forget it. Violetta said she picked up the person's feeling, saw and heard everything, what they were thinking while they had sex. I hope playing with myself counts as sex.

Oh dear, I'm embarrassed again.

I should have drunk more wine. Stop it, Ellen, stop it. Think of Violetta making you feel good when this is all over. Soon, soon, we'll be together, Violetta. Say it, Ellen, don't just think it, just in case she can't read your mind through her feet. And play with yourself. Don't stop. Up and down. Round and round. Wetter and wetter.

"Violetta, I'm okay. Don't worry. Soon we'll be together and can do this for real. Don't worry about me. Look after yourself and don't try to contact me. Remember what I told you on Halloween and stick to it. Stay out of sight, especially now that the hearings are starting. So that I know this shoesex message thing works tell Michael when he picks up the shoes, 'I had to replace the lining. It costs $10 more, but the shoes will last longer.' If it works I'll send you more shoes until we can do this in person. Can you see what I see? Look, I'm enjoying myself thinking of you. My finger is between my legs. I'm fantasizing you're here in bed with me, making love with me. I—I—I love to be eaten."

I close my eyes. My finger works harder. I imagine Violetta naked between my legs, her face buried in my pussy. It's a romantic scene. Candles burn, illuminating the bedroom. From the flickering shadows she looks up, blows me a kiss, licking her lips like a tease. Now it's a dirty scene. She slides her tits across my cunt, all wet and slippery. She squeezes her nipple against my clit, flicking the hard nubs together.

"Violetta, your nipple feels so nice. You know how to

touch me. Make me come with your tongue. Eat me. Eat my pussy."

Violetta buries her face in my cunt. I feel her tongue work in slippery circles, lapping my juices around her face. She nibbles on my clit. I come in ass-shaking spasms. I arch my back and give her every drop.

"Now it's your turn," I tell her.

Don't stop playing with yourself, Ellen. You've got to let Violetta know not to contact the cops. Imagine she's just made you come. You want to repay the favor. Violetta's exhausted. She collapses on the bed. You put your hand between her legs. You play with her. She's wet. Excited from playing with you, making you come. You play with her pussy like this.

Violetta says "I can't wait. I can't wait. Ellen, your hand feels so good."

"Listen to me, Violetta, I don't know how long you'll be able to hear me so I have to tell you this now while I still feel sexy. I know you've seen and heard all the news stories. I had to do it. Otherwise they'd have searched the crime scene and found evidence of you. I couldn't take that chance. By pretending the DK killer was me the case was open and shut."

All this talk is a real mood-killer. Keep yourself wet, Ellen. Think of playing with Violetta. How wet she'll feel. Mmmmmm. That's better. Play with yourself, Ellen. Slide your finger in and out. Spread the come around. Pull the skin back. Wetter. Wetter.

"I hit myself in the jaw with a rolling pin from the DK's kitchen. I almost knocked myself out. I cut myself above the eye with the knife you'd used to slice up the DK. I tore off my clothes. I tied myself up. I did these things because I love you. No matter how much it hurt, I felt wonderful because I knew we'd be together soon.

"I covered myself in Dearside's blood. I know it was a stupid thing to do with all my open wounds. Luckily Dearside had always practiced safe fatal sex. I tested negative for HIV, but we'll be doing HIV tests together for the next few years. Romantic, huh?"

Come on, Ellen, think of licking Violetta's pussy. Imagine sexy thoughts. Keep playing with yourself. Don't stop. She has to hear this.

"You should have seen the faces of the officers first on the scene. It didn't take too much convincing to make them think I'd been in a vicious fight. I told the investigators that I accidentally sliced off his penis and testicles in self-defense. They thought I wasn't tough enough for the job. Broke down under the strain. Let my emotions get the better of me. Violetta, you ought to hear the jokes they tell about me. Half the blood at the scene was from me because I was having a really bad period. Horrible things like that.

"But I can deal with it. This has to be our secret. I know you'll understand. Please, please understand. I did this for you. I love you. I do, and soon we'll be together. We'll do this together. We'll come together. I love you."

I clutch my thighs together, trapping my fingers, but I don't stop.

I come again.

I feel so silly.

I start to cry.

Off with the shoes.

IT'S OVER.

I continue to cry, and come, all the way through the night as I repeat Ellen's wonderfully creative love message. Shoesex is fucking awesome. Normal humans have no idea what a rush it is to be inside someone fantasizing about the person inside them. It's like watching a movie of yourself doing things you never did. Talk about ourselves as others see us. So that's what Ellen thinks I look like. Hey, I'm pretty hot, but my tits are bigger than that.

I can't wait to refresh her memory, but that's going to

have to keep until this witch hunt investigation is over. She's made such a sacrifice for me. How can I not do as she's asked? No matter what bad things and horrible crap I hear about Ellen I promise I'll keep quiet. The world will never know I have taken the first step towards fulfilling my destiny as the serial killer of serial killers.

WHEN MICHAEL DONOVAN picks up the shoes, I give him Ellen's message exactly as she planted it. I even write it on the invoice. I'm rewarded a few weeks later with a pair of stylish low heel boots, delivered again by Michael. The vertical seam from the heel to the pull-on-tab has come unstitched. Once I'm in the boots I find out Ellen intentionally tore it free. As she comes she gives me the inside story of the hearings. Things are going her way. She's up. She's happy. She's pleased she can talk to me through my power.

Before the Internal Affairs announcement two more pairs of Ellen's fingerfuckwear come my way. Michael is a very patient delivery boy. He figures Ellen is killing time by going through her closet, trying to take her mind off the deliberations by doing mindless things. To make him think she's not fixating on me and shoes she has him deliver a bunch of suits to be dry cleaned. She's even cleaning her apartment, he says, adding his opinion that all this cleaning and fixing things is a sure sign she is going stir crazy being cooped up by the press while she waits for the verdict. I know better, but I don't let on.

In this last pair she tells me the announcement will be any day and the next pair of shoes to be fixed will be delivered by her a few weeks after the press gets tired of pursuing her for comment. She knows what the Internal Affairs decision is. They've negotiated a mutually agreeable solution. She does her best to hide the pain from me, but I feel the choked-back tears. There will be a press conference where she reads a prepared statement. After a few more interviews she and I can finally get together. She'll meet me at Shoe Leather.

At least the ordeal is over. Months of San Francisco Police Department hand-wringing and investigations find Chief Detective Ellen Stewart not guilty of any criminal wrongdoing in the Halloween 1990 decapitation and mutilation of Randall Warren III a.k.a. Mark Dearside a.k.a. Laure Dearside a.k.a. The Dildo Killer a.k.a. the DK a.k.a Baby-Face Blond Haired motherfucking cocksucking bastard. She is found guilty of using excessive force and voluntarily resigns from her beloved SFPD. In exchange they let her keep her pension. I keep my freedom and my anonymity. I live to slay another day.

WHEN ELLEN FINALLY comes in just before closing time on a Friday night staying behind the counter is up there in my Top Ten Most Difficult Things I've Ever Had To Do list. She holds a pair of brand-new shoes. They're black patent stilettos with lace-up spaghetti straps that encircle the calf. I want to jump her bones so bad, smothering her with kisses and thanks and licking every part of her body with my tongue, but just in case the press are following her I play it cool.

We have a typical shoe repairer/customer conversation. She thanks me for fixing her other shoes so well. She's just bought these, and they don't fit too well. Can I do anything? She really needs them tonight. I look at the stilettos without seeing them. Sure, I say. Step into the back, and I'll see what adjustments can be made. I look through the front window up and down Ellis. No cameras. No reporters. No obvious cops. Ellen and I look at each other. I lock the front door and turn the Open sign to Closed.

We're naked before we reach the bedroom. We fuck barefoot. Now that we're together we don't need shoesex. I don't want a reminder of the power that made me a serial killer, of the power that cost Ellen her career. Normal sex is a welcome change.

AS ELLEN SLEEPS I look closer at her face, above the right eye. It's scarred. I kiss the ridge tracing the healed gash with my tongue. Ellen stirs. Her eyelids flicker. She yawns, stretches and looks into my eyes. She kisses me, sits up and pushes me to the bed. Her fingers trail from my shoulders, past my tits, to my hips, down my legs to my feet. She lifts my legs up and kisses my toes, licking the bottoms of my feet. I shriek but she keeps shrimping. I'm in tears when she finally stops.

"I'll get the shoes," she says.

She returns and straps the shoes to my feet. They're not for her after all. I didn't think they were her style. I'm going to protest bringing shoesex into our bedroom, but Ellen seems really into it as she lowers herself onto my face. I drown my reservations in her warm thighs. Why should my guilt stop Ellen from having fun? I always love the one I hurt. Being a serial killer of serial killers doesn't have to be all work and no play. What's the point of having shoesex power if you can't have a little fun with it once in a while?

Although, as Ellen's sex kisses my face, I'd be less than honest if I don't mention that my mind isn't totally on licking her pussy. I can't help wondering when all this fucking happiness will be ripped apart by a new sicko who I'll have to kill.

And will Ellen be able to cover up for me again?

Will she want to?

Two

I'M ALMOST TWICE her age.

I tell myself these uncomfortable moments are to be expected, even in a normal relationship involving a thirty-six-year-old woman and a nineteen-year-old girl, let alone one as bizarre as ours. We've known each other a few days, yet our lives have been irrevocably changed. The only explanation is that we were meant to be. I knew it the moment I met her. Violetta is special.

She ignores me.

Maybe she didn't hear.

Her stereo blasts something loud and pounding with an English accent. Maybe she's pretending she didn't hear me so she doesn't have to answer an embarrassing question.

I'll ask again.

I have to know.

I should keep quiet.

No. No. Speak up, Ellen. All those books and talk shows say that honesty in the bedroom is crucial to making a relationship work. What a lot of touchy-feeley garbage. This isn't like me. I shouldn't analyze everything so. I'm just not used to the morning after. It's been so long since I had wild sex with someone I care about. Correction: wild sex with anyone. The SFPD nunnery erased my love life, and Violetta is such a breath of fresh air right up my skirt reminding me that I'm a woman not a cop. I don't want to blow it. I want her to love me so.

"Last night, are you sure you didn't mind?"

She didn't hear me.

Should I shout?

Her head nods in time to the boom-boom beat as she crunches down on her cereal. I made us breakfast. Fruit Loops and coffee. It was all she had in the kitchen, and besides, who am I to complain. I'm no gourmet cook. Fruit Loops and coffee is about my limit, although now that I have more time on my hands I'll be able to eat properly and firm up my flabby thighs. I'll take up running again. Along the beach. This morning when I woke up seeing skinny little Violetta naked next to me reminded me that I was young and fit once before Dunkin' Donuts became my caterer. On her dresser Violetta has many awards for cross-country running. She was an Oakland High School Track Star. Maybe we'll run together along the beach. Run away together.

"What?"

My words must have finally penetrated Violetta's morning haze. She is adorable, mouth open, spiky hair in an unruly mop, sitting in a black tee shirt with the words "Fuck Me And Marry Me Young" emblazoned across her chest. Charming. The shirt barely covers those skinny legs that last night were like an octopus all around me.

"I said are you sure you—"

She signals for me to wait. I pause. She turns the stereo down to a manageable level and returns to the kitchen table. She smiles, sits down, the brown flash between her thighs distracting me from my question. Of course she didn't mind about last night.

"Sorry. I like my music loud. Especially of the morning. Big Audio Dynamite. I bought a CD player at Christmas. Sounds really crisp, huh?"

"You might say that."

She shrugs. She must have noticed the sarcastic look on my face that I tried so hard to hide, the tone of my voice that I didn't really mean to add. Get with it, Ellen.

"Sorry. I'm not that used to having anyone around in the morning," she says, her mouth full of Fruit Loops.

"What about Marsha?"

Violetta's lower lip quivers. She looks down.

Ellen, stupid Ellen.

Remember, you're no longer a cop. Why can't you shut off your inquisitor's brain and stop asking questions?

"I'm sorry. I didn't mean—"

"It's okay. If I were you I'd want to know about my seedy past too."

"It's not that. You don't have to tell me anything."

"No, no, I want to."

She stirs her cereal and speaks into the bowl.

"Marsha and I weren't lovers. We were best friends. The times she stayed over it was like a slumber party, and in the morning we wanted the music loud so we wouldn't have to talk to each other. We were usually all talked out from our all-night gab sessions. All we ever did was talk. Nothing too deep. Just girlfriend stuff. I think we talked so we wouldn't fuck. We could have been lovers. We should have been lovers. I loved her. She loved me. She wanted to fuck me. I knew. I repaired her shoes. I knew what she thought about while she frigged herself on the stage at the Pink Panty. She thought about me doing the kind of things we did last night."

"Why didn't you?"

"Marsha and I were best friends first. If we fucked I

thought she'd find out about my power. I was sure I'd let something slip, and then she'd know that I'd been peeking into her pussy for the last year trying to find the DK. I thought she might hate me. And even if she didn't, it wouldn't have been the same between us. She'd view me as a freak. We couldn't have had sex without her wondering what my feet were up to."

Just like me and last night. Maybe getting Violetta those kinky shoes was too over the top. I'm trying too hard to be young. I wanted to show her that I'm not an old fuddy-duddy, but maybe I just demonstrated how unsure of myself I am and hurt her in the process.

I reach across the table and take Violetta's hand, the one that's been stirring the Fruit Loops. She looks up at me and sniffles. I don't know what to say, so I say something completely gratuitous instead of what I feel. What's awful is that I know I'm doing it and I can't stop. It's the result of all those years delivering too many "Your dear one is dead" messages followed by all the false comfort I could muster before asking "Is there anything else you can tell us?"

"Marsha would want you to be happy."

Violetta glares. Her features sharpen into that same steely broadside she fired at me on Halloween in the interrogation room when I told her that we'd found Marsha dead. I recoil as if she slapped me. My face tingles as if she slapped me. I'm sure I redden. As quickly as she'd reacted, Violetta softens. Her eyes grow round, watery.

"I know that. I know what she felt when she died. She was thinking of me. She was worried that the DK had hurt me cause she thought he was going to be with me that evening. She couldn't believe I wasn't there to help her escape."

Unsaid is that Violetta wasn't there because I'd locked her up, but Violetta's eyes say it all. Will she ever forgive me? She might say she can, but deep inside she'll always carry some resentment. It's understandable. I'm not sure I can ever forgive me. I'd hoped by taking the blame I'd somehow make amends, but how can I ever make up for causing Marsha's death?

Violetta starts to cry. The sniffles turn into sobs. Huge tremors shake her tiny frame, threatening to tear her apart. She looks so small, so vulnerable, not like a killer. I squeeze her hand, pulling her towards me. She sits on my lap, head on my shoulder, crying. Her tears trickle down my neck. I pat her back. I don't speak.

I'm learning.

"WHERE ARE WE going?" Violetta pouts. It's later in the afternoon, and I've dragged her out of her apartment to get some fresh air. That's my excuse.

"To the beach."

"Why all the way over here? Why not Ocean Beach?"

"Stinson is quieter. And it's such a beautiful day for a drive."

"Yeah, right."

Violetta pulls her leather jacket tight around her, flicking the collar above her ears, then she sticks her hands in her pockets. Okay, so it's nippy, and I've got the top down on the Jeep, but the fresh air feels wonderful after all those weeks of being cooped up. It's a bright, breezy, sunny day, mid-fifties with no clouds in the sky and the traffic flows freely across the Golden Gate. I turn up the heater to take away the chill. Violetta turns up the radio. I recognize the song.

"Big Audio Dynamite, right?"

"Hey, yeah, you're learning. BAD II actually, but close enough."

We bounce in our seats to the beat, and I get the notion that maybe things can work out between us. I'm optimistic, but I'll soon know for certain if we're meant to be. And if we're not? Well I'm not going to consider any negatives.

After what Violetta and I went through we're damn well meant to be.

We wind along Highway One past the Pelican Inn in Muir Beach. It's an English-style bed & breakfast and pub that my ex, Catherine, and I came to for romantic getaways before I made Detective and had no life. She was English and said the place reminded her of the country inns of her homeland with big, sprawling four-poster beds, strong, warm beer, roast beef and Yorkshire pudding and greasy breakfasts served in the decadent beds.

The Pelican was where our romance ended. I failed to show for a big night. It wasn't the first time I'd missed a date, but it was the worst. It was our anniversary and things had been strained because of the demands of my career. It was hard for Catherine to appreciate how much harder I had to work to prove myself to all the doubting men who wanted to see me fail because I was a woman and a dyke. The night at the Pelican was supposed to be when we got back on track. I was on a stake-out that dragged on, and as the junior detective I was the stuckee. I couldn't call Catherine to let her know I wouldn't be able to make it. Honestly, I didn't want to call. I knew what she'd say. When I got home the next morning she'd already packed her things and moved out. I found her at a friend's apartment. I tried to talk to her, but she'd have nothing to do with me. Months later I learned she'd moved back to England. I wonder if she heard about me killing the Dildo Killer. There were enough English tabloids at the press conferences. I'm sure she must have seen something, although Catherine wasn't the tabloid type.

"Penny for your thoughts?"

For a nineteen-year-old, Violetta is a perceptive young woman. I sometimes think that the power in her feet makes all of her senses especially acute. There's no point in lying. I tell her all about Catherine and the Pelican Inn. She is merciless.

"We'll have to stop there on the way back, put all those old demons to rest."

"So you wouldn't mind?"

"No, not at all."

She pauses.

"You asked me that question this morning. Or something just like it. I never answered you. You asked me if I minded about something, and we had a tearfest and got derailed. What was it you wanted to know if I minded?"

I breath deep. I can't use the radio as an excuse for not hearing Violetta's question because she actually turns it down so we can talk, not shout. The singer was wailing on about not wanting to be nineteen forever. Just wait until he turns thirty-six and falls in love with a nineteen-year-old.

"The shoes," I say.

Violetta is incredulous.

"Ellen, the shoes are way fucking cool. Of course I don't mind. You have good taste. I love shoes. They're the best present."

"I mean that I—we—"

"Spit it out."

"You know."

"Fucked in them?"

"Yes."

"Not a problem."

"You didn't mind."

"No. Why should I? It's who I am. It's what I do."

"That's my point. That's why I was worried you'd mind me playing with your power. I realized afterwards that it might not be such a thrill to you, after what you'd been through with the Dildo Killer. You said you were worried Marsha would treat you like a freak. I'm worried you'll think the same of me."

"Ellen, don't worry, you're no freak, but hang around me awhile and I'll soon change that."

"Violetta, you know what I mean."

"Violetta Valery."

"Excuse me?"

"If you're going to talk to me like a pissed-off parent then use my middle name. My mom always said Violetta Valery when she was exasperated with me. It's from *La Traviata*, Violetta Valery, with a y not an i-e."

"Pretty name."

"Thanks. Mom and Dad were big opera fans. *La Traviata* was their fave. It means the misguided girl. Appropriate, huh?"

"No comment, Violetta Valery."

"Not bad. I think I'm going to regret confessing that little secret to you."

"You're skilled at changing the subject, aren't you?"

"Who me? No. Gorgeous day isn't it? Too bad 'bout those Niners."

"Do you mind about the shoes?"

"No. And I don't think you think of me as a freak. You knew all about my power before you got involved with me. You've accepted it. It's understandable that you're curious about it. Did you enjoy it?"

"Violetta!"

"Well, did you? Did it turn you on to know that those shoes were recording me eating you?"

"Yes."

"Good. It was worth it then."

"Does it turn you on?"

"Of course, especially when the shoes are strapped on like those stilettos. My power begins playback right away. While you were coming down from coming I was coming over and over again. It was fucking awesome."

"So it wasn't like work for you, using your power?"

"No, not at all. At first I thought it was neat that we fucked without shoes. It was really special, but then when you put those fuck-me pumps on me I was gone. I've always had a pussy thing for sexy shoes. Comes with the territory, I guess."

"You didn't once think that you were being used?"

"Nah. I had a blast. I actually forgot all the crap that's happened. I had sloppy sex and enjoyed it. What can I say? I'm a whore for a cool pair of shoes, and now I have a record of last night that I can play over and over. That's only happened once before, with Jimmy, my first time."

"You lost your virginity with your shoes on?"

"Fuck, is the Pope Catholic? Yeah, I did it on purpose. I wanted a record of when I became a woman."

She giggles, saying woman in a haughty tone. Then as suddenly as she became playful, she becomes serious.

"But my power surprised me. I didn't think it would take effect right away. I think Jimmy thought he was the world's greatest lover, but really, it was my feet that had me flying through space. I won't wear those shoes no more, not since Jimmy was killed by the DK. So it's great that we did what we did last night cause now I can put that nastiness behind me and think of the future. I'm always having to remind myself that shoesex isn't all bad. In fact, it's pretty fucking awesome, and you helped me see what I'd been hiding from. So don't feel bad or worried. Okay?"

"Okay. Do you mind if I ask you a shoesex question?"

"Not at all. I am the world's only expert, so fire away."

"What would happen if you put on those shoes and we had sex while you were reliving last night. Would it erase the original shoesex imprint, or add to it?"

"Dunno, but I'm willing to try. Experimenting is so much fun."

Violetta leans over and kisses my cheek. Her hand slips between my legs, rubbing the crotch of my jeans. She giggles as she realizes she's excited me with all her confessional talk.

"Ellen, you slut."

I feel young again, like a teenager in heat—nineteen

forever. My career cop years vanish like a bad dream. Being with Violetta is a trip to Never-Never land—together we can be nineteen forever.

"Have you ever had sex on a beach?" I ask as coquettishly as I can manage.

"So that's why you brought me here."

"Maybe."

WE PARK NEAR the middle of the beach. We walk down to the wave line, dodging the lapping surf. The beach isn't crowded at all, and it's so clean—nowhere near as much trash as the San Francisco beaches. Violetta skips pebbles. A two skimmer. Three. I try. A one hopper.

"Oh, Ellen, you throw like a girl."

She crouches, a mischievous gleam in her windblown face. She turns and runs. She wants me to chase her. I take off in pursuit and immediately feel the lead in my legs, but I'm not going to give up. Her tiny butt in the tight black leggings she wears looks so squeezable. I want to bury my face in her taut little ass. She weaves in meandering circles, teasing, squealing with delight as I close. She lets me catch her at the top of a bank of sand dunes. I tackle her around the waist. We collapse into the grainy bed. I'm out of breath. I gasp. She clamps her mouth over mine and breathes into me, kissing, tongues colliding. We break apart, our heated breath swirling together. I stroke her hair from her eyes. She looks at me and speaks, not the usual punkish tone, but softer, seductive.

"You might throw like a girl, but you kiss like a woman."

I don't know what to say. Violetta sees me struggling with words. I can tell she does by the way her eyes follow my mouth as it twitches. She shushes me, puts her finger to my lips. I kiss it. I nibble the skin. It's time. I pose the question that I brought her here to ask, her finger between my teeth.

"Would you like to live together?"

I'm so nervous I bite down too hard on her finger.

"Ouch! Not if you're going cannibal on me."

She breaks into song, something about eating cannibal and my love being so edible. There are times I think we speak different languages. She sees my confusion.

"Total Coelo—'I Eat Cannibals.' If we were in a movie, that's the song they'd play as background for this tender scene. At least they should if they had any taste in music."

"Violetta Valery. Be serious."

"Sorry."

"Well?"

"Where would we shack-up? At Shoe Leather? At your place?"

"Where isn't important. And it's not shacking-up. That term died in the sixties."

"I was only trying to speak your language."

"You little cow!"

I roll her over and spank her. She lets me, giggling as my hand enjoys warming her cute, little butt.

"Okay, uncle, uncle, uncle."

I stop spanking, and she twists and sits in my lap, stroking my face.

"That felt good."

"There's plenty more where that came from. If we live together—"

"Oooh, I can't wait. So where would we live?"

"I told you, it's not important. That's a detail to work out. Maybe somewhere else totally new, who knows, but first you've got to want to live together, as partners, as lovers."

She speaks in a gruff, macho voice.

"Man and wife."

I'm coming to understand Violetta. The jokes, the one-liners, all these personas help hide her true feelings.

"Violetta Valery, I'm serious. This isn't a joke to me. I love you."

There, I've said it.

"I'm sorry. I'm didn't mean to spoil the mood. Yeah, sure, I'd love to."

"I know we haven't known each other very long, but we have something special. I know there's differences—our ages, but I—"

She shakes me.

"Hey, I said yes. I accept your proposal."

She switches to a Marlene Dietrich-like movie vamp accent.

"Now kiss me you fool."

We kiss, tumbling down the sand dune, rolling over each other like fighting stuntwomen in an action movie. We come to rest at the bottom of the dune, laughing, sand in our hair, inside our jackets, down our backs. Up our cracks, as Violetta would say.

"Okay, Ellen, where do we set up house? Your place or mine?"

"Let's go for a walk and a talk."

"And later, a pork?"

I shake my head at her flippancy. She's the queen of bad one-liners. I stand and pull her up from the sand. We walk hand-in-hand along the beach. I steer her towards the far end of the beach towards the houses that look out over the sprawling beach and crashing surf.

"Do you want to keep working in Shoe Leather?"

"No, not really. I'd have split a long time ago if it wasn't for hanging around for you to beat the charges, but there is a slight matter of finances. I don't need Shoe Leather to survive. I'm okay thanks to the insurance money from my parents. Add what I could get if I sold the store, and I've got about two-hundred and fifty thousand. I live cheap. That'll last me a long time, but what are you going to do? I don't mind sharing, but eventually we'll need incomes. I only know how to repair shoes and kill people and neither one will make us rich. Hey, do you get the reward money for nailing the DK?"

"Unfortunately not because I was a cop at the time. But in addition to my puny pension I received a nice settlement in return for going quietly. About fifty thousand."

"We can find a nice apartment somewhere until we figure out what to do."

"Do you want to stay in the City?"

"Man, so many questions. My brain hurts."

I point to the row of beach houses facing us.

"Okay, okay, I'll make it easy for you. How about here?"

"Here? Are you kidding? These places must cost a fucking bundle."

"Come on, let's look."

I drag her towards the houses. It's there at the end, exactly where the realtor I'd talked to yesterday said it would be. Hidden by a sand dune, a small two bedroom house, all windows with a small yard and a huge fireplace. The 'For Sale' sign hangs limply from a piece of wood, battered by the weather. From the porch there is a spectacular view of the setting sun.

Violetta is suspicious.

"So what gives? What are you up to?"

"Do you like it?"

"Yeah, it's cute. How much?"

"One point five."

"Million?"

"Million."

"You're delirious. Are we going in to the bank robbing business?"

"No, no, listen to me. Sit down."

We cuddle on the porch. Hopefully something we'll do many times in the years ahead.

"We can afford this place, but it means a bit more sacrifice for the both of us."

"Go on."

"After the Internal Affairs announcement I was contacted by all kinds of talk shows to give them my story. I ignored them. I didn't want to discuss it any more. Then a New York agent contacted me and said he could get me a $2 million advance for the book rights to my story."

"Two fucking million."

"Yes, and that's just the advance. He figures it would be a bestseller, maybe even a movie. We'd have enough to buy this place and never ever have to work again."

"So what's the tiny sacrifices we're both going to have to make?"

"The book, *The Cop That Killed The Dildo Killer*—that's what he wants to call it—will make me front page news all over again. I'll have to do interviews. Go on talk shows, book tours. I'll have to talk about what I did—what we both know I didn't do. Are you okay with that?"

"Are you okay lying to the world? Can you do that to Oprah?"

"For you I'd lie to Donahue."

"You must really love me."

"There's more. We'd have to write the book in a hurry. The agent wanted to get an accomplished writer to work with me, but I said no. I don't want anybody poking into our affairs. I want us to write it, but part of telling my story will be to reveal who he was, what he did, why. It will mean doing a lot of painful research into the Dildo Killer and the victims."

"You mean shoesex research."

"Maybe. As a last resort. I'm sure we can get most of what we need through the police records, but if you're up for it we might learn things no police file will ever tell us. Hopefully you can remember all those speeches he made while he was killing Marsha. If you're up for it I'm sure I can get some of the DK's shoes from his apartment. They haven't yet decided what to do with all his possessions. They can't find any relatives, so there's talk of auctioning off everything for the victims. I'm sure I could get in there. I still have a few friends in the Department."

"Not Michael. He's going to guess there's something up with you and shoes."

"No, not Michael. I could have the New York agent say they want shots of me at the scene for the book. Do it all through public affairs. They'd never dare say no."

"What about the victims' shoes? You said I'd get Marsha's boots back. I never did. If we could get several victims' shoes then we'd really be able to paint a complete picture."

"It might be difficult, but it's worth a try. I can ask about Marsha's boots, but would you really want to put them on again?"

Violetta stands up and walks to the gate. She faces the sun, her back to me as she speaks.

"No, but if I had to I would, just like I did before. I just want them back. She would have wanted me to have them."

"I'll see what I can do."

She turns to face me, serious, not the playful punk she pretends to be.

"All right, since we're having a heart-to-heart we may as well get everything out of the way. We ought to discuss something we've both been ignoring. Let's say we buy this place, and we write this book and it's a blockbuster. Money may not be a problem, but will we live happily ever after?"

"We've overcome so much. There's nothing we can't conquer. There'll be problems, but there's always problems in any relationship. We're meant to be."

"Oh yeah? What if I kill again? Not if. When. What will you do when I kill again? That's why I have my power you know, to kill serial killers, not so we can have kinky sex. Sooner or later there will be another sicko who needs offing, and you may not be able to protect me."

"Violetta, I've thought about this subject a great deal. All the time we were apart, waiting for the investigation to be over, I thought about nothing else but you. Why do you think I covered up for you? Halloween night I made a decision that changed my life. I gladly threw away fifteen years of clawing my way through a system that didn't want me for someone who needed me. And I'd do it again and again and again, as many times as I have to. I'm going to protect you no matter what comes our way. I may not officially be a cop, but I have friends, and I haven't forgotten everything I learned being a damn good detective. I can't predict the future. I have no idea what maniacs we'll come up against, but we're in this together, all the way. We're a serial killer killing team. We'll pool your power and my cop smarts, and this place will be our castle where we'll be safe from harm."

I mean that in more ways than one, but I can't tell Violetta all of my reasons for wanting us to move to this isolated beach. If I can get her away from the City, away from the shoe repair business, then maybe I can protect her from the darkness of her power. All she'd ever have to use it for again would be kinky little episodes like last night. She's told me it's her destiny to kill the bad guys, and anyone who gets in the way ends up dead. She's young and has been to hell and back, and I can see how she'd have a distorted perspective on life. I'm not going to argue with her, but she doesn't have to be a prisoner of her power. I'm going to keep her safe whether she knows it or not.

"Can I play my music as loud as I like?" Violetta asks me.

"Louder."

"Then it's a deal."

She grabs the For Sale sign and rips it from the post.

"Call the realtor. Call the agent. This place is sold."

WE SPEND THE night at the Pelican Inn. I reach the realtor from there and set up an appointment for the next day. For the down payment we need $150,000. I agree to put in the fifty from the SFPD payoff, and Violetta will use a hundred of her insurance money. I call the agent in New

York. He did say to call anytime, as soon as I reached my decision. I track him down at a party for some famous author. I tell the agent he has a deal and to forward the advance ASAP. He says I'll have a contract in two days, the money within two weeks. He tells me to start typing right away. He tells the room full of publishing types that his latest client is The Cop that Killed the Dildo Killer.

Violetta and I sit in the nook surrounding the inn's huge fireplace and get roaring drunk. We stumble up the stairs, drop our sandy clothes to the floor and fall into the four poster bed. We don't have the energy to make love. We cuddle together listening to the surf. This is what it will be like in our little castle on Stinson Beach.

"Are you thinking about her?"

Before I can say who, knowing full well who Violetta means, she adds, "Catherine."

"No, I'm not."

It is the truth.

"It's okay if you are. This was your special place."

"It's now our place."

"Where did you meet her?"

"I gave her a ticket."

"You dog."

"I didn't actually give her a ticket. It was when I was a uniformed cop. She was driving on the wrong side of the road. I thought she had to be drunk. Turned out she was English, just over here to work at the opera house. She was a costume designer. She was lost, in tears. I told her to follow me. I escorted her to her hotel. She asked for my number. We started dating. I saw lots of opera. Turned out to be a preview of our relationship—lots of screaming, drama, trauma and tragedy."

"Did you ever see *La Traviata*?"

"I can't remember. I saw so many. They all ran together after awhile."

"Would you like to see it with me the next time it plays?"

"Of course. We'll rent a limousine and go in style. We'll reserve a box."

"Good. I went with Marsha to the opera for her birthday. *La Traviata*. If you can exorcise your demons, so can I."

I hug Violetta close to me. I pull the fluffy covers over us. We sink into the mattress. I snuggle her. I cradle her feet with mine, rubbing those magical soles with my toes. Her skinny little butt nestles further into my crotch as if we were forever inseparable.

It's a comforting notion. I want it so badly to be true. It's hard for me to believe we've made it this far. I whisper to Violetta my own reassurances.

"No ghosts from the past, no psychos from the future will ever separate us."

She's almost asleep. Her voice spills out of her.

"What about book tours?"

"What?"

"You said that you'll have to go on all the talk shows. You said that your agent was already lining up appearances, book signings."

"You can come along."

"No thanks. I'll stay here and guard the castle. I don't want to travel and meet people. It's safer that way."

"Then I won't go. I'll stay here. I'll be a reclusive author."

Violetta turns to face me. She strokes the side of my face, pulling on the thin blonde strands of my short hair.

"Don't be silly, Ellen. Even though we know a lot of this book is fiction, you can't act like a prima donna novelist. This is true crime stuff. You're the reason people will buy the book. It's you they want to see and hear, the Cop That Killed the Dildo Killer. I'll be fine. Go out and sell lots of books so you can support me in the manner to which I have become accustomed."

"I'll keep the trips to the barest minimum."

"And don't screw around on me because I'll know. Even if you don't wear shoes you'll never be able to hide the guilt next time we fuck. I'll only have to do you as soon as you walk through the door, then I'll put your shoes on, and I'll know if you've been faithful. If Oprah comes on to you, tell her to fuck off. You're taken."

"So, Violetta, is this your way of committing to me? Are we in a monogamous relationship?"

"I have you and my shoe collection. I don't want anyone else."

"Neither do I. I'll miss you while I'm traveling."

"Don't worry, I'll put on the stilettos from last night, and I'll be able to relive our first night as if you were there with me."

"When I'm traveling I'll play with myself and send you the shoes by overnight mail."

"And when you return I'll make you scream so loud you'll wake all the neighbors and scare all the seagulls."

"Why wait until then? I'm not tired any more. It seems like such a shame to waste this four poster bed. Let's pretend I've been gone for two weeks."

"Shoes or no shoes?"

Violetta had worn high tops. I couldn't imagine her naked and sexy in high tops, but then again. . . .

"Come on, make up your mind, or I'll pummel you with this pillow."

"No shoes."

"Are you sure?"

Violetta swings the pillow at me. I deflect the blow with my hand. She jumps on the bed, bouncing with the pillow.

"Pillow fight, pillow fight, pillow fight."

"Violetta, you'll wake the entire hotel."

"Oh shut up. We're going to scare the neighbors and wake the seagulls. Pillow, bolster, whatever. Now, choose your weapon."

We're drunk. She slurs her words. I slur my hearing.

"Shoes your weapon?"

Violetta drops the pillow and rummages on the floor.

"Good idea. Shoes your weapon, why not. I'll take my high top. You take your sneaker. The first one to cry uncle has to be the other's sex slave all night long. Ellen Stewart, I'm going to make your butt all pink and rosy, and then I'm going to lick it better until you howl like a scared seagull woken up by noisy neighbors."

"Oh no you're not."

We wrestle, landing a few errant blows on each other's butts. She gets on my back and I feel her sex all slippery along my spine. She spanks me with her high top and I howl, "Uncle, uncle, uncle."

She drops the shoe and I feel her tongue on my butt. She paints me with kisses, growing bolder, spiraling inwards until she slips between my cheeks to probe my anus. I howl like a scared seagull.

I DON'T REALLY remember too much, except that in the morning when the waiter brings us breakfast in bed we can't let him in until Violetta unties me from the four poster bed.

After shutting the bedroom door she returns to the bed munching on an English banger as rudely as she possibly can. My head isn't too stable. My butt aches. My legs cramp. My feet tingle. They feel strange. I ask Violetta to fill in the gaps. She chuckles as she speaks.

"Sorry, Ellen, right now I can't. It's kind of hazy for me too. I passed out shortly after you, but not to worry, I'll have no problem remembering every little silly, sweaty, screaming, sexy detail."

She flips up the bedsheet and covers.

On my feet are my sneakers.

I stare at my white legs, blue and purple veins cobwebbing my flesh. I sit widespread, the sneakers sadly out of place, mocking the sexiness I thought I possessed. I look silly. Ancient. I feel like a little old lady in tennis shoes. Why did Violetta do this to me? To make fun of me?

As if on cue with my growing embarrassment she starts to laugh. In the distance a seagull joins in—its cries, not the shrill normal seabird soundtrack, but a cackling belly laugh surely aimed at me.

What a fool I've been to think this old, out of shape body is appealing to a young, lithe woman with the powers of a sexual goddess. I've given her everything, and I'm just a joke to her. I feel like one of those sad, middle-aged men who get taken for everything he has by a cute, streetwise hooker who he thinks he's going to save from her horrible lifestyle.

I hurl the sneakers across the room at Violetta. She ducks, and I run to the bathroom. I lock myself in and have a damn good cry.

I may be middle-aged, but I can still act like a teenager.

THREE

"ELLEN, WHAT'S WRONG?"

Sniffles and sobs are my sole answer. Oh fuck, what have I done?

"Ellen, your breakfast is going cold."

"Not hungry."

Her words are faint through the thick wooden door. Her sniffles and sobs are not. They shake, shudder and thunder the Pelican's sturdy walls. What the hell's the matter?

"Ellen, let me in. We gotta talk. Are you sick? Do you need a doctor? You're scaring me. I don't have a clue what's wrong."

"Everything, that's what."

No sniffles, just one huge, blubbery sob. It's the kind of sound the last dying whale would make.

"Ellen, open the fucking door. I've got to take a pee."

Not a sound. Oh Christ, I hope she hasn't killed herself.

"Ellen, open the goddamn door, I mean it. If I have to

get dressed and go downstairs to piss then I'm not coming back. This is ridiculous."

I don't really mean the threat, but it works, which is lucky for me because I have no idea where I'd go if Ellen had called my bluff. I don't drive, and this place isn't exactly on the beaten track.

The lock turns. The heavy metal latch clicks up. The door creaks open. Ellen's sitting on the edge of the bathtub holding a sodden, screwed up tissue to her reddened nose. She doesn't look at me. I lift up the toilet lid, sit down and pee. My tinkling goes on for what seems like forever. I wish it would hurry up and stop because I'm bursting to know what I did to cause this drama, but I don't think it would be appropriate to ask Ellen while I'm pissing. I pass the time looking at my feet, wondering what's up. She's not on her period. Could it be menopause? Man, getting old has got to be a bummer. Joe Jackson had it all wrong. There's nothing wrong with wanting to be nineteen forever, especially if he could see Ellen right now. She looks bad.

Finally, I'm done peeing. As I wipe I ask her in as sympathetic voice as I can muster, "Please tell me what's wrong. I want to help."

I flush the toilet, stand, put the wooden lid down and sit down, my hands between my knees, tugging on the hem of my "Fuck Me And Marry Me Young" Sisters of Mercy tee shirt. Ellen looks at me for the first time since I walked into the bathroom.

"Am I a middle-aged joke to you?"

So it was the age thing.

"What? No. Never."

"Then why the tennis shoes? Why did you laugh at me? Did I look that hideous?"

Whoa, where'd that come from? She's lost me here. I feel like an unwilling passenger on her Runaway Train of Deranged Thought. Tennis shoes? Hideous? What nerve have I touched? I stand and walk over to her. I grab her hands. She looks down. I have to squat to make eye contact.

"Ellen, I laughed because it looked funny, not because you were funny. It was a silly little reaction, you know. It was the kind of sight you'd normally not expect to see, someone who'd been tied up naked in a fancy four-poster bed with tennis shoes on. It was funny. That's all."

Fuck, I feel a giggle coming on. I speak through it, throwing on an I-can't-believe-we're-having-this-discussion face to mask my impending laugh. The situation is really too, too funny for words.

"Look, Ellen, last night we were pretty crazy. We were both drunk off our butts. I wanted to be able to feel what it was like when I tied you to the bed and ate you. The only shoes you had with you were the tennis shoes. I meant to take them off when we were done, but you passed out, and I fell asleep with my head between your legs. The next thing I know the breakfast's at the door. I wasn't laughing at you, but at the situation. It was like something out of a movie."

A farce, I want to add, but I don't dare. The look on Ellen's face tells me I'm treading on shaky ground.

"It's not just last night, Violetta. Sure, the tennis shoes, your laughing was what upset me, but they made me think about things I've been trying to ignore. I'm almost twice your age. I worry about that. At times it's like we're from different planets. What future do we have?"

"Why worry about the future? Let's enjoy the present. We've been through so much in the last few months we shouldn't burden ourselves with worries about what retirement home we're going to end up in."

"We're going to buy a house today. It's a big commitment."

"One I'm willing to make. And so were you yesterday."

"I still am. I'm just scared. I don't want to lose you."

"Ellen, you're not going to lose me, but you are thinking

too fucking much. We have no idea what the future will bring, so why worry about what might or might not happen. In my case it doesn't really matter. Thanks to my power my future is pretty much dependent upon my feet and what sick bastard next needs offing. So I say why give a fuck about the future. Let's enjoy what we've got now."

"That's easy to say when you're nineteen. I'm almost forty. In a few years I'll be all old and wrinkled, and you'll still be in your youthful prime. You might not need me anymore. I don't want to get dumped because I'm past it. Look at you now, all cute and skinny and look at me—"

"All cute and skinny."

"Oh come on. Now you are being patronizing."

"No I'm not. You are cute and skinny and a little out of shape—that's all."

"See, you admit it. I am a gargoyle. I feel so self-conscious around you, especially when we're naked. I can't believe you'll want to hang around me as I turn into a shriveled up old prune."

"Jeez, Ellen, you're talking like you're eighty something with one foot in the grave. There's nothing wrong with you or your body. I love you, warts, wrinkles, cellulite and all. To me, you're perfect."

I try to hug her, but in doing so I squeeze her thighs. Nodules of cellulite appear from the pressure of my grip and her sitting on the edge of the tub. Ellen is quick to react.

"Look, I'm fat."

"No you're not. Every woman gets that if you squeeze hard enough. See."

I turn and squeeze my butt. It's the fleshiest part of my body. There has to be a little cellulite there.

"Not a wrinkle, dimple or depression in sight. God, Violetta, you and your little bird-like body make me sick."

"That's bullshit, Ellen. You're skinny. You're certainly not fat. I think you're gorgeous."

"You're just saying that."

"No I'm not. I hope I look as good as you when I'm pushing forty."

"And I'll be nearly sixty."

"And I'll be fending off all the rich, retired dykes that'll try to take you away from me."

"That's silly."

"No it's not."

I feel like the guy in that Monty Python episode who sits in a room arguing with people, always prefacing every response with an automatic nay-saying. If Ellen wasn't so serious I'd tell her this whole fucked-up conversation belongs in a Monty Python sketch.

"You don't understand, Violetta. When I look at you I see how far I've deteriorated. I was as skinny as you when I was nineteen. That's what hurts."

"For fuck's sake, you are still pretty much as skinny as me. You just need toning. I'm this way because I run a lot. You haven't been exercising so what do you expect. Shit, I grew up in an Italian household. Every sentence was punctuated with food. I've always burned off the calories running. If I had a desk job and ate bad food for fifteen years I'd need firming up."

"That's the problem. What's done is done. I've wasted the best years of my life to be a SFPD slave, and look where it got me."

"Here with me. That's not so bad, is it."

She smiles and squeezes my shoulder. Tension melts from her body. I see light at the end of the tunnel for Ellen's Runaway Train of Deranged Thought.

"Look, Ellen, if being out of shape bothers you that much then we'll start running on the beach outside our house every day. Fuck, we don't have to wait until then. We'll start now. Right now. C'mon, let's go for a run on the beach, and from now on we'll eat healthy. The greasy breakfast has already gone cold. We'll have fruit and cereal when we get back. Just quit feeling sorry for yourself and do something about it. Act like the Ellen that saved my hide. This self-pity crap is not you. Don't look at my naked ass and feel bad, look at it and ass-pire to having one just as skinny."

Ellen laughs at my tirade.

"I love you, Violetta. You should do an exercise video."

I stand and pull her up. She resists. I grab her ass and lift her to me, giving her butt a good old squeeze. It really isn't that flabby.

"I love you too, Ellen."

"I don't have any jogging clothes."

"Shit, Ellen, neither do I. We don't need designer gymwear. Throw on your jeans and tee shirt. We're not going to sprint. We can jog slowly, walk fast, doesn't matter, but we're going to start now. Now, jump to it, Stewart, and don't forget your tennis shoes."

Ellen smiles at me. I think I've braked her Runaway Train of Deranged Thought at Commonsense Station, but in the future I'd better watch my mouth. Man, is she insecure or what? It's kind of frightening. I've never had someone so dependent on me.

FOLLOWING OUR BEACHERCIZE we take a long, hot bath together. Ellen did really well. She's not in that bad shape. I soap her back. She's sitting between my legs. My hands flow up across her shoulders and down to her boobs. She leans back into me, and I lean against the tub. I massage her soapy tits.

"Thank you," she says.

"Oh no, it's my pleasure." I tweak her nipples.

"No, I mean for being understanding. This morning."

"No problem."

"I thought about things while we ran. I've got to tell you, Violetta, I'm scared."

"No one will ever find out. Don't worry."

"Not that. I'm not scared of that. It scares me how much I love you, how much you love me, how vulnerable we are, and yet we still don't know each other. And you have the advantage over me."

"How so?"

"You experience my most secret feelings by putting on my shoes."

"That you've had sex in."

"Right."

"Well, that's a small part of you. Of us."

"But we spend a lot of time doing it. It seems so one-way. Afterwards you learn all about me, but you remain a mystery."

"As I remember, you were the one that invited fuckshoes into our bed."

"I did. Don't get me wrong, I want to enjoy it with you, but I also want to get to know all your secrets too."

"I'll tell you a secret right now. I find tennis shoes, running shoes, sexy."

"Oh come on."

"I do. It goes back to when I discovered my power. I told you about that."

"Your mom's shoes—they were fancy high heels."

"Yeah, right, and the shrink convinced me I'd imagined it all. Which I believed. Duh! I'm talking about when I was fifteen and put on a cheerleader's Nikes. Wham-bam-thank-you-mam, I was inside her sucking off the school's running back, thinking about all the others on the team I'd done. Since then I can't help but look at a pair of sneakers and get hot. So it really turned me on last night to eat you when you had your tennis shoes on. I can't wait to try them on."

Ellen's nipples firm under my touch and my story. She slides her backbone along my pussy. She speaks softly sexual, like a really good phone sex operator.

"If I'd known that I wouldn't have thought you were making fun of me."

"Well, now you know."

"But there's so much about you that I don't."

"Then you'll just have to stick around a long time to find out."

"Maybe you should write it down for me. Just for me. Your life story."

"We're going to be busy enough writing your book."

"Okay, do it after we've met my deadline, while I'm traveling promoting my book. I'll send you shoesex messages like I promised by Fed Ex, and you can send me stories about yourself to keep me company while I'm on the road. Deal?"

"We'll see. I'm more of a reader than a writer."

"It doesn't have to be perfect, just stories about you from you to me. Will you do it?"

"It wouldn't be too cool for some of the things I've done to be put down on paper. They might fall into the wrong hands."

"Don't write about those things. Just give me a few stories about yourself that you're comfortable with so I can get to know you better. Like the cheerleader's Nikes story. I want all the details."

I give in. I know she's right. I've often thought about writing down my experiences, like a diary. It would be a load off to get all the guilt out of me so that I don't drive myself crazy with all those should-have-could-have thoughts. Who knows, maybe I'll turn my story into a novel, change the names and places and crimes. Nobody would believe I was telling the truth about shoesex anyway. It would be a horror-fantasy-erotic-thriller with a really cool soundtrack. It'd be a bestseller.

LATER THAT DAY we make an offer on the beach house, and it's accepted. Ellen's book deal comes through with a big fat advance, and I sell Shoe Leather to the old Vietnamese shoe repairer on O'Farrell. He jumps at my offer to sell. With me out of the way he'll have a lock on the Tenderloin shoe repair trade. Even after he knocks me down from my asking price I make money on the deal. Add these two buckets of money to our savings, subtract the price of the house and we still have a bundle. We stick the remainder of our stash in a joint bank account and plan on living off the interest. We are rich. At least I think so. Ellen is convinced we need more to be totally secure when we're old and gray. I guess people think about stuff like that when they near forty.

Since Ellen and I pay cash for the beach house the deal closes quickly. We take possession in a month. I move my stuff up there in one day. Most of it is boxes and boxes of shoes. Harry from the Pink Panty nudie theater across the street from Shoe Leather helps us move. We could hire a moving company, but we figured the less people who know where Ellen moved to and with whom the better. We rent a U-Haul truck, and Harry does all the heavy lifting. He will not take any cash for it, telling Ellen he is pleased to do a favor for The Cop that Killed the Dildo Killer. I swear, once the book comes out, Ellen could run for President and win.

We don't waste too much time setting up house. There'll be plenty of time for playing happy families once the book thing gets finished. We immediately set up a study looking out across the beach to the restless Pacific, with desks, book-cases, file cabinets, a cork board and a white board. We buy two laptop computers, a scanner and a laser printer and we get down to writing.

Our first research priority is to get the police files. Ellen calls Michael Donovan. They arrange to have lunch in the City at Hamburger Harry's. Ellen and I sit on the beach when she returns, drinking wine, watching the sunset as she tells me all about the lunch date.

Michael and Ellen start with the usual nice-to-see-you-how's-it-going pleasantries. Then Ellen drops the bombshell about us. Michael chokes on his eggburger. She tells him we became friends when she went to pick up the last pair of shoes he dropped off for her. It all developed from there. Ellen said I was so very grateful for nailing the DK after he killed my best friend. I invited her for coffee. Then shoe shopping. Dinner followed. More shoe shopping. Sleepover was spontaneous. Breakfast together meant we could get along. Move in together was inevitable. Simple as that.

Ellen doesn't think Michael suspects anything. He is too shocked, she says. He just keeps saying, "Wow, you two are so different. I'd have never in a million years have guessed you two would get it on. Way to go, Ellen." She says he wished us well, that he was impressed that she was finally getting a love life. He wishes he could do the same, but being a detective doesn't leave any time to cruise guys.

Then she asks him if she can get copies of the DK files for her book. She can go through official channels, but that would take so long. Not a problem, says Michael, but she's not to say where she got them. Give him a few days. He doesn't want any acknowledgment in the book. There's quite a bit of resentment in the department over her megabucks book deal. She asks if I could have Marsha's boots back. Potential big problem, being evidence and all that, but he'll see what he can do. Ellen says she promised them to me. She tells him the publisher wants to do a photo shoot at Dearside's apartment. For that she'll go through Public Affairs. Michael stops eating. Good fucking luck, he says.

NEXT WEEK MICHAEL comes up for a housewarming dinner. We barbecue fresh swordfish. He brings Marsha's boots with him in a big paper bag and the files in another. He hands the boots to me and the files to Ellen. I don't know what to say. I stare at the bag in terror. I know I want them, but now that they're this close they threaten like something with a nasty, contagious disease. Shoes your weapons. No joke. Marsha died in those things. I nearly did too.

Ellen takes the bag from me. She speaks for me.

"Thanks, Michael. Didn't cause a problem did it?"

"Surprisingly no. The case is officially closed. Everything that isn't claimed by victims' relatives or friends is going into storage. I filled out the paperwork saying Marsha wanted her shoes to go to Violetta. Are you all right?"

It takes me awhile to realize Michael's speaking to me.

"What? Oh, yeah. No. Shit."

Ellen comes to my rescue.

"I'll put these away."

She takes the bags into the study. I look at Michael like I'm a deer in his headlights. I offer a completely useless explanation.

"Sorry. They were my best friend's. She wore them when she was murdered."

"I know."

"Oh yeah. You would. Duh. It still kind of freaks me out."

"That's understandable. Look, don't worry about it."

"Thanks for getting them for me. I didn't mean to seem ungrateful. I really want them back. I have all her other shoes, you know. I'm glad you said on the paperwork that she wanted me to have those boots. It makes it official. These were her favorite, you know. She really loved them. She loved all shoes."

"You do too, huh?"

"Yeah, I do. I love shoes. I love the smell of shoe leather."

I can tell Michael thinks I'm strange. I bet he thinks Ellen and I get up to some pretty weird foot fetish stuff. Thankfully, he has no idea about the true nature of our kink. I wonder if he's ever done it in his shoes. Hasn't every gay man in San Francisco, especially one as dishy as Detective Michael Donovan, had at least one quick hand job in a dark alley behind a Castro Street bar? If he slips off his loafers over dinner or while he's relaxing afterwards I have to try a quick slip-on and see if anything registers.

Ellen breezes in.

"Wine anybody?"

Michael and I say yes too eagerly, as though we're both relieved to have something else to put in our mouths besides the possibility of our feet.

DINNER IS COOL. We drink and eat and chat and cappuccino, and Ellen and I are perfect hosts, even though we can't wait for Michael to get the fuck out of here. Those two bags in the study are burning holes in our curiosities. Ellen is really good at not acting distracted. I can't be bothered to listen, but she chats likes she's actually interested in all the comings and goings and he-said-she-saids of the SFPD. I know otherwise. She's thinking about those bags.

Finally, after the second cappo, Michael says he's gotta split. Ellen offers the spare bedroom, but Michael has to be downtown by eight in the morning and the traffic will be a bitch. Some other time.

Yeah, some other time. Bye, drive carefully. Thanks for Marsha's boots. He didn't even take his shoes off. From now on, whenever we have guests we should pretend we're Indian or worried about people ruining our carpet and make our visitors take their shoes off at the door. Then I could sneak a feel at my leisure while Ellen keeps them entertained.

I say good night once more and run into the study as Ellen walks Michael to his car. I ignore the files. I tear open the other bag and there they are, Marsha's thigh-high black patent stiletto boots, all crumpled and shiny and in bad need of a polishing. I hear her voice as if she's standing next to me, cigarette ash raining down. "These boots are killers. Aren't they to die for?"

"NO."

I jump. Ellen's standing in the doorway. She snatches the boots from me.

"Don't put them on. I can't let you."

"Why? That's what we got them for."

"Only if needed. Let's go through the files first. We may find all the background we need in there. We may not need—"

"I want to put them on."

"Violetta, you almost died in those things. They don't come off easily. Remember Halloween?"

"Actually, I don't. Not the details. And that's what we need. That's the stuff that isn't in those files. They can't tell you what the DK said to Marsha about why he killed. I can if I put those on."

"Don't you remember any of it?"

"Some things, but not that I'd be able to quote. That night is a blur. Now that I know sort of what happens, and that I can survive, it won't be so bad. And you'll know when to pull me out this time. Ellen, I have to do it. And if it looks like I'm in a really bad way, just pull them off me. It's not like last time when you had to leave them on me no matter what happened because it was the only lead you had, the only hope of tracking down the bastard."

"I don't know, Violetta."

"Oh yes you do, Ellen. The feet can't be denied. Bad things happen if I ignore my power."

She sighs. She knows.

"Where shall we do it?"

"How about in the bathroom? One thing I do remember is it gets messy. I'll sit in the big tub. Bring a tape recorder. I want you to record everything I say. I'm not sure I'll have the nerve to do this again."

"I'll get some extra towels."

"I'm going to polish Marsha's boots. They haven't been looked after."

I saved some of my machines from Shoe Leather.

They're in the garage. I use the polisher to buff Marsha's boots until they sparkle. Just the way she'd have liked them. Ellen waits patiently in the bathroom. I find her sitting on the floor. She's been crying.

"Don't worry," I say.

"I do."

"Good. I feel better. I feel safe knowing you're here worrying, just in case, just like before."

She helps me undress. I feel like a prize-fighter getting ready for a return championship bout, aided by my long-suffering, trusty coach who isn't so sure I can survive another beating. I sit in the tub. Ellen's made it comfy with a bunch of towels. I pull on one boot. Ellen kisses me. I pull on the other. My soles make contact with Marsha's memories.

TWO PEOPLE, ONE body. . . .

Laure Dearside's tongue slides around my mouth as I lie on the Pink Panty stage. I stick my tongue around her tonsils and let her squeeze my cunt.

"Marsha, I'd like to eat—"

"—Ernie, are you sure we ain't gonna get caught?"

Where the fuck did that come from? Who's Ernie? My memory of Marsha's last night might be a bit hazy, but I know I was supposed to say in Marsha's voice something about loving to be eaten.

"Oooh, I love to be eaten."

That's better.

My favorite song is on, "Peek-A-Boo," by Siouxsie and the Banshees. In time to the beat I grind my hips into Laure's face—

—I'm no longer on the stage. I'm bent over a desk, and I'm black. "Peek-A-Boo" fades. A muffled Madonna song fights with Siouxsie.

That song wasn't out last Halloween. It was big at Christmas. And Marsha would never have danced to it. Something is very wrong. It's like listening to competing radio stations as the stereo scans for the best signal.

"Don't worry, babe, nobody'll be up here. They're all too busy partying and dancing downstairs."

"Well just you get busy, Ernie, I don't wanna lose my job. People will soon miss us."

"I said don't worry, Deeann. I'm the boss now. They're all too drunk to notice."

Ernie lifts up my party skirt. He slides down my panties and pantyhose. They rest on Marsha's thigh high boots. He strokes a thick hand between my ass cheeks, down between my pussy lips. He slides a stubby finger in my cunt.

"Ooooh, that feels good, Ernie, come on, lover, fuck me willya. I feel kinda weird wearing this dead chick's boots—"

"—a little more to the right. Hhhhmmm. Awesome." I can see men watching us, jerking off. They're gonna come, and I love it. The drunks are cheering. Laure makes me wet, they make me wet. I'm gonna come. Look at Laure's fishnet-covered ass. Firm and round. Man, does she have long legs.

I've got two very different shoesex scenes going on at the same fucking time. This is brain-numbing.

Tonight, I'm—

"—Merry Christmas, Deeann."

No, Marsha was supposed to think Tonight, I'm going to wear her like a pair of sunglasses. I remember that thought so clearly. It was so Marsha, but I didn't just now feel it as a part of this shoesex scene. I remembered it. This Ernie and Deeann have stolen Marsha's memories.

"Damn, this feels so good, Deeann. Your long brown legs in them kinky boots look so sexy."

I grip the edge of the desk because the room's spinning a mess, and Ernie's slapping into me like a crazy sonofabitch. I shouldn't have drunk so much, but it is Christmas, and Ernie is the boss now that Ms. Stewart done fucked up. Man, I hope he don't wanna do this kinky shit all the time. I don't much like wearing dead chick's stuff. Especially shit they was killed in, but Ernie really digs—

"—such pretty boots."

Get your hands off my pussy, you fucking pervert. Oh god, just get away from me.

"I told you earlier, you're special, Marsha. You're the first I've ever brought home. You're the first woman since my early, inexperienced days whose vagina I've wanted to fuck. I like you."

Oh god, he's going to fuck me. I thought he wanted to fuck Violetta? Where is she? Has he killed her too? Or just stood her up? God, she'll be pissed. Violetta, I need you. Help me. Call the cops, please—

"—Hey, Deeann, mind if I cuff ya to the table?"

"Sheeet, Ernie."

"Ahh, come on. It's Christmas. Please. You look so fucking sexy."

"Well, okay, but man, you'd better not lose the fucking key."

Ernie doesn't miss a smooth-ass stroke as he whips out his cuffs and slaps 'em around my wrist and to the table leg. He reaches around and squeezes my bubbies. He slaps 'em. I think I'm gonna—

—Get you hands off my tits, asshole.

"I agree with the Marquis when he said that breasts were the source of all evil, and you Marsha, you tried to make more evil, you vile slut. Nature gave you small tits. You tried to improve upon her gift with silicone. You can't meet your maker with bigger appendages than you're allotted. Mister Perfection won't allow—"

—puke. Oh no, I'm gonna throw up. "Ernie . . ."

"Oh, Deeann, you got the nicest titties. I sit in my office staring through the partition window at your straining sweater, dreaming about mauling 'em just like this."

"Hey, Ernie, I don't feel so good."

"Yeah babe, it doesn't feel good, huh. Oh, fuck, I'm

gonna come, babe. I'm gonna come. I love you, I do, but don't tell my fucking wife, okay—

—He's rambling. He's fucking nutso. He's leaving. Maybe he won't kill me. No, he's coming back. What's he wearing? His dead babysitter's clothes? And a Seattle Mariners' baseball cap—

—"Oh, fuck, Deeann, can I buttfuck you? Can I come in your ass?"

I can't speak. My mouth's full of sicktaste. Oh man, what does he want? No, no, not up the poopchute.

"Ah, holy mother of fucking Christ your ass is so tight. I'm gonna—"

—"That's when I made an amazing discovery. His penis grew huge too, and he actually came as he choked to death, as I rutted into him. It was then that I realized that strangling and sodomy were much better than so-called normal sex. I've been a confirmed buggerer ever since, giving my victims perfect orgasms as they die, strangled to ecstasy."

Ecstasy? This is not ecstasy. This is agony—

—"I'm coming, babe, I'm coming in your—"

—"I saved his baseball cap for my collection. I keep a lot of souvenirs of the people I kill. My mother's panties, my father's boxer shorts. I do get quite sentimental. I have quite a wardrobe full. I'm going to keep your bra, to remind me of the nasty trick you played on Nature."

He's stabbing my left breast. I'm going to be sick. I'm choking. I'm drowning in my own—

—I throw up. I try to hold it, but all that banging up my ass, slamming my stomach into the desk.

"Ahh shit, Deeann, couldn't you wait? I'll get some paper towels. You all right? I'll be right back."

Ernie's cock plops out of my ass, and I slide to my knees.

"Ahh, jeeez, Deeann, what a fucking mess. Couldn't you have at least held it until you got to a bathroom? Here, let me get these offa you so we can get out of here."

"I'm sorry, Ernie. Don't be mad at—"

* * *

"VIOLETTA, ARE YOU okay?"

"Fine. Pull the boots off."

Ellen does as I ask.

"Who's Ernie? Deeann?"

"Who?"

"Ernie. Short, fat, Oriental. Deeann, tall—"

"Black, skinny with large breasts. Ernie Tamayo and Deeann Walker. Michael and I talked about them and others over dinner."

"I wasn't listening."

"I know you weren't. And we didn't describe them. Tamayo took over from me, and she's the department secretary. How do you know what they looked like?"

"They fucked in Marsha's boots. During a Christmas party."

"NO."

"Yes. Their fucking blended with the DK's killing of Marsha. It was like when I put on those stilettos with the straps that you bought me on our first night and then we fucked in them again. When I put the shoes on again all the shoesex blended together with pieces from early scenes mixing with the most recent episode. With you and me it was way cool because it was the same basic scene. Mix the DK killing Marsha with Ernie doing Deeann, and it's a headache and a half."

"So some of the DK story is lost."

"Seems so."

"Fuck Ernie Tamayo, that little shit."

I TELL ELLEN as much as I can recall. I take a couple of Excedrins and put Marsha's boots on again, and the scene plays out exactly as before. Marsha's memories of her death are irrevocably damaged, submerged underneath Ernie and Deeann's office party buttlust fest. No matter how hard I try, I can't make more of Marsha emerge. We're stuck with an incomplete picture. After three tries I'm exhausted. Ellen carries me to bed, and she holds me while I cry myself to sleep.

THE NEXT DAY we work through the files. The SFPD did a good job of tracking down Dearside's background. When we add the bits I learned being in Marsha's death boots, we have a pretty thorough profile. The Dildo Killer's real name was Randolph Warren III, Randy for short. He was the only son of wealthy parents from Seattle. He had everything a person could ever ask for. He wasn't abused. He was rich. He was just one of life's evil bastards.

With the cooperation of the FBI and a host of eager police departments around the country, the SFPD detailed Warren's killing career. He may have been responsible for the murders of almost a hundred people in a twenty-year period from when he started at age thirteen. After he killed his parents, the babysitter and her boyfriend, Randy left Seattle for San Jose, where he strangled and sodomized several Boy Scouts and their leader on a camping trip. Newspaper reports spoke of a missing member of the camping party, a youth named Randy visiting from the Northwest. The killings didn't stop. For the next six months San Jose parents lived in terror as Randy abducted, sexually assaulted and killed eight small children.

After San Jose, Randy fell off the planet for a few years. The FBI, working with Interpol, tracked unsolved crimes around the planet matching Randy's M.O. It was surmised that while he was missing abroad he killed more foreigners than Rambo. During his disappearance he took on the identities of Mark and Laure Dearside, eventually surfacing in his home town of Seattle to reduce its population there by a dozen or so. From there he went to Portland, after which he disappeared again. Speculation ran high that he was linked to the San Diego prostitute murders. Then there were his Oakland hooker and Berkeley jogger escapades that occurred during my childhood. After his East Bay stint he spent a short time in Los Angeles before moving to San Francisco to become the Dildo Killer. Throughout these varied kills, he stuck to strangling, butt-fucking and cross-dressing as tools of the trade, yet he was neither gay nor a transvestite nor a transsexual. The Laure persona was simply a disarming camouflage crafted after Laure de Sade, an ancestor of the infamous Divine Marquis, generally viewed by professors of perversion as the guardian angel of the house of Sade.

Warren was not mentally ill. He wasn't a mixed-up schizophrenic. He wasn't a Dr. Jekyll and Mr. Hyde. He was all Hyde. The more we read about him the more we knew that if I hadn't executed Randy, F. Lee Bailey would have had him acquitted on insanity grounds, and that would have been a tragic lie. The things Randy did made people think he had to be crazy, but we knew he wasn't. He was a refined killing machine, and he enjoyed his vocation. As Randy so verbosely explained to the dying Marsha, he epitomized *lustmord*.

After reading the files Ellen and I decide to paint a picture of Randall Warren III as a sane, calculating killer. He was a societal assassin, preying upon anyone who didn't fit his notion of perfection. Much of his speech to Marsha on the subject had been lost thanks to Ernie Tamayo's desire to get kinky, but the limited amount I experienced indicated that Randy liked the sound of his own voice. He enjoyed explaining why he killed his victims.

Unfortunately I'd thrown away Laure Dearside's favorite killing stilettos on Halloween, but in Randy's closet there had to be more, possibly from earlier murders, possibly from when he killed dressed as Mark Dearside.

Time to pay another visit to the Dildo Killer's pad.

FOUR

"How'd you get in here?"

"I walked through the front door, past the reception desk, up the stairs, through the door marked 'Detectives,' wound my way through the maze of desks, paused to say hello to a few friendly faces, and then I walked into your office and found your decidedly unfriendly face."

He scribbles on a pad of paper.

"I'm making myself a note to beef-up our security measures so psychos like you can't come waltzing in here. You could have a knife. Or a gun."

"You mean like Dan White."

"Danny-boy was no psycho."

"I should have figured he'd be a hero of yours."

"Hey, a guy that offs a radical fruit and a fruity-sympathizing mayor can't be all bad."

"Spoken like a true SFPD public servant, Ernie. Do you work at these pearls of wisdom or do they come spontaneously into that Cro-Magnon brain of yours?"

"I ain't got time for this shit, Stewart. Unlike some people, I have criminals to catch, and you're in the fucking way. You're not supposed to be in here. If you want anything, go to Public Affairs, just like any other citizen or ex-screw-up cop. If you stick around here I'll have your dyke-ass thrown out."

"Don't treat me like a pariah, Ernie."

"I'll treat you like a goldfish if I like, Ellen."

Despite his attempt to go one-on-one with me he's still no match. I chuckle at his misuse of words and his mannerisms. Ernie Tamayo possesses a bitchy streak to rival even the campiest of Castro Street queens. I bet he's a closet gay. It's always the most vehement fag-bashers that are secretly homosexual. It's the repression of those perfectly natural desires that makes them so rabid. I bet that's why he did Deeann from the rear. He fantasized that she was a nice young leather boy in chaps.

I momentarily toy with mentioning something about Ernie being a closet gay, but decide against it. Not yet. Ernie has so many weak spots it's hard to know where to start. In the end I go for the vocabulary.

"Oh, Ernie, you may have won a promotion but you're still as stupid as ever. Your reports were always such a joy to redline. Do you still spell perpetrator p-u-r-p-a-t-r-a-y-t-e-r?"

"I did that just to fuck with you. I knew it made you crazy. I know how to spell perp."

"Oh, I see. Do forgive me. You were outsmarting me."

"Yeah, easy to do."

"What's a pariah?"

"What is this, *Jeopardy*?"

"You don't know, do you?"

"As a matter of fact I do, smartfuckingass. It's a nasty little fish that strips the flesh off its victims when it smells blood. Which suits your stinking little dyke bitch picky nature just fine if you ask me. Why you bugging me? On the

– 57 –

rag again, Ellen? Heavy period, is it? I guess I'd better watch out or you might slice me up like the last guy that got in your feminist hag on the rag way."

He sniffs the air around me. As much as I want to slap his pudgy little face, I stay calm. I know I'll be leaving his office with his balls in my hand. So to speak. I didn't bring a knife. Violetta made sure of that. I got so angry over Tamayo's antics with Marsha's boots that I wanted to scare the crap out of him by marching into his office waving a butcher's knife, but Violetta was worried he might not see the humor and shoot me. She even checked my purse before I left Stinson. She really does love me. When we were first together I had a hard time believing she loved me, but the more we're together the more I see she loves me as much as I love her, and it's funny, the more we're together the more we pick up each other's idiosyncrasies. Being in love brings out the best in us. In the bad old days I'd have never thought of scaring Tamayo with a knife, and Violetta didn't know how to spell caution. Thanks to her I'm limited to my razor-sharp wit.

"Ernie, that's piranha, not pariah."

"Whatever. You hairy-legged bulldykes all smell like four-day-old tuna to me. Look, Stewart, it's been real, but don't let the door hit your skanky ass on the way out. I ain't got time to talk fishing with the likes of you, unless you're here to serve me up a pussyfish sandwich."

It's a good job Violetta made sure I didn't bring a knife or Tamayo would be a dick filet right about now. The thought amuses me. I sit down, a big smile on my face as if I were the President of the Police Charity League and this were my annual fundraising visit. Tamayo regards me with disgust and contempt. It will feel so good to humble this little shit.

"For your information, Ernie, I shave my legs and my armpits, and no, I'm not going to show you—"

"But do you shave your pussy? That's what I want to know."

I ignore him.

"And I don't have time to talk about fishing either," I say, the plastic smile disappearing as I make my move. He's oblivious to what's coming. Which suits me just fine. All the more fun to chop him off way above the knees.

Tamayo sits on the edge of his desk smirking. His expression says he thinks he's getting to me. He's unloading all the crap he's ever wanted to dump on me, but couldn't because I was his boss. These days I'm fair game like the hookers he'd bust and harass into giving him a blow job. He's relentless, so I give him enough rope by refusing to rise to his crude barbs. He doesn't know when to quit.

"So you've decided to come over to our side, huh, Ellen? Had enough four-day-old tuna? Need some real dick? About time. Then you've come to the right place after all. What can I do for you?"

He squeezes his crotch and wiggles his tongue at me. For a moment I wonder if I made a mistake at the street corner and walked into the local high school. I can't hold back much longer. I'm salivating at the prospect of deflating his macho pig ego.

"Why did you instruct Public Affairs not to allow me to do a photo shoot at the Dildo Killer's place? The case is closed. It's over. You're only waiting for the court's decision on what to do with the property. It'll soon be crawling with realtors."

"Then get yourself a license and sneak in that way. You got time on your hands now. Oh, sorry, you don't, do you? You must be so busy writing that tell-all book of yours for how many million was it?"

"More than you'll ever make. Is that why you shut me out? Jealous?"

"I don't have to explain myself to you, cunt."

Okay, Tamayo, you asked for it. Only Violetta can call

me a cunt, and then it's usually preceded by horny.

"I'll tell you why, you little ignorant shit. You did it because you are jealous of me. You always have been. You never could stand reporting to a woman, so now you're enjoying lauding your small-dicked authority over me. That's what I think. But have it your way, Ernie. If you don't want to explain your fucked up reasons to me, I'll just invite Deeann in here and you can tell her your ass-fuckingself."

To his credit Tamayo doesn't register any surprise at the mention of his paramour's name or my reference to his preferred method of entry, so I stand up, turn, walk to the door and put my hand on the knob. Deeann sits outside typing away, oblivious to the soap opera I'm orchestrating.

"You know Deeann, don't you, Ernie?"

"Course I fucking do. You know I do."

"I mean in the biblical sense."

"What the fuck are you getting at?"

He's irritated. His higher pitched voice betrays him. I've touched a tender spot. Time for the kill.

"Of course you know her in the biblical sense, as in carnal knowledge. Let me refresh your memory. You were quite drunk that night."

I assume the fucking from the rear position favored by Ernie. I mimic his weasel voice. "Oh, Deeann, you got the nicest titties. I sit in my office staring through the partition window at your straining sweater dreaming about mauling 'em just like this."

I pelvic thrust, bend and squeeze my fingers around an imaginary pair of tits. The look on Tamayo's face is priceless. He glows red then pale. His lower lip quivers. I bet he doesn't know whether to laugh or cry. I straighten up and reach for the door knob.

"Sit down."

I turn the door knob.

"Ellen, please—I got a wife, kids."

– 60 –

"Okay. If you insist. I'm all for family values."

He's defeated. I can tell by the way he says sit down without a sophomoric epithet. No time for any more cat and mouse games.

"I want you to call Public Affairs immediately and tell them you have no objection to my photoshoot. In fact, they're to expedite the request so the photographer can get in there tomorrow before the DK's things are cleaned out and the realtors make the place look like a model home."

"Or?"

"I'll see that the press hears about your predilection for fucking secretaries up the ass in crime scene evidence. They'd love the bit about the handcuffs. As would your wife and kids."

"You have no proof."

"You don't know that. Walls have ears. Evidence storage rooms have cameras."

"You're bluffing. Who's going to take the word of an ex-cop who was drummed out of the force for slicing up a guy because she was too afraid to do her job? Sounds like sour grapes to me. You have jack shit. I made sure Deeann and me weren't in view. I even checked the tapes."

"Then you admit it."

"I admit shit. What's this really about? Do you want it up the ass too? It could be arranged. I wouldn't mind doing you in the evidence room just like I did Deeann."

"Oh, Ernie, you're so stupid. Too bad you didn't check for this tape."

I pull out the microcassette recorder I hid in my purse. Tamayo cringes. He comes back fighting.

"Did one of your faggy friends tell you about Deeann and me?"

"You don't need to know how I found out."

"It was fudgepacker Donovan, wasn't it?"

"No, it wasn't. You were probably too drunk and horned-up to notice, but he wasn't even at the department party. And if you do anything nasty to make his life any more difficult than it is I'll use this tape against you whether you let me in to the DK's apartment or not."

"If you think I'm going to let you blackmail me forever—"

"Ernie, just shut up and listen. I'm the least of your worries. Did you know that Deeann's ex-husband is a Navy Seal? You didn't, did you? She doesn't talk about it much. She confided in me when I interviewed her for the job. He's a real psycho. Beat her senseless a couple of times. He refuses to think their marriage is over. That's why she moved out here from back East. The last guy he suspected of enjoying Deeann's favors ended up being eaten by bears. No one believed it. Just couldn't prove anything from what little of his body was found. Those Seals know a million ways to kill. If I were you, Ernie, I'd watch my back, especially during fleet week. Can you imagine what he'd do if he found out you got Deeann drunk, made her wear a pair of hooker boots a young woman was killed in, handcuffed her to a desk and then fucked her up the ass until she puked?"

"Okay, okay. Enough. I get the picture."

Victory is mine. I stand up, a broad smile beaming across my face. I pause at Tamayo's door. I enjoy this moment. I wish Violetta were here to enjoy it with me. Maybe if she puts on my shoes she'll be able to sense the joy I'm feeling. It's definitely not sexual ecstasy, but it would be worth a shoe feel because I am just about as happy as I can be.

"Shall I have Deeann call Public Affairs for you?"

"I'll take care of it."

"Do that, Ernie, and stay out of my way, and Donovan's, and we'll all get along just fine. Cross me, and I'll be all over you like a school of hungry piranhas. That's piranhas as in flesh-eating fish. Not pariahs as in social outcasts. Have a nice fucking day, you ignorant misogynist. That's misogynist as in hater of women. Ignorant as in Chief Detective Ernesto Tamayo."

I walk out of Tamayo's office, his balls figuratively in my hand. Even though I can't wait to tell Violetta all about my victory and have her try on my shoes, I spend a few moments chatting with Deeann. It's innocent female gossip, but Tamayo doesn't know that. He squirms in his office, unable to take his eyes from us.

UNLIKE ON HALLOWEEN we go in through the front entrance.

The SFPD Public Affairs flunky punches in the alarm code and opens the heavy double metal doors. I smile smugly at Violetta. The security code's been changed from the one she learned by being in Marsha's boots. She sticks her tongue out at me. She was all for sneaking in through the garage using the DK's old 696969 code and avoid dealing with Tamayo. I maintained that the department would change the security code to prevent just that kind of occurrence. Who knows how many people knew about the code and would take advantage of the investigative lull to sneak into the DK's apartment and snag a few souvenirs?

Violetta was willing to give covert operations a try. She really didn't want me going downtown to do battle with Tamayo, but I figured the department may have the place watched, and it wouldn't do for either one of us to get caught trying to sneak in. And besides, I wanted to take Tamayo down a few notches. God, that felt good. It's been a day since I made him squirm, and I'm still glowing. Unfortunately, Violetta couldn't register even the slightest flush of satisfaction when she tried on my shoes. Doesn't matter how strong the emotion, her shoesex power seems only to work with matters sexual.

Winning the argument to do battle with Tamayo was the first time I'd prevailed over Violetta. She's very strong willed, as am I, but we're getting along just fine. Thanks to Violetta's refusal to let me wallow in self-pity I've gotten over my age difference insecurity, and she's learning that sometimes I do know best, even if I am an old fart.

She helps the photographer's assistant carry in the camera gear. Violetta pretends to be part of the crew. I told my publisher I wanted my 'assistant' to surreptitiously wander around taking candid file photographs of the DK's place while the shoot was underway. He thought it was a great idea and suggested that Violetta be disguised as one of the crew. He clued in the photographer to the arrangement, who didn't mind the extra pair of hands, especially when I told him how many stairs he'd have to haul his equipment. My job will be to keep the SFPD Public Affairs flunky busy catering to my star needs while Violetta goes in search of guilty shoes.

That's not on my mind right now. Honestly, I'm scared walking up these stairs. It's like that scene from *Psycho* when the detective gets knifed walking up the stairs. I expect the ghost of Randy Warren III to come flying at me, screaming that I didn't kill him, and he can't rest in peace until the truth is known. I can only imagine what Violetta must feel like. She's behind me, carrying a crate of lights. I hope she doesn't drop them. I'd scream the place down.

We make it to the top without any paranormal visitations. I calm down. Just a little. Actually, a lot, because Violetta seems calm too. I expected her to be on edge, and that worked me up, but she is so relaxed. Too relaxed. Is this the lull before she explodes? I'm getting nervous again.

"Where would you like to set up?" asks the flunky.

"Definitely the bathroom. We have to have that. That's where it all went down, right?" says the photographer.

"Yes," I say, eyeing Violetta. She shows no outward sign of wanting to bolt. I know I can do this. I can go back in there. I can. I can.

"Then let's set up in there first. Lead the way."

The flunky moves to usher us in the direction of the bathroom, but Violetta heads him off and sets out as if she knows where she's going. Which she does, but she wasn't supposed to act like she did. We went over this so many times. I can tell by the look on the flunky's face that he's puzzled.

"That's right, through there," I yell after Violetta. She doesn't even turn back. I look at the flunky. "I sketched them a map when we discussed the shoot. I didn't want to burden you with being a tour guide." The flunky nods in apparent acceptance of his reduced role, then adds, "Well, if there's anything you do need, be sure to ask. Chief Detective Tamayo was very insistent that we extend every possible courtesy."

"That's so nice. Do thank him for me."

I walk into the bathroom. I know it's been cleaned just like any other crime scene, but I half expect it to be awash with blood and gore.

It's sparkling clean, like one of those bathrooms used in advertisements for miracle cleansers. The brightness is disturbing, accusatory, like interrogation lights. I whisper to Violetta as she unpacks crates.

"Are you okay?"

"Fine. Just proving an old police saying."

"What?"

"The murderer always returns to the scene of the crime."

"Violetta Valery."

She laughs. "Relax. No one heard."

The flunky walks in and watches the beehive of activity. He dodges out of the way of the photographer and his regular assistant who are busy setting up lights. Violetta hands off equipment to them as if she's been doing this all her life, but I still want to distract the flunky from even looking casually at her.

"Been long with the department."

"Two years. I was in the Mayor's office before that."

"Oh."

After a few more pleasantries I'm at a loss for more distracting chat, but luckily the bulk of the setup is quickly completed.

"Why don't you go take those test shots and light readings we talked about, for the other locations," says the photographer right on cue to Violetta. He's learned his lines well. Violetta on the other hand improvises, saying her lines like a bad actress.

"Yes, why don't I take those test shots and light readings we talked about, for the other locations."

There are times when I could shake her. She takes everything so flippantly. Or so she'd like people to believe. I know she pretends everything's a big joke just to disguise the scared little girl who lives inside her. She was supposed to say "Okay, I'll be right back." She winks at me, and I pretend not to notice. I don't want to encourage her. She grabs the oversized camera bag and slips past the flunky. He pays her no attention. He's engrossed with being at the execution site with The Cop that Killed the Dildo Killer.

"Let's do your makeup. How do you usually look?" asks the photographer.

"Like this."

"Oh."

"I don't wear much makeup."

"Oh."

"Is that a problem?"

"Not really, we'll do a subtle job. We'll need to dull the glare on your skin. Now that you're a star I might suggest splurging on a makeover. With all the appearances you'll be doing you'll need to look your best. Wouldn't you say?"

He stares at the flunky who finally realizes he's being spoken to.

"Yes, yes, I guess so."

"I must say, the suit is very stylish," says the assistant.

"Thanks. Vi—I bought it especially for the shoot."

That was close. I'd better watch myself and not get too

chatty, because naturally I want to tell people the things Violetta and I do together, like when she took me shopping for clothes.

"It has the perfect balance between power and femininity. The padded shoulders are so you. Don't tell me, Bebe— right?"

"Right."

"I can always tell."

The flunky looks bored, so I ask him what he thinks of my suit, and he parrots the photographer's assistant, adding a few typical Public Affairs say-a-lot-mean-a-little comments. Thankfully, by then the powdering and painting are done and the photographer has me sit on the edge of the tub for the first shots. Then stand in the tub. Straddle the tub, looking over my shoulder. Face the camera, stretch, arms on the shower rail. Sit on the toilet, lid down. Stand, pulling back the shower curtain. I feel like I should have a scrubbing brush in my hand and say something like "Eliminate those pesky mildew spots with just one swipe."

In each pose he has me turn my body one way, my head another. Look happy. Look sad. Look worried. Look thoughtful. Not hard to do. I can't keep my mind from wondering about Violetta's search. She's been gone so long. I hope she doesn't get trapped in a shoefuck. How would we explain that to the flunky?

"Excellent, excellent. Wonderfully pensive expression," says the photographer.

"Oh, yes," says the assistant.

"That's the cover," says the flunky.

I do feel better. I'm more comfortable posing, perhaps because I don't hear Violetta screaming and the photographer's very good at relaxing me with his compliments and suggestions. I don't feel so self-conscious any more. I don't think of this bathroom as a bloody scene in which I bathed and bruised myself. It's my stage, and I feel like a star. I could get used to this adulation. I'm ready for my close-up.

The photographer's also very good at occupying the flunky with little questions like "What did you think of that shot?" and requests like "Could you hold this?" or "Move that." All this busywork makes sure the flunky doesn't wander off and disturb Violetta.

The door opens. Violetta walks in. We all turn to look at her.

"Got the fuckers," she says as if all she really were talking about was a bunch of irritating test photos and light readings, but I know different. I can tell from the steely expression on her face that this time she's not in a joking mood. She wants out of here. She wants to put those fuckers on her feet.

The photographer ignores her. The flunky looks at her as if she's a rude little punk.

"Would you mind getting my notebook out of the Jeep," I say to Violetta, eager to get her and the fuckers out of here. "The keys are in my purse."

"Sure."

She swings the bag on her shoulder and strides out.

"What's next?" I snap at the photographer.

I'm eager to get out of this place too.

WATCHING VIOLETTA WHEN she's in an unknown shoefuck is terrifying. I want to rip the shoes off her feet, but I never do. It's like watching somebody sleepwalk. Doctors say more damage can be done by waking up a somnambulist rather than letting the sleepwalk end naturally. I feel that way about Violetta when she's in a shoefuck, although I have no foundation for my apprehension. There are no shoesex doctors to advise us. No books to read. No late night talk shows to call up and ask for advice. It's just the two of us, out there in shoesexland taking one step beyond reality.

Just look at Violetta shaking. It's horrible. It's such a contrast to when we play by ourselves. Then there's no fear, just sexiness, like when we made love with Violetta wearing those spaghetti-strapped high heels I bought her for our first night together. Then it was such a turn-on to play with Violetta's power, layering sex act upon sex act. Now it's the other side of shoesex—hate-making, not love-making, and it scares me because it's out of our control. I don't believe we know the boundaries of her power, what she's capable of when she's under its influence. We do know that there's no fun involved when she's inside a killer. It's all sexual violence and murder, and I feel so useless being a towel holder, an observer. I'm a cop. It's in my nature to intervene. I can't detach myself from Violetta. I love her. It's my duty to protect her.

I've been trained to prevent crime, and even though I know that a crime isn't really happening when Violetta puts on the DK's shoes, to her it is happening. It reminds me of *The Strange Case of Dr. Jekyll and Mr. Hyde,* where the idealistic doctor tries to conquer evil but ends up succumbing to it and committing horrible crimes. I find myself expecting to read in the morning paper that the DK crimes have started again. It's irrational, I know, but this whole shoesex thing defies logic. So how am I supposed to act? When she's in Randy Warren's designer dress shoes killing someone it's awful hard for me not to stop her. I want to keep her safe, and even though I know the Dildo Killer came to no physical harm during the murders, what will it do to Violetta to be him, to know how to kill, to enjoy killing as a sport? Will it change her? Will she become addicted to murder like she is fuckshoes? What would coptrained me do then? Could I stop her?

On the drive back from the City, Violetta said putting on the DK's shoes wouldn't permanently affect her. She told me to remember back to the day before Halloween when she put Laure Dearside's killing stilettos on for the first time. She said it scared and disgusted her that she felt the thrill of the kill, climaxing as she relived murder after murder, but she soon got over it enough to come to the police within a few hours. Not that we listened, she added. Violetta can never resist an opportunity to rub my nose in the police department skepticism that lead to Marsha's death. Will Violetta ever forgive me for not listening to her? I knew better than to bring up the subject, because she'd say she has already, but comments like that one indicate the wounds are still open.

So don't worry about me becoming hooked on murder, she told me. Now that I have a cop by my side who listens and loves me, and I know what to expect. I'll be fine. This is just a job. Don't take it so seriously. I can handle it. It's cool.

As I watch her skinny naked body writhing and thrusting and punching and spasming, I'm not so sure. The blank look on her face is horrifying. She's covered in beads of cold sweat that I'm afraid to wipe away. Her mouth moves and unintelligible grunts escape. As much as the noises are frighteningly inhuman, I'm actually glad of it. I couldn't stand to hear Violetta say the hideous things the DK said to his victims. I'm reminded of the first time I saw Linda Blair in *The Exorcist*.

It's going to be a long night. Violetta wants to try on all the shoes she found so we can close on the book research. Or so she says, but I think there's more to it than that. It's the shoes. She's addicted to fuckshoes. She can't resist a virgin pair to slip onto her feet. There were three pairs of fuckshoes in the DK's closet—the expensive dress shoes that Dearside wore when he was a smart young man out on the town looking for some rough trade, a pair of engineer's boots that Dearside wore when he cruised the gay bars looking like a leather biker boy and a pair of five-inch plat-form heels that belonged to Melanie Courtland, the first victim.

I knew the shoes were Melanie's. The DK collected sou-venirs of his victims' perceived imperfections. He took

Marsha's bra because he wanted a reminder of how she had her small breasts enlarged. He took Delores Cochran's leather jacket because she was a blustery leather dyke. He took James Purcell's rock star sunglasses because he was such a poseur. Melanie was short, just four feet eleven, and from the brief flash Violetta got when she tested the platforms, a short woman was being groped by Laure Dearside in an upscale lesbian bar.

I'm not looking forward to Violetta wearing Melanie's shoes. At least when she's inside the DK I know she won't die. Back on Halloween when Violetta tried on Marsha's boots for the first time she stopped breathing. I pulled off the boots and gave her mouth-to-mouth. She coughed and came around. We thought it was the vomit that caused the breathing problem, but her breasts burned painfully where the DK stabbed Marsha and her jaw was stiff from being punched. When Violetta put Marsha's boots on again a few weeks ago and was sitting up in our bathtub she didn't stop breathing, but the physical pain was still there, although it was reduced and she recovered quickly. She said the less severe effects were because she's more in control of her power now, but I can't help wondering how much of the lessening of the effect of Marsha's death was due to Deeann and Tamayo's muddying of the shoefuck waters.

Violetta has no idea what happens to Melanie Courtland. I do. I was the first detective on the scene. I filed the report on her. Violetta says she doesn't want to know what happened to Melanie or any of the other victims because it could cloud her perception of the events and what she learns about the Dildo Killer. She didn't want to read the crime scene and Coroner's reports until she'd had the opportunity to experience the crimes firstfoot, as she likes to say.

I admire her dedication. I've told her so, and I've also told her that Melanie dies a gruesome death, but Violetta won't be dissuaded. She figures that if she survived her best friend's death nothing could be worse. She has no idea. What happens if Violetta dies when Melanie dies, just like she comes when the original wearer comes? Will I be able to save her? Mouth-to-mouth won't cut it this time. The DK cut off Melanie's feet and stuffed one into her mouth and the other into her vagina while he sodomized her with his trademark Mister Perfection dildo. Cause of death was due to the combined effects of the blood loss from the wounds and strangulation with the vibrator's cords. We were never able to ascertain whether she was wearing shoes when he cut off her feet. We thought maybe she took off her shoes when she arrived home. There were several high-heeled platforms lying near the entrance to her apartment and none had blood on them. I hope for Violetta's sake that a night of dancing in high heels made Melanie's feet ache so much that she kicked them off when she got home and we learn nothing new about the DK's killing ways.

"Is the tape rolling?"

I start at the sound of Violetta's croaky voice. I give her a drink of water to soothe her throat, and then I hug her, happy to have her back with me. Hearing her voice instead of that animalistic grunting is such a welcome relief, even if it is raspy.

"Are you okay?"

"I feel fine. Fucking A considering I just fucked the eyes out of a gay priest, fucked him up the butt, carved Jesus Sucks The Devil's Cock In Hell on his back with a crucifix that I pocketed as a souvenir, strangled him to death with the Mister Perfection's power cords and came buckets of come as he died."

She bursts into tears, and I hold her, telling her she's okay, she's safe, and all the while I'm being her comfort I'm thinking is this quest for information worth the pain? Why don't we just make up stories about Randy Warren III for the book? Why does it have to be accurate? No one will know the difference. Heck, the whole damn book is predicated on a big lie. Why worry about getting the details right at Violetta's expense?

"Because I have to," says Violetta when I suggest this solution after she's finished spilling her guts into the tape recorder. I argue we have enough background information from the priest's murder. We can make up the rest. Killing a gay priest gave Mark Dearside every opportunity to espouse his killing for perfection philosophy. He thoroughly enjoyed taunting the priest in much the same way that his idol, the Marquis de Sade, did in his writings.

Violetta refuses. "If it were just the book, I might agree with you, but it's not. This is about my responsibility."

So I was right.

"My power allows me to know this sicko better than himself. What I learn about the DK will allow me to do a better job of killing the next creep. There were so many times in the year leading up to Halloween when I could have had him, but I denied my feet. Then people around me, people I love, died. I will not take that chance with you. Fate wanted me to find those shoes, and I'm going to wear them. It's all part of some grand plan of Good versus Evil. It's bigger than you or me. Getting dirt for the book is a nice by-product, but it really is incidental to my motivation. I'm destined to be a serial killer of serial killers. Shoes are my weapons."

I play dumb. I don't want Violetta to suspect that I am going to do all I can to thwart the future use of her power to kill more serial killers.

"But we got them for the book."

"I know we did. I know that's what we talked about, and that's what I thought too, but when I searched the DK's closet and found them I realized the real reason. There will be another killer to be killed. Ellen, it's inevitable."

Not if I have anything to do with it, I want to tell her, but when Violetta gets this way there's no reasoning with her. She's possessed, just like that child in *The Exorcist*.

– 73 –

Burdened, more like. Burdened with a strange power no human should ever be asked to handle. No wonder she believes all this fate and destiny and Good and Evil stuff. If I'd experienced what's she's endured by the age nineteen I'd be superstitious too. "Okay," I say, "But promise me, don't go being a hero. We're in this together." She agrees, and I resolve to myself to keep the serial killers at bay. Violetta has to be given a chance to lead a normal life, a love life with me. I'll be damned if some magical power is going to come between us, and I won't be disposed of so easily as her previous loved ones. I know what I'm dealing with.

Good versus Evil. So be it.

Violetta and I are eternal.

End of story.

If any serial killer wants to disturb our peace, then look out. The Cop that Killed the Dildo Killer will have a truer sequel: *The Cop That Killed Even More Serial Killers*.

FIVE

"THAT'S IT, ELLEN. I'm sorry. There's not much new stuff at all, just the same old speeches, a ton of butt-fucking and come-drinking from condoms, excessive violence, Mister Perfection's grand entrance and the victim's desperate pleading for mercy. Then comes his painful death while various killing episodes flash through my mind as I have a really good laugh and jerk off into a condom in front of his pulpy mess of a face. Oh, and the souvenir was the dude's oversized belt."

Ellen looks at me with the closest thing to motherly concern she can muster. She pulls the DK's engineer boots off my sweaty feet and clicks off the tape recorder. A worry wrinkle furrows her cute brow. She knows how to make me feel guilty, and let's face it, I don't need any help in that department. I immediately regret the callous way in which I summed up my latest DK shoekillfuck. I've always parroted that Harrison Ford line from *Blade Runner*—I'd rather be a killer than a victim, and that attitude's really starting to show. I don't feel sympathy any more for the victims. They're just collateral damage casualties in the war between Good and Evil.

Fuck, have I become too jaded by walking in a killer's shoes?

I really do sound like Deckard, that burned-out killer of replicants.

I've just offed a fat Japanese businessman who thought he was picking up a cute go-go boy from the anonymous darkness of The Studly Mine. Instead he got a blind date with Mark Dearside. Consequently he never had a chance to go back to the Land of the Rising Sun to say *sayonara* to his cute little wife who had no idea about hefty hubby's homo habits. At least that's what chunky-san said to the DK when he begged for his life. What will my wife think? She doesn't know. She'll lose face. Dearside loved that last pleading. He joked that once he'd fucked the poor bastard's eyes out at least hubby and wifey would now have something in common. They'll both have lost face. A real thigh slapper that one. Oh that Dildo Killer, he was a right cutup. He promised to do a thorough facial destruction job.

He did.

I did.

And all I can say is that it was the same-old, same-old shoes, sex and violence. Yeah, I'm getting too jaded. Time to be a victim again. There's nothing like being on the receiving end of Mister Perfection to stimulate the sympathy glands.

"Look, Violetta, you're tired. Why don't we call it a night? You may be missing stuff."

"I'm not, Ellen. Tired or missing stuff. I know I didn't say it too eloquently, but I think we've learned as much as we're going to from the DK's shoes. I'm in his groove. I know his thoughts, motivations and worse of all, his jokes. The only surprise is what nastiness he'll inflict upon the poor victim. Who was he by the way?"

"That was number twenty, Innoye Matsoshi. He actually died of a heart attack before the DK finished him off."

"Maybe that's why Dearside wasn't so inspired once he got into the hardcore violence. He gets off more when they scream and squirm. Once Innoye realized begging wasn't getting him anywhere he just jiggled and farted a lot."

The image of Innoye's big flatulent butt rolling around against my Greek god thighs as I pounded away flashes into my head, and I can't help laughing. The DK really got off on it. Old Innoye was a gigantic gasbag. There were times I was convinced that if he hadn't been tied down he'd have zoomed around the room like an uncorked balloon. It was grotesquely funny and smelly. Somehow Ellen has to work this into her book—she uncovered the DK's diary or some such crap. I tell her to turn the tape recorder back on, and I recount Innoye's fart Olympics and the DK's rapture at catching such a prolific rasper. Randy Warren's big inspiration was the Marquis de Sade. It's where he got his alias Mark Dearside. He also got his love of farts from Sade. He regaled Innoye with the story of how the Marquis paid prostitutes to fart in his mouth. Right on cue Innoye let rip, and the DK practically came. Fuck, did the fart stink bad, but Dearside was in heaven.

Ellen tries hard not to chuckle with me.

"Violetta, you're terrible."

"Oh come on. If you'd seen Innoye's huge ass vibrating with every thunderous blast, you'd laugh too. It was awful funny. And you know the worst of it? Amongst all the wobbling flesh the DK had a tough time finding Innoye's a-hole for Mister Perfection."

"Violetta Valery."

"Okay, Mom, I'm sorry."

I wipe the tears from my eyes. Ellen watches me closely. There's that worry frown again.

"Tears of laughter," I say. "They are. Honest."

"Are you sure you don't want to take a break? The shoes will still be here tomorrow."

"Nah, I'm fine. Let's go from the huge to the tiny. Maybe we'll learn more from Melanie's platforms. She was the first victim so maybe the DK wasn't in such a rut."

Ellen yawns and stretches.

"Let's take a rest. I really am very tired."

"No. I want to do this now. I won't be able to sleep if I don't. If you want to call it quits, go ahead, but I'm not stopping until I'm done."

"Okay, okay, if you've got the energy, fine. I'm staying by your side through this. You know that. It's just that Melanie was a victim—"

"Exactly. Like I said, she was the first so we may learn something new about why Randy Warren the Third became the Dildo Killer."

"What I was trying to say was that Melanie was a victim, and we don't know that you'll be okay when you're a victim. We were lucky to get through Marsha's boots without losing you. At least when you're the DK we know you'll live."

"I'll be fine with you here."

"I may not be able to help. He hurt her horribly."

"I know. You've told me all I need to know."

"But you don't know the details. You don't want to know, but if I told you I'm sure you wouldn't want to put on those shoes."

"Then you don't know me very well. I would put them on no matter what horrible or disgusting things went down in them. It's what I do. We may not learn as much if I'm waiting for the other shoe to drop—"

I raise my eyebrows. Ellen doesn't laugh at my silly joke.

"Shoe to drop—get it?—oh well. Wasn't very funny, was it? Look, Ellen, I can't let the horrible things the DK did stop me. There's something important in those shoes. I feel it in my feet. I wouldn't have found them otherwise. If it's one thing I've learned about my power is that there's no such things as a random event. Everything happens for a purpose. Those shoes contain the DK's first kill and his last message to me and it won't be cluttered by other killings. It'll be a pristine shoefuck because it was to the death and no one's worn those shoes since. Until I found them. They've been waiting for me all these years, don't you see?"

Ellen sighs. She knows I won't give in.

"It's just that I want to protect you from harm. I love you. It's so hard to see you put on those shoes knowing that you'll experience what happened to Melanie. Do you have any idea how useless that makes me feel?"

"I feel safe knowing you're here to help me, so don't feel useless."

"There's nothing I can say or do to stop you, is there."

"No. I can't stop myself if I wanted to."

"Then I'll get a cup of coffee, and we can get started. Want anything?"

"Water's fine for now. Afterwards we'll bust open a bottle of champagne and celebrate, okay?"

She smiles at me, it's almost a grimace, as though she doesn't think there'll be an afterwards or at least a desire to celebrate. I call after her.

"I love you, Ellen. Thanks."

I understand why she's worried. I'm scared shitless I'm not going to make it out of Melanie's shoefuck alive.

The DK was an efficient killing machine, and yet it was easy for me to slay him. It must have really pissed him off to be done in by a neophyte murderer. Mad enough to want revenge maybe? He was always one step ahead of me. What if Melanie's platforms are a trap? Is this shoekillfuck the DK's way of getting revenge? A booby trap? I don't even laugh at the obvious double entendre given what he did to Marsha's tits.

Fuck, I'm scared.

*   *   *

TWO PEOPLE, ONE body...

"I love your shoes."

Loud music. Did she say she loves my shoes?

"Excuse me?"

She's leaning closer. Her long blonde hair is swishing across my face. She's so tall, fair, beautiful.

"I said I love your shoes."

"Thanks."

What's she doing on the floor? Oh my God, she's stroking my shoes. Polishing them? With her blouse? She is. She is. She's using that long, filmy material like a rag. What now? Oh no. It can't be. Yes, it is. She's kissing my feet.

This is so kinky.

This is so embarrassing.

Is everybody watching me?

Relax, Melanie, no one's paying attention. They're all into their own little scenes. Those women are having sex in the corner. Those two are kissing, almost wrestling. Most of the room's watching the spanking show. My God, this place is wild.

Oh, oh, her hand's sliding up my ankle, my calf, behind my knee, higher, along my thigh. Look at her. She's beautiful. She's smiling. Smile back. Oh shit, I must look stupid. Her hand's on my crotch. Pussy likes that. Backwards and forwards, wet, wetter. Oh my God I'm soaking my panties, my pantyhose, her fingers.

"There was a scuff."

"What?"

"So I rubbed it away."

Oh, my shoes.

"Thanks."

"Like this."

Harder, quicker, working my clitoris between her fingers, through my pantyhose and panties.

I'm going to come.

Burning up. Oh, God, I'm sweating.

She's laughing. She's leaning forward. Her lips are parting. Her tongue's sliding across her bright red lips. I'm staring, opening my mouth.

What a kiss. She's sticking her tongue in and out like a
dildo.

I'm coming. Little tremors in my pussy. Bigger as she
kisses me, groping my clit. It won't stop and neither will
she. If it weren't for her kissing me, I'd be screaming.

I'm moaning, growing louder, spreading through my
body. I'm buzzing with sex.

Back arching, legs are weakening. I'm collapsing onto her
hand.

My first public sex, and I've only been in San Francisco
three months. Score.

Melanie, what would your mother say?

We're not in Pine Gap anymore, that's for damn sure.

She's backing away. Teeth biting my lip. Ouch.

No, don't go. She's reaching out her hand, touching my
lips with her fingernail. My pussy tastes good on her finger.

"Beats shaking hands, doesn't it?"

I'm nodding. She's laughing. She does that a lot.

"I'm Laure."

"Melanie. Pleased to meet you."

"You're sweet, Melanie. Care to dance?"

Yes, no, maybe later. She's heading for the dance floor.
Okay. Yes.

We're dancing to Madonna.

Laure's leaning closer. She's shouting in my ear.

"Do as Madonna says. Get into the groove."

Hands all over me, coaxing me to move. Okay, I can do
this. I'm so turned on. I like dancing. Dirty dancing. Laure's
turning around, backing into me and grinding her butt.
What a hard ass.

She's so tall.

I'm so short. Even in five-inch platforms. She's so sexy.
All legs. This is so cool. Wave your hands, Melanie. And

snap your fingers the way they do in videos. Be as sexy as you can.

Laure's turning around, straightening. She's biting my fingers, licking them.

"Would you like to get out of here?"

What should I do? I've never done anything like this before.

She's whispering in my ear.

"I'd like to make love to you all night long if you'd let me."

Oh, wow. I can't believe this is happening to me. It's time I did it. Melanie Courtland, stop acting like a scaredy-cat chick from Podunksville, Flyoverland.

"I'd like that, Laure. I have an apartment in the Marina."

"Roommates?"

"No."

"Excellent. Lead the way, Melanie of the Marina."

The air outside Jezebel's is cold, but I'm feeling like it's a midwestern summer's day. She chose me.

"I'm parked around the corner. How about you?" Laure asks.

"I don't have a car. I took a taxi."

"Perfect. I'll be your chauffeur."

She must be amazingly rich. Her car's a Porsche, the expensive kind. Soft seats. Fancy stereo. Loud. Pounding.

"Sisters of Mercy."

"Who?"

"Sisters—never mind. Just listen and look cute."

Louder. Stupid Melanie. Sisters of something. Record store time tomorrow.

Her long legs slide through the gears, clutching, braking, accelerating. Her legs are twice as long as mine. I'm so short.

"What are you looking at?"

"Your long legs."

"Why thank you. Your legs are pretty too."

"They're too short."

"Not in those heels. They look spectacular. Almost perfect."

"For sure?"

"Absolutely, and after tonight, you'll feel perfection."

I'm shuddering. Touch my pussy again, only this time skin on skin.

"I can't wait."

"Neither can I. You know, you're my first."

"Really? You seem so experienced."

"Appearances can be deceptive."

Shit, was that my street? I should have been paying more attention to the road.

"Oh, turn right here."

She's squealing the car around the corner. I love being so reckless. Darn it, there's no parking on my street.

Here we go, just a block away.

She's getting out. Nice butt. And a Gucci bag.

"I like to have a change of clothes for in the morning."

"You want to spend the night?"

"Yes, of course. I don't want to rush this moment, Melanie. I'm not a one night stand kind of girl. I don't want to fuck and run. Tonight's very important to me. I want it to be the first of many."

"Me, too."

I'm falling for her. She's so full of wonderful contradictions. I like complex people. They're always sophisticated and worldly. Like I'm going to be. Look out, San Francisco, Melanie Courtland has arrived.

Laure's looking so sexy by the streetlights, like something from a perfume commercial. I'm staring, but so what. I'm sure she knows and likes it. She's moving off toward my apartment. She's stopping, turning around, holding out her hand.

"You're so cute."

Don't wake the neighbors. It's late. Turning the key in the lock softly, softly. I'd better take off my shoes so I don't make too much noise on the hardwood floor. My feet are killing me. I can't wait to get naked with Laure.

Squeeze the door shut.

"Nice place."

"Thanks."

Shoes-off time.

"Don't do that." Nails biting my wrist. Ouch, Laure. Nice ouch. "Leave them on. You look sexy in them."

"I was worried about the noise, you know, the neighbors."

"Oh don't worry, you'll be horizontal very shortly."

She's laughing again. Join in. Laugh too. It's okay. Who cares. We connect. I can just see us going to art galleries together and spending long afternoons drinking strong coffee in North Beach.

Better impress her.

"Fuck the neighbors." Oh God I can't believe I said that.

She's smiling again, nodding. I'm scoring points.

"Melanie, I don't want to fuck the neighbors. I want you all to myself."

She's laughing at her joke. I'm joining in.

"A drink?"

"I'd love champagne."

"I only have wine. Is that okay?"

"If I can drink it from your pussy it will be."

Into the kitchen.

"Make yourself at home." Only white Zinfandel, but at least it's Gallo. Two glasses. Shit. They're dirty. Fingerprints and lipstick stains. Lousy dishwasher. Can't give Laure a dirty glass. A quick wash'll fix that. Mission accomplished. Unscrew top. Drain bottle. Done.

Don't spill a drop. Take it easy.

"Here we are."

Laure's bending over, rummaging in her overnight bag.

Posing for me. Sexy. I can't wait to bury my face in her pussy and have her wrap those long legs around my neck.

I'm so turned on.

"Here you go, Laure."

"Enjoy the view?"

"Yes. You have a lovely ass."

What's wrong. What'd I say? She's not smiling anymore. She's sneering. The wine?

"I hate white Zinfandel. Only cheap little imperfect short sluts drink piss like that. And Gallo? I have never been so insulted. Put that slop down now, right away."

"Ha-ha-h—" This has to be a game, right? She's a top. Okay. I can deal with that. "I'm—"

"I'm not joking. Do as I say, cunt."

What's up with the threats. If I'd known she was that picky about the wine she drinks I'd have run out to the liquor store. Okay, forget the wine. Out of sight, out of mind.

"I'm really sor—"

She's spinning on her heel so fast like that Saturday morning cartoon figure. What was his name?

Metal zooming towards me.

Her fist.

"—ry—"

I can't stand. I'm falling. Scream. My jaw won't move. God, the pain. I can't get up. Oooh, cold. She's pouring the white Zin on my face. Oh Jesus that stings.

My eyes are tearing.

Can't focus.

Is that a dick between her legs?

SCREAM.

A gurgle.

Must scream. The neighbors are light sleepers. They'll hear the noise and call the police. They'll rescue me from this nightmare.

That's it. This can't really be happening.

Scream. Nothing. It is a nightmare. That's why I can't scream. It's a bad dream. Wake up. Wake up.

"Wake up, Melanie. I don't like my dates to fall asleep on me."

My head—upwards. Neck—back. A gloved hand slaps my face. Rubber smell. It's like a hospital. Scream. Try.

"Save your breath, my dear, short Melanie. You'll only choke on your delightful little panties which I've thoughtfully balled into your throat."

Coughing.

"Don't try spitting them out. It's useless. They're strapped in with one of the legs of your pantyhose."

Kicking. My leg won't move. Oh God. Paralyzed, bent over something. My vision—blurred. Where am I?

Laure grabs my hair, yanks my head upwards. My jaw—wobbling. The pain—killer.

"Hello, Melanie, it's me, Laure. It's no use struggling. I tied your arms and legs to your adorable little sofa with the other leg of your pantyhose. I had to cut through the slut-soaked crotch to split them in two, so I don't think you'll be able to break free. You'd need a knife, and well, I'm just not that stupid. I am thoughtful though. I know how sensitive you are to your—shall we say, imperfection—so I took the time to put your shoes back on you. Your feet wouldn't have touched the ground otherwise because you're so fucking short."

She's blowing me a kiss and letting go of my hair. My head falls.

Her high heels clicking on the floor.

Follow her movements. What's she doing? Oh I feel sick. The pain in my neck. Why me? What did I do to deserve this?

"Now, Melanie, I want you to know you're going to die, but first I have to amuse myself with you, and in the process I'll help you attain perfection."

What?

Die.

Dead.

Murdered.

No, I don't want to die.

Thrashing. Can't break free. Wimp. Fight. Do something.

Can't.

Crying, sobbing, begging. Please, please, please, let me go.

"Oh don't grovel so. It's not becoming. Welcome death is the only success you'll ever know in your meaningless life. You might be the first of a new series of victims, but you remind me so much of that last prostitute I killed in Oakland before I moved to San Francisco. What was her name? Ah yes, Nikki. Little Nikki she called herself. So small. So cute. So pathetic. She begged too. She had the nerve to say she had a child, as if that would sway me. Have mercy. Think of my baby, she blurted. She showed me a picture of the little brat in a delightful cross she wore around her neck. How could I take the child's mommy away? Easy. I strangled her, possessed her bottom and hung her from the ceiling fan, and I took the cross as a souvenir of her sorry life. It was after Nikki's obnoxious pleadings that I decided to gag my victims. Your ridiculous soap opera lives are of no concern of mine. You don't have a child, do you? An invalid aunt? A retarded brother? A disabled mother? An alcoholic father? Any of the above? All of the above?"

Shaking my head. Why bother? Just stop taunting me.

"That's good, but it wouldn't make any difference if you did. I've never shown any mercy. Not when I killed my babysitter. Or her boyfriend. My father actually begged me to spare my mother. Can you believe that? I must say, I was rather ashamed to be a part of that gene pool, but I have more than made up for his weak shortcomings. Since

I began my crusade I've perfected fifty-nine useless people. You're the sixtieth and the first to be dispatched by Mister Perfection. I hope you're honored."

No. Shaking my head.

Face slapping. Doesn't hurt. Beyond pain. She can't hurt me anymore.

"Rude short slut, how dare you not appreciate the importance of this moment. I've planned tonight for years. My killing career has been a rehearsal for this moment. I was destined to kill you and all those that will follow. It all began when I found that delicious double-dong in a smutty store on Hollywood Boulevard in Los Angeles. I couldn't believe my luck. I'd migrated southwards to avoid the Berkeley jogger murder investigations. Imagine my delight when I'm browsing through the shelves with no specific purchase in mind, and I'm presented with the sex toy incarnation of my philosophy of the bedroom and life next to a complete set of the divine Marquis' work. It was as though he were sending me a message, a command from beyond the grave to begin perfecting useless people just like you. Now, don't you feel special? No need to answer. I'll take your pathetic whimpering and shaking as a resounding yes.

"For several years I experimented on the occasional degenerate until I'd perfected my technique and accumulated a sufficient arsenal of dildo weaponry. I've been very careful, buying Mister Perfections and other nasty devices in various disguises, by mail order, from a number of stores throughout Southern California. I moved back to the Bay Area where there are such fertile concentrations of victims, and tonight I'm declaring war on all imperfections. The short, the fat, the tall, the weak, the stupid, the boring—no one will be safe."

The rusting of material. Static charge of nylons. Must be undressing. This is it. Say a prayer. Our Father who art in—

"Now, my dear Melanie, look up."

—Heaven. Hallowed be thy—

"Oh dear, you are going to be difficult."

—name. Thy kingdom come—

Unzipping my dress. Yanking my head backwards. Knotting my hair to my bra strap. My hair. My neck. The pain.

"Well, at least breasts are useful for something besides being the source of all Evil. I'm so glad you wore a bra. That's better. Now, look at me."

—Thy will be done—

She's lifting the hem of her skirt. Her pantyhose pushed down. An erect cock sticks out. I think it's a cock. It's very small. She's stroking it.

"You are an imperfect slut, Melanie Courtland. I am Laure Dearside. I am perfect. It is my duty to eradicate all imperfections. The very fact that you gaze on my perfect beauty denigrates it. This shall be the first of your punishments from which you will evolve into the slime and muck from which you came, making the world a more perfect place for me and my dear, dear brother, Mark."

She—he—is sliding a metal cylinder over—his—her—its cock. Aiming it at me. Cylinder—spikes. No, no, no. Not my eyes. Not my eyes.

"Closing your eyes will do no good. The eyelid offers no protection against my Steely Dan. Be brave. Watch as you attain perfection."

Squeeze my eyes shut even tighter. She's laughing at me. "You're so pathetic."

She's gripping my head with her hands. Vice-like. I can't move. I can't struggle.

"Take solace, my dear Melanie. If you think this is painful, just you wait. After I'm done with your face, Mister Perfection will possess your anus and your vagina."

—In Earth, as it is in Heaven.

Amen.

I'm at peace.

Steel against my cheek. The dildo up to my eye socket. Inching forward, scratching my face. So much for prayers.

I'm quaking.

She's thrusting.

Screaming bile and choking on my retching.

She's alternating, left and right. Oh dear Christ, my head's exploding. First one eye and then the other. Searing, burning pain. Screaming. Gagging. Vomit is dripping from my nose, mixing with what's dripping down my cheeks. Struggling, but it only makes the pain worse.

How stupid I was not to think she'd hurt me as much as she could.

Time slowing.

Pain growing.

I'm imaging my face, bloody holes where blue eyes once were. A voice coming through the numbing rush in my ears. "You shouldn't have moved to San Francisco, Melanie. I knew you'd end up like this."

That's what Mother will say at my funeral.

My funeral? So scared of dying just a few moments ago, but now I'm more worried about not dying. What if Laure leaves me like this? I'd kill myself. Jump off the Golden Gate. I want to die. Please kill me.

Throbbing pain.

It's Mother again. "I warned you, Melanie, but you wouldn't listen. You had to move to San Francisco because of your deviant lifestyle. Well, I hope you're happy now."

No, Mother, I'm not.

White hot heat down my face. White light. Death.

I can't feel anymore.

Dying. Is that the white light? It is. Thank you, thank you, thank you.

"Hmmmmm, a fine face fuck. I had quite a wonderful orgasm. Don't worry. I practiced safe sex. I wore a condom inside my Steely Dan."

She's laughing.

Fainting.

Hollowness.

Slapping me. Where's the white light? I can't see it. Where is it?

"Say hello to Mister Perfection, too short Melanie bitch. I'm sorry you can't see this. I must remember in subsequent perfectings to show my victim the guest of honor first. He is spectacular with two big, swollen, vibrating cockheads. He's huge, and all the veins bulge. He's at least two feet long and two, maybe three, inches in diameter."

Hands on my ass, probing. Ramming the dildo inside. My bottom's exploding. Pooing myself. She's bending the dildo around. My insides are twisting. Thrusting the other end into my pussy. Never felt anything so big.

My ass and pussy—one massive hole. Vibrations up my spine. Shaking. Head's ringing. Buzzing. Louder.

More words. Doesn't he know I can't hear anymore. Wires wrap around my throat. Flesh constricts. Tighter. Roaring. Blackness.

"I—shall—save—your—shoes—as—a—monument—to—your—imperfection."

She's working with the straps on my shoes. My feet swollen. Ankles too. She can't undo my shoes. Hah, hah, Laure. Even the perfect fail.

Silence.

Where is she?

Click of heels.

Breath against skin. Wires tighter. Whispers.

"You—can't—cheat—Nature—imperfect—slut—I'm—taking—your—shoes."

Sharp cold metal down my face.

Scratches down my spine.

It's a knife. A knife. Over my bottom. Down my legs, to my ankles. A knife.

Burning tears my skin. Sawing backwards and forwards,

tearing, flesh disintegrating. The pain, the pain, each stroke something from the fires of hell.

"Now you'll be even shorter, imperfect slut Melanie."

Her voice is clear. I'm calm. The pain? Gone. Numbness. Am I dead?

Fuck you—can't speak. Think it. Fuck you, Laure and your little dick and your sick brother Mark. You can't hurt me anymore. I've won.

"What was that? Did you want to say something."

Warm metal slices. No gag. Cough my panties out. Words come.

"Fuck you and your little dick."

"Why how rude. After all I've done for you, Melanie. I'd say you've really put your foot in your mouth now."

She's laughing. Prying my mouth open. Bite her—jaw won't work. Ramming something into my mouth. One. Two. Three. Four. Five. Five little piggies.

Wire—neck—tighter. Pussy—empty. Oh no. One. Two. Three. Four. Five little piggies.

There's the white—.

"VIOLETTA. VIOLETTA. NO."

Ellen's standing over me, a knife held limply in one hand, Melanie's shoes in the other. I look down at my feet. There's blood everywhere.

I can't feel my feet.

I scream.

SIX

I MUST LOOK like Norman Bates to poor Violetta when I finally free her from Melanie's tightly-bound platforms and she comes out of the shoefuck.

I don't know which one of us is more afraid, but her scream at least shakes me out of my rookie-like freeze. It doesn't take me long to realize I've acted stupidly. I panicked. It's as simple as that. Thanks to a few months of being in love, years of police training was lost in a matter of seconds.

I know exactly when I started to lose it. I hated watching bruises swell around her eyes. I knew what the Dildo Killer was doing to her. I tried to stop her from thrashing as he toyed with her, but she couldn't be calmed. When her ankles swelled and she began to choke I had to intervene. I struggled with the straps but I couldn't budge them. The shoes wouldn't come off. Violetta's ankles were turning a ghastly color, her skin was cracking, so I tried to cut the straps with a pair of nail scissors, but the patent leather was too tough.

I ran into the kitchen and grabbed the first knife I found. It was a carving knife, and it probably wasn't too smart of me to go for something so big, but I was hysterical. I wasn't thinking like a well-trained ex-cop. I was a woman in love scared of losing her lover. I knew blow-by-sick blow what was happening to Violetta. I had been the first detective on the Melanie Courtland crime scene. One of the beat cops was throwing up by the front door. There was blood and gore everywhere. I remember thinking that the thing tied over the chair couldn't possibly have been human. I did my job like a good cop, and then weeks later when I read the Coroner's report I was violently ill. It all came back. All the feelings I'd suppressed overwhelmed me.

Those horrible reminders went through my mind as I pried through the ankle straps, only now Violetta Cutrero's name was substituted for Melanie Courtland's. I chastised myself for letting Violetta have her way, and I became more panicked, slicing away at the shoes with greater force. The bindings gave way after a few strong slices and one shoe came off easily. Violetta slumped. She was breathing, but seemed to still be under the shoefuck influence, so I attacked the other shoe. As I sawed off the straps her free foot kicked out and the knife skidded off the shoe and stuck into me.

The wound wasn't that deep, but it gushed. It was a strange feeling. Watching my own blood drip down on the unconscious Violetta pulled the floor out from under me. I almost passed out. If she hadn't come to and screamed, I would have keeled over on top of her. That I was holding a knife just doesn't bear thinking about.

Violetta said the first thing she thought was that I'd chopped her feet off to save her from dying, the way a wolf will gnaw its foot off rather than be caught in a trap. No wonder she screamed.

DESPITE ALL SHE'S been through in Melanie Courtland's shoes, once she realizes it is me that is injured, Violetta sets aside her pain and comes to my rescue. She makes me sit down. I watch my blood drip on the floor, and I feel so useless. As bad as my hand throbs, I think my ego has been damaged more. Here I am, determined to protect Violetta from the side effects of her powers, and yet it is me that needs help. To her credit, Violetta doesn't slap me, like I've done in many similar situations throughout my police career. I've never been very patient with hysterical women. She steadies me, strokes my hair and holds me close to her. She cleanses and bandages my hand before she cleans herself and nurses her wounds. All the while she talks softly, calming me down from the waves of cold shock that wash over me. It is a side of her I've never seen. She's always seemed the vulnerable one, and yet here she is as steady as I am shaky.

She wants to call an ambulance, but I refuse to consider it. I don't want to attract attention. Drawing from another facet of my policing experience, I know knife wounds after midnight don't get treated as kitchen accidents. A black and white's usually dispatched as well because it's either domestic violence or a gang fight and the paramedics don't want to go in alone. In our neighborhood they'd eliminate the gang trouble and figure rich lesbian bitch fight. The Cop that Killed the Dildo Killer doesn't need that kind of publicity. We've lived an anonymous existence in Stinson, and I am determined to keep it that way.

Stinson is an isolated community. The local medical center is only open during the day. It takes us an hour to reach the nearest hospital emergency room. We drive over the hill into Greenbrae. I steer with my right hand while Violetta shifts gears. I didn't realize she didn't know how to drive. Now is a hell of a time to find out. With so much pain it's difficult to concentrate on the winding road so we drive very slowly. I hold my bandaged left hand elevated in the late night chill.

While the bruised, battered, hobbled and exhausted Violetta waits in the Jeep I tell the emergency room doctor I was preparing a late night oyster snack, and I slipped with the shellfish knife. The young MD recognizes me, and we exchange a few witticisms about how funny it is that I had injured myself in the kitchen when I'd managed to escape the Dildo Killer in the bathroom. Several hours, numerous excuses and twenty stitches later Violetta and I team-drive home with the sunrise chasing our backs.

BACK AT THE beach neither one of us can sleep. Adrenaline still pumps. We sit on the porch, wrapped in blankets, cuddling close to each other's curves. We share a giant mug of brandy-spiked milky coffee. The cool morning breeze on my bandaged hand feels good. Or maybe it's the pain killers the doctor gave me. It's probably all these things—Violetta, the ocean air, the pills and the hot toddy. I feel pretty darn good.

"I never realized you didn't know how to drive," I say, just wanting to chat.

"It didn't come up. It's usually not the kind of thing prospective partners ask each other."

"I just assumed. I thought everybody in California knew how to drive."

"Well I don't, okay? When most kids were begging for a car I was working in Dad's shoe repair store searching for fuckshoes. I rarely went out. The world came to me. Sometimes I took BART to San Francisco and buses around Oakland. I didn't need a fucking car. I was only interested in foot power. Cars are only good for backseat sex or drive-by blow jobs. And after Mom and Dad were killed in a car, you couldn't get me near one. Then I moved to San Francisco, and you should know that for an ordinary person a car's a liability there. It either gets ripped off or becomes a ticket magnet. Parking costs a fortune. I stuck to cable cars, trams, buses or my own two smelly feet."

"Do you think you ought to learn to drive now that we're living over here?"

"I don't plan on going anywhere."

"What if we have another emergency? What if I'm not here? Then you're stuck. I can teach you. You did great shifting gears when I clutched."

"Maybe. I'll think about it."

"We shouldn't waste any time. I'll be on publicity tours in a few months. What if something happens when I'm traveling?"

"I'll have to rely on the cruelty of strangers."

"Be serious. I worry."

"Don't. And I am serious. Cars scare me. I'd rather take my chances with a nutcase than a car. Mom and Dad would be alive if they hadn't missed the A's fan bus to Candlestick. They took their car and look where it got them. Flattened under the collapsed freeway. So if I get stuck, I'm staying put."

"Violetta, that was a freak accident, an earthquake."

"Yeah, so? You're saying I need a car in case of an emergency and those are the kind we get in California. I'm saying I don't need to drive. I'd stay among the ruins."

"Violetta, I worry. We're so isolated here. It took us an hour to get to the hospital. And it's not just natural disasters or weirdoes that concern me. What about when I go on my trips. Don't you want to come and see me off? And pick me up?"

"That's not fair."

"You can't take a bus to or from the airport from here. A taxi would cost a fortune. If you had a car you could pick me up at the airport, and we'd have sex in the backseat."

"Not if we're driving. If we took a taxi we could do it to pass away the commute."

"We'd distract the driver. No, if you picked me up we'd park somewhere and make up for lost time. Isn't that romantic? Sexy? C'mon, indulge me." I broke into a favorite old song of mine, "I can see paradise by the dashboard light."

Violetta winces at my attempt at rock and roll.

"Jeez, Ellen, enough with the classic rock, okay? If it'll shut you up, you can teach me to drive. Okay? Satisfied? And you can fuck me in the backseat if it'll satisfy your long lost teenage fantasy. And whatever car we get for me, it had better have an awesome sound system so I can play my music loud. And don't get the wrong idea. I still don't like cars or driving. I'll be your reluctant chauffeur, and not that often. Only when I have to."

I hug Violetta, smothering her with kisses. What can I say? I'm high on Violetta and thanks to the ocean, pills and booze and our recent adversity I don't mind showing her all she means to me. With my help, we can banish the ghosts from the past and have a future together.

I need this small victory. Violetta's near death experience in Melanie Courtland's shoes terrified me, and I have to talk about it.

"Neither one of us understands your power, and it scares me. When you have shoesex you come. It's exactly like the original thing. You thrash and moan and move as if you're having sex, but when you're experiencing sexual violence you feel the pain, but the injuries are muted. You suffer bruising where the original wearer was mutilated. If the injuries are reduced, what about the pain?"

"As far as I'm concerned it's the same agony."

"I'm not so sure. You didn't die. There's no way to know if your perceived pain is the same as that of the victim, but if you'd actually experienced the same level of horrors as Melanie Courtland, I wouldn't have had to visit an emergency room right now. I'd be IDing your body at the morgue."

"Can we talk about something else?"

"I'm sorry. I just thought it would help if we got it off our chests. Let me just say this, and then I'll shut up. I think I figured it out. Maybe it's because shoesex is just that—shoe sex. Your power is designed to transmit sexual feelings, not violent ones. Violence during sex is transmitted but only on the sexual wavelength. From my encounter with Tamayo we know it doesn't work with simple happiness without sex. Shoesex must be like a radio tuned to receive a specific station. Interference can get through, but it's masked by the primary signal. What do you think?"

Violetta shrugs her shoulders.

"I think those painkillers are making you loopy."

"Don't you want to understand your power?"

"No, Ellen, I don't. Whenever I think I've got it figured out then my power surprises me, usually in a bad way, so I've given up trying."

Violetta seems so comfortable and safe in my arms, our fingers entwined, wrapped around the same coffee mug. I want to keep the demons at bay forever. I hug her with my good arm and she winces. I've been focusing so much on my pain I'd forgotten how badly she must feel.

"Do you need to see a doctor?"

"No. I'll be okay in a few days and several long, hot soaks in the Jacuzzi. Once the bruising goes down I'll feel much better."

"Just look at us. We look like we've been in a dockwork-ers' bar fight."

"Did we win?"

"Yeah, you should have seen the other guys."

We laugh, and I can tell it hurts her, so I take the op-portunity to make one more point.

"One thing's for sure, Violetta, no more victims' shoes. I'm putting my foot down there. Hah-hah."

She doesn't object. This is a good sign.

"You're getting more and more like me every day, Ellen, using silly jokes to make uncomfortable points."

She's right, but it's no joke. We've got more than enough information about Randy Warren III and all of his incarnations. While she waited for me to be stitched up in the emergency room Violetta sat in the Jeep and filled two cassettes about the Melanie Courtland incident. Add that to her experiences in the DK's shoes, plus the information in the police files and we have enough background to write several books. Whether we can do one by the looming deadline is another matter, but for now that pressure can wait.

"How about a hot bath?" I ask her.

"That's another of my quirks you're picking up. Changing the subject whenever you get exposed."

"And you're sounding like a know-it-all cop."

"Then we're made for each other. They say people look like their pets after many years, or that couples who've been together for decades look and sound alike. If we're picking up each other's habits after only a few months then we're an ideal match."

"Violetta, how sweet. I knew from the moment I met you that underneath that tough exterior lurked a sentimental softy."

"Well it was love at first sight. I threw up at your feet and you threw me in jail."

"Seems like a lifetime ago, but you're right. It was love at first sight. You changed my life. Within two days of knowing you I gave up everything I thought I believed in. You gave me back my life. You're very special, Violetta."

"A lot has happened, hasn't it? We've done, seen and survived more in these last few months than most couples ever see in their lifetimes."

"We're over the worst of it."

"Are we? I hope so. I'm not so sure I can do this killing

thing again. Last night really scared me. I'm only nineteen. I'd really like to see twenty."

Violetta's lip quivers. She looks down. I lift up her chin with my hand.

"Hey, it's over. I'm not going to let any harm come to you. You changed my life. I can change yours. You're safe with me. Now how about that bath? You'll feel way better. You've been riding on fumes. It's okay to unwind and relax. Let's go."

I stand and hold out my good hand. She chokes back tears and forces a smile.

"A bath would be nice. Every muscle in my body aches."

"Come on. I'll run it for you. I have one good hand to scrub your back with."

I fill the claw-foot tub with steaming water and a chemistry set of salts, herbs and bubbles. The bathroom smells nice. While the tub's filling I throw away the blood soaked towels. I make sure all the blood splatters have been wiped away from the tile. I want to throw away Melanie's shoes, but Violetta might get angry. Shoes, even ones with horrible memories, are special to her. They're like shrines. So I wipe them clean and put them next to the garbage can in as suggestive manner as possible without sticking them in there. When Violetta comes in all scrawny and pink and naked and bruised she seems relieved that I've disposed of the mess. She deliberately doesn't look at the shoes. I pour her a glass of wine. She takes a sip and slides under the water to her ears. I sit on the side of the tub admiring her body. Even with bruises, she is gorgeous. Then I tell her.

"I want to throw away Melanie's shoes."

I expect her to jump out of the bathtub chattering like the dolphins that leap out of the Pacific at sunset.

She stays calm. She speaks, but doesn't look at me.

"Wait until we've finished the book."

"You're not going to wear them again. No way."

"You never know."

"No, Violetta."

"Ellen, listen to me. I don't want to put them on anymore. I don't want them around either. They're a reminder of all that's bad about my power, but you can't throw them away. It doesn't feel right. Call it superstition, but if you throw them away something horrible will happen to you. I can't let that happen. When the time is right, I'll throw them away, and not before. You've got to trust me on this. It's my power. I have to live with it."

"Promise me you won't put them on without me being there."

"I promise. With any luck I won't need to wear them ever again. I remembered everything that happened. It was so clear."

"Did you learn anything new?"

"There was a lot more background. He gave so many details of earlier killings."

"Was there anything significant? You thought the shoes would contain a special message."

"I'm not sure. There was so much. One mystery's been cleared up. I found out why he took Nikki's cross, the one I liberated from his souvenir closet."

"I'm not following you. How did we go from Melanie to Nikki?"

"Oh, the usual. He was bragging about earlier kills. Nikki begged for her life because she had a kid. In the cross there's a picture of the kid. She showed it to him. Randy thought it was very irritating that she'd plead for her life because she was a single mother and there was no one to look after her kid. He strangled her, buttfucked her and took the cross. Melanie was pleading, so the DK told her it would do no good, using Nikki as an example. It's all on the tapes. And more. While you were being stitched up I filled two cassettes. We're going to have to figure out how to get all we've learned into the book. We can't exactly say how we know this stuff. Any ideas?"

"I could say we found the DK's diary. Or why give any substantiation at all? Maybe we don't have to say how we know. If anyone asks we can say we're protecting our sources. Journalists do it all the time. This isn't a court of law. We don't have to tell the whole truth."

"They'll ask. Of course they will. It'll be the first or second question out of Oprah's lips."

"Then I'll be evasive. I've had years of experience with people who don't tell the full story. I've learned from the best liars in the world. I can pull the wool over Oprah's eyes, don't you think?"

"Sure."

Violetta submerges herself under the bubbles. When she surfaces I hand her a towel to wipe away the water and bubbles from her eyes.

"You know, Ellen, we could leave out a lot of the details."

"We could, but I think it would be a shame. We know things no one else knows. The cross thing will have people in tears. It'll show Randall Warren for what he was. Let's leave the details in. I don't mind lying. If pressed we'll say we found the DK's diary."

"What if they ask to see it."

"Then you'd better get writing."

My answer is a splash of soapy bath water.

THE NEXT FEW months are dedicated to finishing the manuscript. We have precious little free time. What we do have we spend on driving lessons and occasional tired sex, but mostly our life revolves around writing.

As we work our way through Randy's killing career we develop a detailed chronology of his murders, starting in 1971 in Seattle when he killed his babysitter and ending on Halloween 1990 immediately after his ninety-eighth victim when Violetta executed him. We line one wall of the study with victims' names, dates of the crime, locations and

Randy's M.O. We constantly refer to the wall as we work on the book, making sure we have our chronology correct. As the deadline approaches we are under so much pressure to finish the book we hardly have any time to ourselves. Gone are the driving lessons and the tired sex. Now it's just writing, editing and rewriting. We complete the manuscript a week early. We called it a night after killing a bottle of champagne, or was it two? I can't remember. I wake about three in the morning, my head spinning. Violetta isn't in bed. I find her in the study staring at the chronology.

"What are you doing?"

"Something's bothering me. Look."

Violetta has scribbled various notes next to Randy's killings. My head is fuzzy. My eyes blurry. I can't be bothered to read her chicken scratch now.

"Did we get a date wrong? We can fix the manuscript in the morning before we Fed Ex it. Come back to bed."

"No, look closer. There's no error. This has been bothering me for months now. I couldn't put my finger on it until we were done with the grunt work, and I could think straight. This is the message the Dildo Killer left me. Look."

I rub my eyes and peer at the notes. They describe various events in Violetta's life—Violetta Conceived, Violetta Born, Violetta's First Birthday, Mom and Dad's Anniversary, Violetta Discovers Her Power, Violetta Loses Her Virginity, Mom and Dad's Death and so on.

"Wow, what a bunch of coincidences."

It is a stupid thing to say, but in my defense let me say my mind is still curled up in our nice, warm, empty bed nursing a budding hangover.

"Ellen, you know there are no coincidences. Things happen for a reason. Everything is connected. It's fate. Look, Randy began his killing when I was conceived."

I speak through a yawn.

"You don't know that date exactly."

"Maybe not, but Dad always joked he and Mom did it

on January 12 so I'd be born on the Italian-American's favorite holiday, Columbus Day, October 12. Randy made his first kill—the babysitter—on January 12. He killed a small child in San Jose the day I was born."

I don't want to get drawn in to this line of thinking. I always believed that Lee Harvey Oswald acted alone. I don't want Violetta consumed by conspiracy theories, but I have to admit to myself, this is weird. Time to play the skeptic.

"There are so many killings that had nothing in common with significant events in your life."

"Yes, but every significant event in my life is related to a killing. Without fail."

"What are you saying?"

"Somehow, Randy Warren and I were related."

"Like a long lost brother given up for adoption? Come on, Violetta, that's so farfetched it's impossible."

"Not physically like a relative, but as in Good and Evil. I think I was given my power to stop him. It was my destiny."

"And you did."

"So why didn't my power disappear?"

"I don't know."

I know I sound exasperated. I don't want to, but we've been down this road so many times.

"Look, Violetta, forgive me. It's just that we've been over this, and no amount of talking is going to change the fact we don't know why you still have your power. Maybe it will go away with time. You've said you think you have your power to kill other killers. There's no way to know. I wish I had the answer, but I don't."

"Yeah, I know, but seeing all these dates lined up started me thinking. Maybe I don't have to be a killing machine. Don't you see? I could be free. Maybe that's somebody else's job. Maybe the Universe works to correct itself. Evil breaks out, so Good is created to combat it. For every killer, there is a designated executioner."

"So maybe you can live a normal life and not spend it chasing murderers. Is that what you're saying?"

"Yeah, wouldn't that be nice?"

She yawns.

"Wouldn't it?" I catch her yawn. "Let's go to bed and sleep on it."

I like this line of reasoning. I want her to stop right there on a positive note, so I take Violetta's hand and lead her back to the bedroom and under the covers. I spoon her, trying to make her fall asleep. It's not working. I can tell from her breathing she is wide awake.

"It could mean something else," she says.

Oh no, here it comes.

"Hmmmmm."

I know very well what she's talking about, but I don't want to feed her paranoia. If I don't respond, maybe she'll give up and doze off.

"Not losing my power. It could mean that Randy's Evil isn't over. He might be dead, but his Evil lives on. There's unfinished business out there."

Now I'm awake. I stroke Violetta's hair. I kiss her neck. It's time for me to play mother hen.

"Look, Violetta, you're working yourself up for nothing. You said yourself you can't figure out your power. It always surprises you, so you don't try to understand it. Do the same with this thing you've discovered. Yes, it's creepy the way all the dates line up, but that doesn't mean that you're locked in some kind of eternal battle. Randy Warren is dead and so are the things he did. Maybe you've still got your power so you can enjoy yourself. Have you ever thought of that?"

"No."

"Well maybe you should. Maybe the good fairy lets you keep your power as a reward for all the nastiness you endured in stopping Randy's Evil. Now you can shoefuck yourself silly without a care in the world."

"You think?"

"Sure. You've more than paid your Karmic police dues. It's just as probable as Randy's Evil living on. And a lot nicer."

"Fuck, yeah. Could we be that lucky?"

Part of me says no way in hell, but I'll never let Violetta know that. She needs a cheerleader.

"Yes, of course we could. Why don't we start right now? All we've done for the last few months is do serial killer research and write."

"And have driving lessons."

"Shut up. Let's make love."

"You mean fuck."

"Yes, let's fuck."

"Okay. I love it when you talk dirty."

Violetta climbs on top of me. I know how to bury this bad power thing once and for all. I push her off.

"Just a minute."

"Fucking tease."

"I'll be right back."

I scurry out of the bedroom, bypassing the bathroom. "Where are you going?" Violetta yells after me. "You'll see," I yell back. I'm not going to give her a choice in the matter. I find what I'm after in the study. I wipe the dust off the shiny surfaces. I force my feet inside Melanie's platforms. They're a tight fit, but now that the straps have been sawn off I can work my toes in deep. I wouldn't want to walk very far in these toe crunchers, but that's no concern. I don't plan on being on my feet very long.

I teeter through the hallway, using my hands against the walls to steady myself on the five inch heels.

"I'm waiting," Violetta says seductively as she hears me coming. "This had better be good."

I flounce into the bedroom doing my best imitation of a

naked stripper strutting her stuff. Violetta wolf-whistles, her shrill welcome tapering off as she sees the shoes on my feet.

"I thought—"

I don't give her a chance to object.

"I know what I said. And I meant it. No more victim's shoes. But this is better than throwing them away. We're going to obliterate what happened to Melanie with our own good fucking. Remember how Tamayo and Deeann doing it in Marsha's boots weakened the memory of Marsha's murder? That happened with a one time quickie. We have all night to make love over and over until Melanie and the memories of the bad side of your power are laid to rest."

She smiles.

"Ellen, you're wonderful."

I dive on the bed. We roll our bodies together, limbs entwining, pussies rubbing, pubic hair slicking with our wetness. We kiss. I squeeze Violetta's tiny breasts. She bites my nipples. We make love—we fuck—for hours. She eats me. I eat her. We eat each other. She fingers me. I finger her. We finger each other. Orgasms come like the distant crashing of the Pacific. Inevitable, constant, never-ending, some are tiny little ripples, others are loud, splashing monsters.

In one abbreviated night full of passion we make up for months of nun-like dedication to work. My body melts into the sheets. I loll, my eyes refusing to stay open one more second. Satisfied, exhausted, I fall asleep, Violetta's head resting on my cum-soaked butt.

IT'S LATE IN the day when I stir. Violetta's sitting on the edge of the bed, her back to me. She bends, pulling off a shiny blue platform from her foot. I start, sitting up wide awake. She turns, looks over her shoulder and smiles.

"Mission accomplished. Not a trace of Melanie or the Dildo Killer."

I hug her. There are tears in her eyes.

"That's the nicest thing anyone's ever done for me, Ellen. You gave me back the fun in my power."

I kiss her forehead.

"The fun has only just started, Violetta. Get dressed. We're going shoe shopping. And you're driving."

SLINGBACKS

SEVEN

"'...'A TERRIFYINGLY INTIMATE insight into a serial killer's perverse reality.'"

"'After reading *The Cop That Killed The Dildo Killer*, all I can say is thank you Ellen Stewart for ridding the world of this monster. I sleep sounder now.'"

"Oh, oh, listen to this one. This is good. 'Stewart's captivating romp through Randall Warren's various killing sprees reads like a best-selling crime fiction novel. It's a real page turner. The scary thing is, it's all true.' If they only knew."

"Yes, well, they never will know, will they? Here's a good one. 'The world needs more cops like Ellen Stewart. Then we'd have less sickos like Randall Warren III.' We should send that one to Tamayo, the Chief of Police and the Board of Inquiry."

"They must be hating life right about now. Look at all these reviews. Ellen, you're a fucking star."

"That makes you a star fucker."

"And proud of it too. You're number one on all the best-seller lists, and we're going to live happily ever after. Do you have to go on this publicity tour?"

I knew the answer, but I had to ask the question, like when a kid says "Do I really have to eat my Brussels sprouts?"

"I have to. You know I have to. The deal with the publisher requires that I support the book for the next six months. That was why I got such a big advance so we could buy this place outright, remember."

"The advance isn't refundable. If we don't sell one goddamn book we're cool."

"Technically, but we've got very little left in the bank. Wouldn't it be nice to never have to worry about working again? Most people never get that chance unless they win the lottery. We're lucky. With just a little bit more sacrifice now we'll live in luxury for the rest of our lives. My agent thinks I could make ten million easy off the combined sales and ancillary rights, but he needs me out there selling the heck out of it. We make almost two dollars off each book sold. That means to cover the advance we'll have to sell one million books. I might be on the best-seller list but we're nowhere near that many sold. Yet."

"Yet can't be very far away. Look at all these reviews. *The New York Times*. *The Los Angeles Times*. *People* goddamn *Magazine*. The fucking *Wall Street Journal* even mentions you as one of the publishing industry's hopes to lead it out of the doldrums. 'Finally a major publisher gets it right with a multimillion dollar advance for a tell-all book. Ex-lead detective Ellen Stewart's must-read story of the hideous serial killer that plagued San Francisco, and as she reveals, many other places, promises a major return on investment for a publisher that has in the past spent wildly, but not wisely.' You can't lose with press like that."

"All the more reason to capitalize upon it now, while I'm hot."

"You sound like your agent."

"It makes sense. This time next year I'll be in the bargain basement."

"Yeah, right."

"I'll only be gone for five days. I told them, no trips longer than a week. They're working with me. Won't you? I don't want to be away either, but moping isn't going to change things. It makes me feel bad, and I already feel rotten for leaving you. Even if it is only for a few days. We've talked about this over and over."

"Yeah, well, that was then. This is now. For real, not some hypothetical topic of conversation. You're going away tomorrow."

"If it bothers you that much you should change you mind and come along. I could hide you in my hotel room."

"Nah, I don't have a passport."

"I'm only going to New York."

"Exactly. A different country. I'll stay here and keep the home fries burning."

"Fires."

"No, I mean fries. I plan on surviving by eating nothing but potatoes while you're being wined and dined, and you know how I burn everything. How am I going to live without you to cook for me?"

"There's plenty of stuff in the freezer, and what do you mean, burn everything. You're a good cook."

"Ellen, wise up. I'm playing the martyr and cracking jokes because I'm so fucking sad. I'm going to miss you. Tomorrow will be the first night in six months that we've been apart. I know it's in our best financial interests, and that you're obligated, and it's only five days, but I still don't have to like it."

Ellen stops sorting through the publicity packet and itinerary that her agent Fed Ex'd so she'd have it to look over on the plane. Glossy photos of Ellen from the DK's apartment shoot scatter. She ignores the fallen images of herself and hugs me.

"I'll miss you too."

I pick up the Fed Ex box and the pictures.

"I guess your Fed Ex fuckshoe delivery will have to do. Just make it a juicy one."

"You bet. And you hold up your end of the bargain too."

"I will. I'll write so much I'll put Stephen King to shame."

"You know, that's the one thing about this trip I'm really looking forward to. I can't wait to read your stories. It's so nice of you to do that for me. I'll read them every night just before I fall asleep. It'll be like you're in bed with me."

"Don't have nightmares."

"They'll be sweet dreams of you."

Ellen kisses me on the forehead. There, silly, everything's all right now, the gesture seems to say.

"What shoes should I wear for my first shoefuck message to you from my publicity tour?" Ellen asks. She holds out her hand. "Come, help me choose."

I select a little open-toed slingback action, moderate heel, perfect for late-spring frigging in the Big Apple. Then I help Ellen pack. She's doing *Good Morning America* and a Barbara Walters interview as well as a bunch of bookstores, radio stations, newspapers and magazine interviews. Between our clothing uncertainty she packs enough outfits for a month. She fills one bag with shoes, a thoughtful mix of the practical with enough sexy extras to send a pair or two back to me. We call it an early night and cuddle. Ellen wants to get all passionate because she's going to be gone, but I don't want to celebrate her leaving at all. I just want to lie there because I don't want to send her off as though I'm not going to see her again. We should just treat this little PR jaunt as though she were going into the City for lunch. A five-day fucking lunch. Then I think, wouldn't I hate myself if something happened and I never saw Ellen again, so we fuck like bunnies and fall asleep all come-sweaty.

THE FLIGHT'S AT ten so we get a major early start given we're fighting traffic all the way. The shoe suitcase fits easily under the hood, but it takes both of us to lift her big suitcase into the backseat of my Bug. After I passed my driving test on the first go we bought a bright pink 1974 VW for my emergency transportation, and Ellen leaving is an emergency. Nine-point-nine on the Violetta scale. I don't know what I'm going to do on my own for five days. I don't much feel like writing my life story for Ellen. I'd rather tell it to her in person, curled up in her hotel bed-room, but I'm afraid to go along on these trips. Too many people might ask questions, and I'm not as good of a liar as Ellen.

We kill time at the airport eating crappy donuts. So much for the healthy diet, but what do I care? I feel like a con-demned woman waiting for my ten a.m. execution when United Airlines Flight 62 to New York's JFK airport takes off. We dally as long as possible, even to the point of the airline having to make an announcement for Ms. Ellen Stewart to proceed immediately to Gate 14.

Parting is not such sweet sorrow. It fucking sucks. Juliet was a stupid cunt anyway. How would she have felt watch-ing her main squeeze walk down a corridor to a plane that could crash, to a city full of beautiful, sophisticated people who'll want a piece of her. It is not sweet sorrow standing there with my chin quivering, trying not to cry so that Ellen won't run back down the corridor likes she's done twice before to comfort me. She waves. I wave, a forced smile stretching my face. She turns the corner. They shut the gate. I plaster my nose to the glass and wave at the little airplane portals unable to tell who the fuck is waving back. Once the plane pulls away I go in the bathroom and have a good cry. Christ, I'm a baby. She's only going to be gone for five days.

Five days. And nights. And notice I didn't say fucking days and nights. I'm so upset I can't even speak properly.

I feel like waiting at the departure gate for the five-day duration until it becomes an arrivals gate. I feel like I'm a dog in one of those Disney movies about an abandoned animal who faithfully waits in vain for her owner to return, but they never do so the poor animal goes in search of them through all sorts of harrowing adventures. Christ, I'm a sorry case. This pathetic image of myself as Old Yeller convinces me to get my ass home.

Driving out of the airport I feel sad, hollow, alone, empty, depressed, a veritable human thesaurus of melancholy. I need familiarity in my life, so on the way back to Stinson it's inevitable that I stop off in the City at Tú Lan and have a hot, spicy Vietnamese lunch with a Saigon 33 chaser. I buy enough dishes to last a month. Some of them I don't even touch. They're just packaged up, and I take them to go. This restaurant was my hangout with Marsha. We'd come here for lunch and dinner. We had some of our best chats over Tú Lan. I wish she was here to comfort me. I do not like being alone.

I drive by Shoe Leather, only it's not Shoe Leather any more. It's Saigon Shoe Repair. The Pink Panty is still there. I toy with going in to see Harry, but I'd have to put on a happy face and tell him how great things are or he'd worry. He's such a nice guy. He deserves better than me raining glumness over him, and anyway, I just want to go home and be miserable. On my way to the bridge I stop off at Tower Records on Columbus and buy a bunch of depressing CDs. The Cure. Morrissey. An old Sisters of Mercy that I never bothered to get before now. Perfect slit your wrist music. It's a bright sunny day as I cross the Golden Gate, but it may as well be a foggy soup as my little pink Bug rattles to the sounds of doom and gloom. When I get home there's a message on the answering machine from Ellen. It's barely intelligible. She used the in-flight phone so it sounds like she's talking into a flushing toilet about loving me and missing me and calling me as soon as she gets to the hotel.

Which she does. We talk for an hour before she has to have dinner with her agent and publicist. She feels like royalty. Or a rock star. A limo picked her up at the airport and an assistant went over her schedule as she sipped champagne. She has a suite at the Plaza. She's too excited. I'm happy for her. After she hangs up I go for a walk along the beach, wondering which pair of fuckshoes I'm going to play with tonight. It should be a pair of Ellen's, or those strappy numbers she gave me for our first night of fuckage, but I just can't get myself in the mood because I'm feeling nostalgic. Maybe something from the past will do the trick? Maybe some of Marsha's. I never worked my way through all the ones she left me. I could put on Mom's sparkly high heels and have a once around the hotel room with her and Dad. Or if I really want to wallow in a sea of misery how about putting on little Nikki's rhinestone platforms and having Dad fuck his regular hooker up the ass before he slaps me around a bit? This is too fucking sad. I burst into tears and the seagulls laugh at me in that cackling fashion they reserve especially for stupid humans.

In the end I don't do any fuckshoes. That's how bad I feel. I just listen to my sad tunes over and over. Ellen calls me when she gets in from dinner. She's exhausted and a little tipsy. She has to be at the GMA studios early. She'll never be able to sleep. She's caught up in the whole Toast of the Town scene, but even so she wants to know how I'm doing. Fine, I lie. I'm really very miserable, but I don't want to dampen her mood. I'm so fucking considerate. She's planned a surprise for me, she says all coy. What is it, I ask, knowing that we'll go through the obligatory It Wouldn't Be A Surprise routine. We do. Just watch the show tomorrow, she says. Be sure to set your alarm and the

VCR, she reminds me. As if I'd forget Ellen's big moment.

Our big moment. That's right. It is *our* big moment.

I don't sleep much. In between empty-bed tosses and turns I try to write a story about my shoesex power for Ellen, but I never get past one lousy sentence. I finally fall asleep before I'm supposed to get up, but I'm so restless I actually beat the alarm clock to wakefulness. I have my morning coffee and wait through all the banal GMA gabbing about weather in places I couldn't give a fuck about, then Joan Lunden's smiling face holds up *The Cop That Killed The Dildo Killer* and asks us all to welcome Ellen Stewart.

I cheer. Ellen looks stunning, a real fox, a bit flushed, but sexy as a new pair of stilettos.

Speaking of which. . . .

Move the fucking camera down. I want to see her shoes. What pair did she choose for her national debut?

She crosses her legs, and I see.

The open-toed slingbacks. What a slut. No wonder she's flushed. She's laughing and joking and serious when required and the world's falling in love with my Ellen. How could they not? She is simply the most gorgeous woman on the planet. It may be only seven in the morning, but I'm horny as hell, so I rub myself watching Ellen on the boob tube. Joan asks all the standard Dildo Killer questions, and Ellen answers them just fine. Very fine. She handles the vigilante justice questions diplomatically.

"You're something of a heroine. Aren't you worried that others will follow your example and take justice into their own hands?"

"I go to great lengths in the book to point out that I didn't plan to take justice into my own hands, and that others shouldn't try to emulate my actions. What I did I did in a fight for survival. It's unfortunate it has become a rallying cry for lynch mobs, but I can't be responsible for that. It's more a reflection of how fed up people are with the justice system."

Nicely dodged, Ellen. Then Joan moves on into what it's like being a lesbian cop, and Ellen lands a few more good jabs at the macho pig powers that be, and I land a few good strokes in exactly the right place.

"What of your personal life? Was it difficult to maintain a relationship through all this turmoil?"

"When I was a cop it was impossible. I felt like I had to be better than the men I competed against. I sacrificed my home life to always be the one there when the department needed a warm body. During the Dildo Killer investigation I was consumed with catching the monster. I wouldn't have been good company. I was obsessed. It became very personal. That's why he came after me. He said so."

Oh nice touch, Ellen. Excellent style points for consistent lying.

"And now? Has your life calmed down since you were, shall we say, retired?"

The camera zooms in on Ellen. I rush over and kiss the screen, then I lay myself down spread-legged wide and beat a tattoo on my clit.

"Retirement's fine. Yes, now it's much better. I've found the love of my life. We're very happy."

Ellen looks right at the camera. It pulls back to let Joan into the picture. Ellen crosses her legs. The slingback dangles.

"That's wonderful, Ellen."

Damn right it is. I come, and I'm not even wearing shoes. Joan wishes Ellen the best of luck and recommends that everyone rush out and buy the book. Ellen smiles at the camera. It's as if she's smiling right at me, saying, Violetta, I know you were fingering yourself while I was on national television displaying my feet and the shoes you chose for me.

All warm and squishy and happy from a great jill off, I

know today will be a better day. Full of inspiration I start writing my stories for Ellen. I begin at the beginning when I first discovered my power. Words flow like my juices just did. I tell her about being ten and dressing up as the Bride of Frankenstein for Halloween when I slipped on my Mom's shoes and found Dad on top of me doing things with his "Love Monster," as my mom called it. And yes, just to make sure I don't forget anything I put those sparkly high heels on again and see and feel it all again.

"WE SHOULD BUY stock in Fed Ex," I tell Ellen, all out of breath. I'd only that moment returned from dropping off the overnight package for her. I hear the phone ringing as I fumble with the house keys. She has a few spare minutes at her hotel before going to a dinner with an Editor from *Time*. She's going to be on the cover next week. But that's not what she wants to talk about. She wants to tell me she'd mailed the shoes from GMA, right after the show. I tell her she looked awesome, and I played with myself. She gets a big kick out of that. She won't tell me what she did in the shoes to make them fuckshoes, but I have a pretty good idea. I tell her I'd just sent off the first installment of my sordid life story. It'll be at her hotel by ten tomorrow. The shoes will be at the beach likewise, she says. She has to run. Duty calls.

I go back to typing. This life-story business is a rush.

ELLEN'S SHOES ARRIVE the next day. I had been right in my shoefuck suspicions. Ellen, the horny little cunt, had played with herself before the GMA interview, slipped a pair of Ben Wa balls up her pussy and a small butt plug up her ass. Every time she changed position in the interview chair little tremors of pleasure flashed through her. During the interview she thought naughty things about Joan Lunden's legs and brought herself off in the bathroom right after the show thinking of me.

I swoon. I'm retarded in love.

In those slutty slingbacks I feel Ellen's exhilaration, the rush of being a star and her desire to share it with me. I come in the GMA green room bathroom, my hands lodged between my legs as a publicity flunkie waits for me outside, eager to rush me to the next appointment, probably thinking that I'm in the bathroom because I'm so nervous. Afterwards I have a good laugh. Ellen brings a whole new meaning to the various recommended techniques for conquering stage fright.

I'm spazzed with happiness. My power allows me to be there with her, enjoying Ellen's fifteen minutes of fame as if it were my own. Throughout her summer public relations odyssey my power becomes a means to keep us together. I relish this good aspect of what not so long ago I viewed as a horrible burden solely for catching killers. It's strange. Ellen's trips apart from me bring us closer together because she gives me back the fun in my power. I love her more with every pair of shoes she sends me. Thanks to Ellen's masturbatory daring, in addition to Joan Lunden, I sit through intimate chats with Barbara Walters, Larry King, Johnny Carson, Donahue, Oprah and dozens of lesser media gods. I pass the ordeal of a four-hour book signing with a smile on my face and a wetness between my thighs. I admire Ellen's self-control. The lengths she goes to keep me inside her are amazing. Love makes us silly.

And in return I pour out the history of my power in print and send it to Ellen. The more she includes me in her daily grind, the more I tell her about growing up an Avenging Angel Sex Goddess. Writing my life story is a blast. I don't leave anything out. I initially was only going to tell her the cute little stories, but the more I write, the more I want her to know it all. Ellen gets the good and bad. Telling her the horrors I endured somehow belittles them, renders them just stories to be passed on. I particularly enjoy getting Nikki out of my system. Putting on those gaudy platforms and having my dad do me up the butt and slap me has always haunted me. Now I can say it doesn't bother me. Well, maybe a little, but at least I'm not frightened of those shoes anymore. They're actually pretty cool. Maybe one day I'll get Ellen to wear them when we fuck so Nikki can rest in peace, just like Melanie Courtland.

When I'd finished serializing my tale I'd compiled quite a tome. During one of the breaks in Ellen's travel schedule we box up my stories and place them and the computer disks in a safe deposit box. We don't want the truth falling into the wrong hands. Ellen is now a high profile public figure. The press pay attention to her moves, who she's seen with. There's going to be a movie about her. The film rights were sold to the Disco Slut herself, Onna Nomad, for an astronomical amount of money of which we get fifty percent. Fresh on the dancing heels of her multi-platinum obnoxious disco crap records, Onna has platinum blonde ambitions to be a serious movie star. The Disco Slut wants to play Ellen. There's talk of a meeting in Hollywood sometime in the next month so Onna can get to know The Cop that Killed the Dildo Killer. I told Ellen it was cool as long as Onna didn't choose the music for the movie. I'd hate to see the death of the Dildo Killer done to a disco beat. I offered to be the soundtrack selector. Ellen said she'd mention it to Onna, but I think my dear sweet Ellen was just humoring me.

I GO TO one book signing. It's in San Francisco at the downtown Books Inc. Ellen knows I am there. We drive in together, but don't act like a couple. I hang around at the rear of the store. The line stretches around the block. There are cops in line that want a signed copy. It's an amazing spectacle. I join the intestinal snake of patient fans and wait the six hours it takes to get to the front. It's frightening how popular she's become.

She plays it cool as I stick the book on the table in front

of her. She smiles at me as if I were just another adoring fan.

"Hi, to whom shall I sign it?"

"Oh, I don't know. Just put, 'To my biggest fan.' "

She signs with a flurry of her Sharpie, and I'm whisked to the checkout counter by a frazzled assistant where I shell out twenty bucks of which two are coming back to us. After worming my way out of the crush I read the inscription: "To My Biggest Fan From Your Biggest Fan. Happy Twentieth Birthday, Violetta. All my love, Ellen, October 1991."

My birthday isn't for another week. We hadn't talked about it, so I'm extra happy that she remembered.

I'm not so happy on the drive home.

"What shall we do on my birthday?"

"I've already made a few arrangements."

"What? Do tell."

"It's a surprise. Just plan on going out in style. All I'll tell you is that I've rented a limousine. Be prepared to leave at five. I have a one o'clock signing in Oakland, but I'll be back in time."

"What?

"I know it's a bother. I told them I wanted nothing on that day, but the publicist's assistant set it all up without checking with her boss and now the publisher and the store have run ads, so I can't back out. It's from one to three. No matter what, I'm leaving on the dot. I'll be back in time for the limo and our night out. You could come along if you want. Just like today. That was sneaky of you to wait in line."

"Like hell I will go back to Oakland. Didn't you read anything I wrote to you?"

"I read everything. You know I did."

"Then you should know I'm not going back to Oakland ever again."

"I just thought—"

– 125 –

"I wrote to you 'I've never been back to Oakland since, and I never fucking will.' I didn't say that for fun or effect. I meant it, and you know why. How could you even think of going there? Bad things will happen if you go there. The place doesn't exactly hold some of the best memories, you know."

"Well, neither does San Francisco, but you got over that."

"That's different."

"How so?"

"I can't explain. It just is."

"I can't cancel this signing."

"I'm not asking you to."

"Good."

"Good."

We don't speak the rest of the way back to Stinson. I know I'm being childish, but so fucking what. I don't know what pisses me off more, the signing on my birthday or Ellen assuming I'd go to Oakland with her, or her agreeing to do a signing there in the first place. Before the Jeep comes to a halt I jump out and run down the beach. I'm steaming.

Ellen finds me by the wave line. I'm skimming pebbles. I ignore her. She skims a pebble alongside mine, so I stop throwing and turn to face her. She's the first to speak.

"I'm sorry, Violetta. I should have thought more about all of your bad memories. We've recently done so well at putting the past behind us. I just didn't think it would be an issue. Forgive me?"

I realize how stupid I've been.

"I'm sorry too. I acted like a brat."

We kiss and make up, but I don't go to Oakland. No fucking way.

THE BIRTHDAY SURPRISE is a limousine ride. All the way to our mystery destination Ellen hums that damn "Do

You Know The Way" song, and I don't fucking get it. I mean, San Jose. What the fuck's in San Jose? Once we pass the City and we're on the 280 going south I give up trying to figure it out. I bet we're going to drive around the Bay in one big circle and end up back in the City. She has me completely fooled, until we pull up outside the San Jose Center for Performing Arts, and I see its sign announcing *La Traviata*.

"Back at the Pelican I promised you I'd take you to see *La Traviata*. It's not quite the Opera House, but it is your favorite opera. And this production is supposed to be excellent. San Francisco Opera was doing a Mozart thing, so I thought you'd prefer this. Even if it is in San Jose."

"Ellen, it's perfect."

I'm in tears as I dive on top of her and we kiss, rolling around the expansive seat of the stretch limo. My formal thrift shop dress rides up my thighs, but I don't care. What are limos for if not for love wrestling. The driver opens the door and gives a polite cough after he's treated to a great view of my ass. I'm sure he's seen every conceivable backseat entanglement before, but there just ain't no graceful way to dismount, so he gets a crotch shot too. And not just the driver. The good citizens of San Jose waiting patiently in line for the doors to open are shocked as I stumble out of the car in a state of disarray, giggling like a drunk rock star. If only I'd been clutching a super-expensive empty bottle of champagne, or better still, an empty Jack Daniels bottle, the image would have been killer perfect.

Ellen and I can't stop laughing as we make our way arm-in-arm to the door. She scored a private box. We cry through the entire opera. It is beautiful. I think of Mom and Dad and their gift of the record just before they were killed, and I think of Marsha and the time I took her to see *La Traviata* in San Francisco for her birthday, and I think of Ellen, my dear sweet beautiful Ellen, who makes me think not of the past, but of the future.

Our future.

My demons are buried.

"This is the best birthday I've ever had. I mean it. I know people say that kind of shit, but I do really mean it." I tell Ellen this as we enjoy a late supper at Rue de Paris, a— surprise, surprise—small French restaurant near the theater. "I feel like I'm finally over the bad things of the past."

"Me too," she says as we clink champagne glasses.

We fuck all the way back to Stinson. Ellen wears her slingbacks.

I HONESTLY BELIEVE we are over the past and Halloween confirms it. Ever since the Halloween after my tenth birthday October 31st has never been very much fun for me. This year is the one-year anniversary of my trick-or-treating the DK into lots of tiny little pieces, the one-year anniversary of Ellen taking the blame. I expect something nasty to happen, but Ellen, as she vowed, keeps the monsters at bay.

She even tells Onna to take a hike. The Disco Slut wants to have a meeting in LA to discuss the movie during the day. Ellen isn't going to take any chances on getting delayed and leaving me alone, so she tells Onna's people she can't do Halloween, but she'll meet the next day. It turns out Onna really wants to meet Ellen on the anniversary of the DK deed, but Ellen stands her ground. The Nomad minions suggest that Onna will fly up to meet with Ellen, but Ellen says no, she has a prior personal commitment. Am I ever flattered. The agent can't believe Ellen's balls. I can. After all the blustering it's arranged. Ellen's flying down for lunch tomorrow and will be back late Friday night. No problem.

WE SPEND HALLOWEEN drinking away the memories and carving psycho-face pumpkins. We don't dress up. We turn out all the lights and no little ghouls ring our doorbell.

That's one of the advantages of being so isolated. We don't get uninvited visitors. In honor of the occasion we don't talk much, just stare at the roaring fire as we guzzle wine. We're both kind of lost in our own thoughts, our own reminiscences. Ellen stops drinking way before I do, because of her travel plans, she says. She doesn't want to meet Onna Nomad with a hangover. It's Onna's business if she wants to have a hangover, I joke, getting drunk enough to enjoy silly grammatical jokes. I don't have to be anywhere tomorrow so I keep knocking back the vino. I want to obliterate myself so I don't remember all the bad Halloweens. Ellen is there for me. She holds me as I tie a big one on. If a bitch of a hangover is all this Halloween gives me, then I call it a huge fucking success considering my track record.

A huge fucking bitch of a hangover it is. By the time Ellen has to leave for the airport I'm over the barfing stage, but I'm in no condition to drive. She tells me to sleep it off, and she'll be back from LA by the time I wake up. She'll drive herself to the airport. Ellen kisses me on the forehead, and then on my lips, even though I've been sick and didn't have the energy to brush my teeth again. And then I remember how last Halloween she kissed me after I'd been sick surviving what the DK did to Marsha, and I realize how much I love Ellen. In sickness and health. Never a truer word. Have a safe trip.

IT'S DARK. THE phone rings me awake. I'm disoriented, but I manage to pick the phone up. It takes me a few moments to realize I'm speaking into the wrong end. Rather than turn the phone around, which would have been simpler, I contort my body so my mouth is in the right place.

Clearly, I'm not at my best.

"How are you feeling?"

It's Ellen.

"Better. Yeah, better."

"Just waking up?"

"Yeah, I've been asleep since you left."

"That's good."

I yawn. "How was the meeting."

"Good. Great actually. I'll tell you all about it later. Look, if it's okay I'm going to stay over down here. Onna wants me to meet with the scriptwriters tomorrow. She's set up a breakfast meeting. Is that okay? Will you be all right?"

"Sure. I'm just going to sleep some more."

"Make sure you eat something. Some toast or cereal."

I yawn again. "I will. Have fun."

"I'll be home in the early afternoon."

"Cool."

"Good night, Violetta. I love you."

"Love you too, Ellen."

And I fall soundly asleep.

I WAKE BEFORE dawn and down a big, fat bowl of cereal. I go for a morning run, the sweat and salty air purging my body of the last remaining alcohol toxins. I pick up the newspaper from the porch and place it on the table while I shower away the skank.

Wrapped in warm, comfy towels I brew an eye-popping cup of coffee and work my way through the *Chronicle*.

I never finish my drink.

There is a story written just for me. I read it twice to make sure I'm not hallucinating, my brain perhaps suffering some delayed reaction from too much alcohol and too little food. I'm sober. No matter how much I blink it is still there in accusatory black and white.

CINDERELLA KILLER STRIKES
AGAIN IN OAKLAND

The first killing was on October 12th, my birthday.

The second killing was on October 17th, the anniversary

of my parents' death. The anniversary of me discovering my power.

The third killing was on October 31st, Halloween.

I dress in a daze and throw together a bag of a few things I think I might need—my shoe leather trimming knife, a change of clothes, a bunch of cash and several pairs of fuckshoes that hold memories of my days in Oakland. Don't ask me why I did that. I just figured I'd need them, like they're my weapons against whatever Evil I was going to face.

I should have known my power couldn't be denied. Avenging Angel Sex Goddesses can't retire. Despite my resolution, I fucking will go back to Oakland, because I'd rather be a killer than read about any more victims.

EIGHT

I KNOW I'M in trouble when they mention *Magnum Force*, but they're supposed to be the experts so I keep my mouth shut.

Which is difficult to do when *Death Wish* is invoked. I was never a big Charles Bronson fan.

"I think we want to give it that *Star Chamber* feel."

"What do you think, Ellen?"

Onna has been eyeing me throughout my exposure to April and Jerry, the scriptwriters assigned to the movie by the studio. I nibble on a pastry while I deliberate how blunt I want to be. Onna and I enjoyed a late night which had delayed the start of our meeting. Breakfast became brunch. We're eating and meeting in a conference room at Paramount Studios. I thought we'd rendezvous at a restaurant or the hotel but a catered meal behind studio walls was preferred for security reasons. Onna told me that even though the rights to *The Cop That Killed The Dildo Killer* had been secured by the studio and her, we could expect several similar productions by other studios. It was important to act fast and keep the plot under wraps. Which is a bit confusing to me since by the publisher's latest count over two million people had bought the book and therefore know the plot.

So I decide to be blunt.

"Forgive my ignorance, why does our movie have to be like these other movies? They were fiction. This is fact. Why not give our movie *The Cop That Killed The Dildo Killer* feel. That's what you paid all the money for."

April and Jerry look at each other with raised eyebrows. They turn to Onna who smiles as if she's been through this discussion before.

"That's a good point," April says.

I smile back, feeling like I'm making progress.

"But," Jerry says.

"But," April says.

"But," Onna says.

I do not say "But." I wait for the punch line. They all look at me like I'm supposed to fill in the blanks. I keep on smiling. Jerry can't take it any longer.

"But this is film. Not real life. Real life is boring. Too many details. Everyone's read your book. And it is fantastic, but—"

"It's too real. It would take days to show. We have to condense. Cut." April says.

"Viciously," Jerry says.

"Okay," I say. "So why do you need me? Why don't you get Clint Eastwood or Charles Bronson or Warren Beatty and make a standard good guys, bad guys, cops and killers movie?"

The scriptwriters put their pens down on their pads of scribbled on paper. Bran muffins are savaged. Onna intervenes.

"Ellen, this is your story. It is a unique story. It's a true story. We don't want to make another tired old film with

– 133 –

has-been actors, but this is Hollywood and everything is derivative. By citing other movies that may have a minute similarity, it helps refine the story into something that can be told in two hours, but more importantly the studio heads who supply the money only think in terms of past projects. They're not too imaginative and need reference points to feel good about their budgets. It's a game."

Don't I feel stupid. Onna continues.

"But Ellen, as long as I'm connected with the project, this movie will be unlike anything that's been done before. After spending an entire day and evening with you I think I have a feel for what you went through. We shouldn't concentrate on the action, macho guy, big gun movies, but more on films that deal with the obsession a cop is prey to when chasing a notorious villain."

April nods. Jerry sees this and does likewise.

"I see," I say.

Onna leans forward.

"It would be different if we were shooting a documentary, but—"

April leaps to her feet as if Jerry had stuck a Mister Perfection up her skirt. She interrupts Onna with a shriek. Decapitated bran muffins scatter everywhere.

"That's it, Onna, you're a genius. We tell Ellen's tale as if it were a documentary. As if a camera crew followed her throughout the investigation from the first murder to the last and on in through the investigation. We show her moments of strength and the self-doubt. We could even shoot a lot of hand held stuff in black and white, as if we were looking over her shoulder. We tell Ellen's story as if it were true. Which it is. So a documentary feel is a perfect style, and it hasn't been done before in this genre."

"I like it," Onna says.

"It's very good," Jerry says through a smile that leaves no doubt he wished he'd thought of the idea first.

They all turn and look at me.

"I think it's great. I like a documentary feel. It's a true story and should be told like one."

"Bravo," Jerry says, leading the cheer. There's applause all around for the success of our brainstorming. Everyone is pleased, especially me. I've earned my consulting fee. The production company is paying me more per day than I earned in a week of being a cop, and all I have to do is be myself. According to the deal my agent negotiated I'm supposed to be available from concept stage through principal photography for advice on matters of accuracy. Six to nine months is what they think it'll take. I'll even get a trailer and a chair with my name on it and a production credit.

Being a star is fun.

"Let's take a short break," Onna says. "I think we're really getting somewhere, so let's have a stretch and come back and take an hour or two to get down to specifics before we call it quits. Is that okay, Ellen? I know you have to catch a plane."

I look at my watch. It's eleven-thirty. Violetta should be up by now. There are flights every hour to San Francisco. "Sure, can I use a phone?"

"Follow me," April says. She shows me into an office. "Just dial nine for an outside line. And by the way, I'm so glad you voiced your opinion in there. All those other ideas were Jerry's. He's so into the macho cop thing. He wouldn't listen to me, but now I have a really good feeling about the documentary direction. I just know you and I are going to work well together. If you have any suggestions, don't hesitate to pass them on to me. I really admire you and what you've done. You're an inspiration."

"Thank you," I say, smiling at her as she shuts the door. Over the last few months I've become very adept at handling flattery. At first I was bothered by such overt adulation, feeling like I had to deny my thrust upon greatness with you're-too-kind-but-I-only-did-what-anyone-would-do-in-similar-circumstances comments. Endlessly circuitous conversations of greater flattery would result. Now I just absorb the praise with a smile and move on. The only person whose opinion matters to me is Violetta. With her I listen. She's my anchor to reality, and it's time for a reality check. I do miss her. I shouldn't have let her drink so much, but it was Halloween and she needed to forget. She was determined to get blasted, but if she hadn't drunk so much she could have come down to LA with me, and we could have gone out shopping once the meetings were finished. Maybe next time.

I ring our number, but there's no answer. The machine picks up after two rings, which means there are other messages. Violetta must have the phone turned off. There's a way to retrieve the messages, but I'll be damned if I can remember how.

"Hi, Violetta, it's me. If you're there pick up. Pick up. C'mon, pick up, sleepy head. It's big movie mogul Ellen calling. Oh well, you're probably asleep or on the beach or in the shower. Things are going well here. It's a riot. I'll tell you all about it when I get back. It's almost noon. Figure about two more hours big shotting it, and with the flight and the drive I should be home by five. Hope you're feeling better. I'll ring you again when we're done to let you know I'm on my way. Miss you. Love you. Can't wait to see you. Bye."

I open the door and encounter a lurking Jerry, who just happens to be coming back from the bathroom. I bet he's been pacing the hallway waiting for an opportunity to accidentally run into me.

"Ellen, I just want to say I'm simply thrilled that you're so easy to work with. I must admit I was a tiny bit worried, I mean, you are the Cop That . . . well, you know, I just want you to know that I'm all behind the documentary idea. I was never too keen on the action idea myself, but April likes those gruff heroics. I'm ecstatic that you spoke up. If you have any ideas, come to me. I feel like we're in tune."

"Thanks," I say, "I'm looking forward to working with you too."

He smiles.

"This is going to be big. Can you spell Oscar?"

"O-s-c-a-r."

For an instant Jerry looks at me as if he's not sure whether I got the point of his question, but his calculating brain realizes that he'd better not make me feel stupid, so he laughs at my joke.

"O-s-c-a-r indeed, Ellen. You're such a wit. What a sense of humor. It's a breath of fresh air."

I head back to the conference room while he's still dumping praise. Jerry bolts ahead of me to open the door, beaming as he follows me in. I think he's trying to display to April and Onna that he and I had been having a private chat. It's amazing. I've finally found a place with more ass-kissing and internal politics than the SFPD. But the food is a hell of a lot better. Magically, breakfast has been removed and lunch has replaced it. Sushi, pasta, Thai food, champagne and herbal tea. As we munch, April and Jerry map out the three acts, following my book's development quite closely. I offer my opinion on the things they want to cut out. Everything's moving along very nicely until Jerry takes a detour.

"I know we're going for the truth feel here, but I just want to throw out an idea. May I?"

Onna gives the nod. Jerry continues.

"Well, Ellen, forgive me, but it's always something that's bothered me about your book."

I'm petrified he's going to suggest that I didn't actually kill the Dildo Killer, that my lesbian lover did, and I covered up the crime so we could live happily ever after in our isolated beach house love nest. Can you spell fraud? E-l-l-e-n S-t-e-w-a-r-t.

"It's the whole vigilante/copycat thing. Can't we play up the overwhelming fear you must have that your action will spawn vigilante justice or even other killers who want to be killed by you?"

April is quick to jump in.

"Jerry, we agreed to stay out of the fantasy realm."

April smiles at me. I'm poker faced. Onna sips champagne. Jerry stands and waves the *Los Angeles Times*.

"But it's not fantasy. Look here. 'Cinderella Killer Claims Third Victim.' "

"Let me see that," I say. I haven't paid much attention to the news lately. I've been skipping the front section for book reviews. Jerry passes the paper round the table. It reaches me via April via Onna. Each person adds a sound byte as the article passes by them.

"Oakland."

"Johns."

It's a small article, no more than two paragraphs in the *Around The State* news section. Three male johns killed in Oakland in the last three weeks. The murderer forces the victim's feet into stiletto heels, hence the Cinderella moniker. I look up. Everyone's looking at me. I'm sure I'm pale and getting paler.

"I was just in Oakland. For a book signing."

Jerry is oblivious to my discomfort.

"And wasn't the first Dildo Killer victim's feet mutilated?" He says, proudly displaying the yellow sticky tagged page of my book where I deal with Melanie Courtland's murder, and my shock at arriving on the scene.

"They were cut off and inserted into various parts of her body," I say in a guilty monotone, confirming what they already know from reading my story. Jerry closes the book and puts on an enthusiastic face.

"I think we have a copycat here who wants Ellen to track him down. We're so lucky. It's a whole new angle on the celebrity/fan stalker thing. It's a wonderful opportunity. We could end the movie with someone reading the book, becoming infatuated with Ellen and deciding to do these horrible crimes. Can anyone spell sequel here? Crime goes on, and we're. . . ."

I'm not listening any more. I don't want a sequel to what Violetta and I have been through.

"I need to use the phone," I say as I stand. "I'll be right back."

The room is still as I walk out. Jerry has the frozen shrugged shoulders and look of "Was it something I said" amazement about him.

THERE'S STILL NO answer at the beach house, but I don't leave a message. Instead, I call Michael Donovan at home. He picks it up on the first ring. I interrupt his hello with a "Hi, it's Ellen."

So not as to appear rude I work my way through the preliminaries of how are you, and how I'm doing, and where I am, and with whom I'm meeting, but I've never been one for small talk.

"So what about the Cinderella Killer?"

"So that's why you called me. And I thought you just wanted a friendly chat."

"Well, are you involved?"

"I'm helping the Oakland police, but you know how they are. They say they can handle it. They don't need SFPD help. I gave them all the stuff on Melanie Courtland—"

"Do you think they're related? My book and the murders?"

"It's possible some sicko read what the DK did and decided it'd be a nice way to off some johns. You can't be sure, but it's being considered very strongly. You were pretty graphic in your book. Where did you get all that info? It wasn't in the police files I gave you."

"If I tell you I'd have to kill you," I laugh and change

the subject real quick. "You know I just did a book signing in Oakland, on the 12th."

"I know. That was the date of the first murder."

I think of Violetta's significant dates. I don't like where this is heading or the disturbing fact that I haven't been able to reach her. My heart pounds like a machine gun.

"The 17th and 31st," I say with the silly hope that by speaking quietly I'll be wrong. Michael has no trouble hearing.

"Yeah, that's right, that's when the other killings were."

Oh no. Oh no. Violetta and I are over the past. We are. We're sure we are. We celebrated it.

"How much of a DK copycat do we have? Was there any evidence of sexual mutilation?"

"No dildos. The murder weapon was a knife. The johns' throats were slit and then they were dressed up in drag—wigs, lipstick, the whole lot—and their feet were mutilated, toes and bits of the heel chopped off, and what's left gets stuffed into hooker pumps. It's a real butcher job. Nothing precision. No body parts have been found. A page from an old copy of *Cinderella* is stuffed in their mouths. All of the victims had just visited prostitutes before they were murdered."

I hope Violetta hasn't read the newspaper. She can't find out about this until I'm back. All that shoe and foot symbolism. She'll freak. If it's a small article maybe she'll pass it by. She doesn't always read the newspaper.

"Are these details out in the press? The *LA Times* had barely two paragraphs. No real specifics."

"There was a press conference yesterday after the third victim was found. I don't think any of the gory details were released, but you know how it was with the DK investigation. Things have a way of leaking out."

"Yeah, I know."

"I should warn you. In fact, I was going to call you, but you beat me to it. The Oakland cops are taking the copycat idea seriously, so your name and the book are being mentioned in not the best of lights. When you get back you may want to call the Oakland police and head them off. I'm surprised they haven't already tried reaching you. Harrison's running the investigation. Tell him anything you remember about the signing. If there is a copycat out there he was probably at your appearance. He could be killing to get your attention. Do you remember anyone acting weird? Anyone overly attentive, hanging around, lurking, even fawning over you."

"Michael, that was three weeks ago. I do three or four signings a week. Nobody sticks out in my mind. They're all a blur."

"The surveillance tape has been requested from the security service. Check with Harrison. He could run it for you and see if anybody jogs your memory."

"That's a good idea. I'll give Harrison a call when I get home."

"Do that. If I speak to him first I'll tell him we've talked and to expect the call."

"And Michael. . . ."

I pause, unable to decide whether I should ask him to look in on Violetta. If she's heard of these killings there's no telling what she'll do.

"Yes?"

I decide not to say anything. Michael's a friend, but he's also a cop. I don't want him getting too close to the truth. If Violetta's going off the rails and he shows up, who knows what she'll do. What she'll say. I have to get back to Stinson. Now.

"Thanks. I owe you lunch. How's Tamayo treating you?"

"Strangely enough he's being nice. Almost too nice, if you know what I mean. Kind of worries me. When this case came up he assigned me to be the liaison with the Oakland cops. "

"That's how it should be."

"I know, but I was so amazed. I thought for sure he'd give it to one of his cronies."

"Well, don't nominate him for any awards just yet. Watch your back."

"Oh I do."

"And give Ernie my regards."

"Yeah, sure. He still cringes whenever he hears your name."

"And so he should. Look, I've got to rush. Bye, Michael. I'll ring you when I get back after I've talked to the Oakland cops."

"Bye, Ellen. Say, could you do me a favor?"

"Sure. Anything. Name it."

"Could you get me Onna Nomad's autograph?"

WHICH IS ABOUT all I have time for once I get back in the conference room. I announce my hurried departure and make my excuses, saying I'd called a SFPD friend and there's to be an Oakland PD briefing this afternoon on the Cinderella Killer, which my friend will get me access to. Actually, he's the one that wants the autograph. Would Onna mind?

"Absolutely not," she consents with charming *noblesse oblige*.

I give her Michael's particulars. She doesn't have any photographs with her, but April says she has Onna's latest CD in the car, which she doesn't mind giving up for a good cause. I promise I'll pass on what I learn from the mythical briefing to Jerry and April so they can work it into the script. I try to look enthusiastic, as though these killings are such a great opportunity for us. I struggle to hide the worry churning my guts. It may not be too wise, but I knock back a glass of champagne.

While April's retrieving the CD I call Violetta. Still no answer, but this time I leave her a message and tell her that

I'm on my way back now, and to please wait for me at the house. I try not to sound too panicked, but I tell her that I have some news to go over with her, and we need to figure out what we do. I almost said bad news, but I checked myself, emphasizing the we—as in the both of us need to solve this problem. I only hope she hasn't done something cavalier, like go off to Oakland on her own. Given Violetta's hatred of the place I don't think I really have to worry about that possibility. It's the others that disturb me so.

Next I call the airline. United has flights every hour out of Los Angeles to SFO, so I make my reservation for three. It's one-thirty right now. I'd never make the two o'clock, even with the courtesy of Onna's chauffeur driven limousine. Jerry warns me that even celebs have to bow down to the fickle gods of LA traffic. Even on weekends, traffic's a bitch. Onna accompanies me to the airport, which flatters me, but I hate having to wear my game face. My face muscles strain from hours of enforced smiling. I'd love to be alone to relax and call Violetta on the limo phone. Then it dawns on me how used to my star status I've become. There are people on this planet who would commit worse crimes than Randy Warren III just to have the chance to be in Onna's company, and here am I wishing I was alone. So I try to make the best of it. We make small talk and she hands me the signed CD. It's a greatest hits record called *The Immaculate Deception*. She's signed it "To Detective Michael Donovan. If ever I need the long arm of the law, I'll know who to call. Love, Onna."

"That's very nice of you."

"It's nice of him to help out. If you give me his address I'll have my publicist send him a photograph on Monday."

I scribble the SFPD address on a piece of paper, worrying about Violetta the whole time. It's tough to think about anything else, but I try. I'm sure receiving a photo of Onna delivered to his desk will bolster Michael's reputation, but damn, I do hope Violetta is okay. Why wasn't she in when I called? Why did I have to come to LA when the news of these killings broke? Maybe Violetta's right. Evil is constantly looking for a way to destroy Good.

And Violetta is Good's secret weapon.

"Are you good friends?"

"The best. We've been lovers for over a year now. She's seen me through some very difficult times."

Onna's eyebrows raise skyward. Her head tilts back and she laughs.

"I meant Detective Donovan."

Stupid Ellen.

"Sorry. I was thinking of someone else. I promoted Michael from the uniforms. He's a good detective. He's gay, but I didn't promote him because of that, but I think we naturally gravitated towards each other. He saw the difficulty I had dealing with the male elite, and he's faced many of the same obstacles, but he overcame them just like I did."

"So who is this 'she' that monopolizes your attention? If I'm to play you as well as I can, I have to know all about you. You didn't say anything about a partner last night, although I had learned from some of your interviews that— how did you put it on *Good Morning America*—"

"The love of my life."

"Ah, yes, the love of my life. I envy you. Tell me about her."

"She doesn't like publicity. She's much younger than me—just turned twenty. We're very happy and I'd like to keep it that way by respecting her privacy."

"Is she the La Traviata to whom you dedicated your book?"

"Yes, it's her favorite opera."

"That's very romantic. I wish I could find that kind of love. It never seems to work out for me. Men don't know how to be comfortable with a strong woman."

"Many women don't know how to be comfortable with a strong woman."

"Yes, that's true, isn't it?"

The conversation stalls as does the traffic. Onna pushes ahead. The traffic doesn't.

"Ellen, you know we are going to have to address your private life in the movie. The book, the movie is as much about you and your personal odyssey as it is the crime. You are the attraction. There's no way around it. You talk about how the pressures of police work made your relationship with the costume designer fall apart long before the Dildo Killer case, and how you had to maintain a front during the investigation that you were a lesbian in a stable, long-term relationship."

"Yes, the Mayor's office thought it in the best interests of the department if I didn't look like a dyke on the prowl."

"That's a dynamite angle. They'd never do that to a single guy."

"No, but they might to a gay."

"Good point, but don't you see, the audience will want to know what got you through the Internal Affairs investigation. Was it this mystery woman?"

"Yes and no. We weren't involved at that time more than a casual hello, but I wanted to be and was afraid to try because of my job and what had happened before. I'll tell you a secret that I didn't put in the book. I was relieved when I was asked to resign. It meant that I'd no longer have the jealous mistress of my career to interfere with finding the love of my life. I could finally have a life."

"We have to work that into the film. It's too crucial. How did you meet her?"

"You're going to laugh."

"I won't."

"She was my shoe repairer."

"That's amazing. And you just hit it off?"

"Yes. On the surface we're so different, but we clicked.

She's a young punk. I was on the rebound from being jilted by my career. She made me young again."

"That's wonderful. Let me talk to April and Jerry and see what ideas they have for working it into the script."

"Look, no offense to them or you, but it's her life. I don't want it discussed. I promised to keep her out of this. Can't we do that? I wasn't involved with her during the Dildo Killer investigation or the initial aftermath. Whenever I took my shoes in for repair, yes, I thought she was cute, and we had this crazy kind of rapport, but it was only after all the dust had settled that I got up the nerve to ask her out for coffee. So I don't see that it's really pertinent to the story. That's why I didn't put it into the book."

I didn't mention Violetta's interrogation in the book, omitting her role when I referred to all the wackos that came forward with bizarre Dildo Killer theories. Someone would have to dig very deeply to find that Violetta and I met during the investigation. Wanamaker, the cop that initially interviewed Violetta and ridiculed her, blew his brains out because he couldn't stand the guilt of letting the DK get away. The only person who currently knows I knew Violetta before and now is Michael, and he's cool, but I don't want to give the Tamayos of the world too much ammunition. I hope Onna buys my cover story. I've practiced it often enough. Violetta and I refined it in case of nosy media, so I was comfortable with the lie having had lots of practice in recent months. It seems like truth to me.

"If it's that important to you."

"It is."

"Well, I'll drop it. It'll stay between you and me. It's enough to know about the longing you had for a normal life. We can work that motivation into your character without going into specifics. Thanks for telling me. It'll help me play you so much better."

"Thanks. We appreciate it."

We hug like sisters.

"I'd like to meet this mystery woman someday. Maybe when we're up in San Francisco filming we can all have dinner together."

"That would be nice. I'm sure Violetta would love that."

"Violetta, what a pretty name. You're very much in love, aren't you?"

"Yes, we are."

And right now, very much afraid.

ONNA'S LIMOUSINE DROPS me off at the terminal. We kiss cheeks goodbye. The moment I step out onto the pavement I'm hit by a brusque, damp chill. Through the tinted glass it had been impossible to notice, but ocean fog had eclipsed Hollywood's sunshine. At the gate I'm told the flight is delayed thirty minutes until the marine layer thins.

Thirty minutes becomes an hour of ringing Violetta to no avail while the fog thickens. Angry at the world I march up to the check-in desk and press the harried counter person for a better estimate of when I can expect to leave.

"It's impossible to tell. The tower said it would be clear by now, but the wind has dropped due to—"

A weather report I do not need.

"That's not good enough. I must be in San Francisco immediately. It's an emergency."

"Ma'am, there's no need to shout. Everyone is in the same boat here."

"At this point I'd settle for a plane."

"You'll just have to wait with everyone else until a plane can take off. I'm sorry."

I've never put my fame to use in trivial situations. This isn't a trivial situation. Violetta could be in trouble, so I felt justified in uncorking the VIP bitch.

"I'm not everyone. Do you know who I am?"

He looks down his nose at me.

"Ma'am, it doesn't matter who you are. I've told you. Everyone is in the same boat. We have celebrities flying with us all the time, and no matter how famous you are, you can't control the weather, and neither can we."

I pull out a copy of my book and stick it under his turned-up nose. He cracks a smile.

"Oh, so you're The Cop that Killed the Dildo Killer. Pleased to meet you."

"Likewise, and if you don't help me get back to San Francisco in a hurry my next book will be *The Ex-Cop That Killed The Airline Check-In Clerk.*"

He gives me a contemptuous look.

"Are you threatening me, Ma'am? Because if you are I'll have you know I just have to pick up this phone, and you'll have a nice long chat with airport security, and I promise you won't see San Francisco tonight."

There are times when I think life was so much easier when I had a badge instead of a book.

"No, I'm not—"

I peer at his name tag. Ass-kissing time.

"Jerome. I was only trying to make a joke. It's been a long day. I know what I said wasn't very funny or smart. I just want to know my alternatives. Now, why don't you find a way to get me home ASAP while I sign this book for you."

"I already have a copy."

"Then you'll have two. One signed by a very grateful author."

"Could you make it to Patrick?"

"Of course."

"We'll have you on your way in no time."

NO TIME IS taking a gamble that the marine layer won't clear, and that a limo to Burbank and a Southworst flight to SFO is faster than waiting. Instead of arriving at four-fifteen I arrive in San Francisco at six-thirty. As I make my way through the arrivals area I'm determined to try phoning Violetta one more time. Maybe if she's been out all day doing something like God knows what, she'll be back now ready for dinner with me.

I never complete the call.

As I punch the digits of our number I turn and see the newspaper rack. Bold headlines. CINDERELLA KILLER STRIKES AGAIN IN OAKLAND.

No way could Violetta have missed it. Unless maybe she didn't read the newspaper. There are some days she doesn't touch the *Chronicle*. She's not a big morning person. Unless I open it the newspaper usually sits there all rolled up in plastic. Maybe she didn't even look at the *Chronicle*.

Or watch television.

Who am I kidding?

I buy a paper. The article doesn't give the exact details of the foot mutilation. That is good. But it does say the victims were dressed in drag with stiletto shoes forced onto their feet. That is bad.

I don't bother to read the rest.

I sprint to my Jeep and gun it out of the parking structure. I have to get home as fast as possible. Assuming Violetta has read the article how would she have reacted? I couldn't believe she'd go to Oakland. But where would she go? Why didn't she answer the phone? Was she sitting on the beach in shock? Was she terrified in the house, afraid to move? What if she put on a pair of fuckshoes to gain clues from past crimes and was trapped, and I'm not there to pull her out?

I turn onto 101 North and floor the accelerator, honking and swearing at every slow bastard only exceeding the speed limit by ten miles-per-hour. It's almost seven. With any luck I'll be home by eight and Violetta will be waiting for me, wondering why I left so many messages when all she'd done was go out for the day.

Fuck.

Red and yellow flashing lights.

The Cop that Killed the Dildo Killer is about to get a ticket.

NINE

I SNEAK INTO Oakland the back way. I'm not about to drive anywhere near the Bay Bridge feeder road that collapsed and squashed Mom and Dad, so I exit the freeway in Berkeley at University Avenue. As I urge my sputtering little pink Bug up the hill, I keep telling myself I really want to do this going back crap. I think I can. I think I can. I think I can turn around and go back to Stinson. That's my home. Not this rattrap full of stale reminders of a life I'm afraid to remember. Something bad will come of this, I know, but worse things will come of ignoring the warning signs. That I also know too well.

Oh fuck, I'm so scared. My heart races in time with the Bug's engine. My palms sweat and slip on the steering wheel despite my white-knuckled grip. I'm not even playing music. That's how fucking scared I am. Not even some old Clash or Sex Pistols to pump me up. Just the sound of my own forced breathing and the putt-putt of my trusty little car.

I turn right on San Pablo and head towards Oakland.

After a few more blocks of Berkeley bizarreness I see the downtown Oakland skyline lurking through the morning haze. It doesn't matter that the two very different cities run together. I know exactly where Berkeley ends and Oakland begins. It's about twenty blocks ahead, two years ago. My pinkness flashes through intersections as red lights yield green. The lights remind me of a mechanical Moses parting the asphalt seas to suck me across the city limits and take me back to a promised land to which I promised I'd never return. And what do you know, two years later, here I am. City of Oakland: Elevation and Population spray painted over with the latest graffiti scrawl. There's no fanfare. No Welcome Home Violetta parades, just my own uneasy feelings that I'm making a terrible mistake.

I haven't been back since October 19th, 1989. Two days after the earthquake. One day after I found out that Mom and Dad hadn't been safe in Candlestick watching the World Series after all. I look around me at the funky little shops, the run-down apartments, the menacing alleys, the people hanging around.

Nothing's changed.

I still hate the place.

Coming back is not so smart. I know this, but when have I ever worried about following the wisest course of action? If I'd been wise last Halloween then the DK would have been acquitted by now on some technicality because I'd have turned him over to the cops instead of my knife. Adding its own strange punctuation to this rationalization, a police car overtakes me with its lights flashing and sirens blaring. More mental alarm bells sound as the siren recedes. What will Ellen say? She'll have a cow, that's what, a prize fucking heifer. I know I promised her I wouldn't go off on my own killing crusade, but I really don't have a choice. These Cinderella Killings are an invite and my dance card is empty. It may be a new killer with a new name in an old setting, but this is unfinished business. The Dildo Killer has a hand, a foot, a dildo, something, anything to do with these murders. I know it. My feet know it. Ellen will be mad, but she'll understand. She always does.

Ellen. Oh fuck, I didn't even leave her a note saying "Gone to Oakland to kill a serial killer. Be back for dinner." What the fuck was I supposed to do, lie? "Gone to Oakland to visit friends." Or "Thought I'd go into San Francisco and have a blast down at Fisherman's Wharf." No way. She'd see right through me, and now that I've not been there to answer the phone she's going to wonder where the hell I am. Too bad I don't know how to reach her in LA, but even if I did, I wouldn't call her and tell her I'm going to Oakland on official shoefuck business. It'd worry her sick. She'd rush back and probably get in an accident. She doesn't think I can look after myself. Actually, it's not that. She knows I'm not weak or stupid. She knows better than anyone living what I'm capable of. She just wants to protect me from the big, bad world, which is kind of cool. It's neat to have someone looking out for me, but I have responsibilities I can't shirk. I'm an Avenging Angel Sex Goddess, the serial killer of serial killers, and there's one on the loose in my old hometown. Which I take very fucking personally.

Since I didn't leave Ellen a note with some half-assed excuse I'd better call and leave her a message so when she gets home she'll know where I am. I'll tell her the truth. Honesty is best. Most of the time. So I stop near a 7-Eleven and use a pay phone.

"Hey, Ellen, how are you? I hope LA was fun. I'm dying to hear all about it. Was Onna cool? Look, this is going to sound strange, but I'm in Oakland. I know I said I never fucking will go back, or words to that effect, but I think you know why I'm here. You've probably seen the newspaper. The Cinderella Killer. Don't worry. I'm not going to do anything stupid. I don't even know what I'm going to do. I'll probably be back before you, and I'll erase this message so you don't hear what a dweeb I am. Look, I'm just going to look around and see what I can learn, and then we'll put out heads together and figure out how we nail the bastard, okay. It's almost eleven. Can't wait to see you. Bye. Don't worry. Bye."

I feel like a real shit. Ellen deserves better than my Don't Worry Be Happy excuse. Once she gets the message I bet she'll wish she never pushed me into learning how to drive. If I'd had to take the bus to Oakland I may have thought twice about running off to do battle. I'd have probably waited for her to come home and the both of us could have done a John Wayne. I never wanted a driver's license. I told her only bad things come from cars. They're like guns. People use them in the heat of the moment. Public transportation is a real cool-downer. See, it's all Ellen's fault that I've returned to the scene of the original crime.

Yeah, right. Low blow. The fault's all mine. If I hadn't gotten drunk on Halloween I'd have driven her to the airport and would have been obliged to pick her up. I wouldn't have run off to Oakland and left her stranded at the airport. Or would I? I haven't been thinking too clearly since I saw the article in the *Chronicle*. Yeah, well, all this what-if shit is so much mental masturbation. Stop jerking yourself around, Violetta Valery. That's what Ellen would say. But she was the one that stayed over an extra day in LA because things were going so fucking well. If she'd come back on time none of this would have happened. We'd be together figuring out what to do, instead of me on my own, scared shitless, pointing fingers in all the wrong places.

I'm doing this self-flagellation routine because I feel bad about not letting Ellen know my plans. When I dialed our number I could tell by the length of the beeps that there were other messages on the machine. Ellen has probably called to see how I was doing and is worried sick since I didn't answer. She probably called a bunch of times. I should have at least stayed at home until she rang. I'd have told her I was okay, was going out for awhile, and then bolted. When shoefuck duty calls I stop thinking. I bet I've fucked up her day with Onna Nomad.

I wish I'd bothered to learn how to use the remote message retrieval feature of our answering machine. It has something to do with pressing # and a number for so many seconds, but which fucking one? I guess I could try every # number combination. I probably have enough change in my hundreds of pockets. Maybe Ellen left a number where she could be reached. If I could get into our machine I could erase my message and tell Ellen directly.

I sort through my pockets collecting coins from various parts of my anatomy. I have a dollar in spare change, enough for five tries, but I don't even make one call. I'm distracted by the paper rack and the Cinderella Killer headline. I buy a *Tribune* for fifty cents and give the rest to some homeless guy who looks at the handout with disdain. The local Oakland rag is full of Cinderella Killer stories, anecdotes, denials, rumors and real details. There's way more info than in our paper. I should have known that the *Chronicle* wouldn't have covered a poor relative across the Bay story with any thoroughness. The *Tribune* has a whole special section, but it's not that feature that captures my attention. It's the subhead immediately below the main block letters that I can't take my eyes off.

POLICE REFUSE TO CONFIRM REPORTS OF FEET MUTILATION

The report goes on to say that the *Tribune* had learned the victims' feet hadn't simply been stuffed into small stiletto heels, but that parts of the victims' heels, toes and soles had been hacked off to force the feet into the shoes and that the body parts had not been found. That's why the name, the Cinderella Killer, had been chosen, because in the original fairy story before it became sanitized that's what the evil stepsisters did to make their feet fit into the glass slipper, but they were betrayed by a trail of blood. Supposedly a page from an old copy of the story was stuffed into each of the victims' mouths. The police refused comment on the report, citing their long-standing policy of not providing crime scene details of ongoing investigations.

There follows an interview with a Berkeley psychology professor who goes into great detail about the symbolism of the fairy tale, and the type of person who might use *Cinderella* as killing inspiration. The person probably has a repressed foot fetish and is acting out the self-hatred he or she feels for a sibling. The fairy tale probably triggers a strong childhood memory of abuse and sexual identity confusion. Depending upon the exact nature of the memory, the killings will probably stop now that three 'ugly sisters' have been slain, until some new trauma resurrects it at another time.

Oh yeah, I know all about repressed foot fetishes, don't I? All this foot stuff hits too close to home. Shoesex is somehow involved. These killings are aimed at me. There can be no doubt. They're in my old neighborhood. They involve shoes. Like hell they'll stop because three victims have been offed. They'll stop when I slay the killer, and not before. Don't need a doctorate to know that. There's definitely unfinished business here. The DK is involved. Look what that prick did to Melanie Courtland's feet. Foot fetish mutilation indeed. That professor has no idea. I do. He hasn't been on the receiving end of a psycho's knife. I have. The DK didn't have a foot fetish. He had a killing fetish, and I bet so too does this CK.

Horrendous memories of my time in Melanie's platforms flood my body. I feel faint. I need a sugar rush and a jump start, so I buy a coffee from the 7-Eleven, stir in a few packets of the sweet stuff and catch my breath in the Bug. I skim the rest of the *Tribune* reports as my batteries recharge. It's all such typical crime reporting—the victims' profiles, hooker comments, pimps' denials, police statements, concerned citizens' outrage, civic response, learned theories. I've seen it all before, so many times. It reminds me of the prostitute murders that happened when I was ten. They're fresh in my mind from all the research we did for Ellen's book. I even have little Nikki's shoes with me—Mom's sparkly high heels too. Those two pairs of shoes are my only link to Oakland's past, so I brought them along. Why, I'm not sure, other than they may contain a clue I could use to catch the CK—something I may have overlooked because I was so occupied with the DK. Yeah, right, like I'm about to put them on in the middle of San Pablo Avenue and have a shoefuck for old time's sake. Sometimes I'm really lame-ass. I have no idea what I'm doing here.

Knowing fuck-all never stopped me before.

So I focus on the victims. Nothing stands out. No similarities, just three horny guys who came and then went for good. They were all white, but that probably doesn't mean anything. Most of the hookers' customers are white. What about locations? The *Tribune* was thoughtful enough to print a map with the murder scenes indicated by high-heeled shoes. Cute. All three johns were killed along the MacArthur Boulevard stroll. I figure why not take a look, so I putt-putt north a few blocks and worm my way along the street to the first killing site.

As do many other murder groupies.

Even though there's nothing left to see there's a steady stream of gawkers. October 12th's event happened behind the Tiki Motel, in an alleyway full of dumpsters. I park the Bug and walk a few blocks, and as soon as I get there I wish I hadn't bothered. Not because of the smell of rotting garbage, but because Japanese tourists are lying down where the body was found, and they're taking each other's pictures. Even I think that's sick. It's almost as bad as putting on a dead person's shoes and stealing their sex life.

The second murder was a bit more bold and personal. It happened in the rear parking lot of The Paradise Motel, which is fairly well lit according to the paper. Thanks to fuckshoes I can vouch for that. The victim was found in his car. Now this is fucking eerie. I know this place. This sleaze-bag motel is where Dad did Nikki up the butt a few days before she was murdered at that same motel, probably that same room, on the 17th of October, 1981. The day I discovered my power. The day Nikki dropped off her sparkly shoes at Cutrero's to be repaired. Okay, we've got major fate going down here. I've walked in those platforms many times. She brought me and Dad to the Paradise. She brought Randy Warren III to the Paradise, and Nikki was the last hooker killed by him, at least in Oakland. And now I'm back for another murder. This situation is too fucking weird for words. It reeks of fate and destiny. Unfinished business, oh yeah, I can smell it, like shoe leather.

I park the Bug on the street in front of the Paradise. I pick up my shoulder bag of shoes and march up towards the motel. Getting to the lobby is tough. There's a constant parade of rubberneckers wandering around the motel. Some religious nutcase marches up and down the street with a sign warning all sinners to repent. I push past him and he calls me a harlot doomed to Hell unless I change my sinful ways. I'm flattered. At least I don't look like one of the murder groupies. I don't need to see any more corpse posing, so I go straight to the motel's lobby. Well, it's not really a lobby, more of an alcove. I can't help but stare at the peeling paint and the stained carpet, imagining Nikki renting a room all those years ago. I feel strangely in awe of this place. The Paradise holds a special significance for me, like Graceland to Elvis fans. My dad shot his wad up Nikki's butt here. I want to pay my respects. It's a fucking shrine, okay?

The guy behind the counter slams open a sliding glass window, and before I can say anything he jabbers off a bunch of Indian-English and points to a sign. It's the room rates. Monthly, weekly, daily, hourly. And they've all been hastily increased with a felt pen.

"No rooms for one hour."

"Excuse me. Is that no hourly rooms or no rooms of any kind for an hour?"

"You don't hear so good. Come back one hour. We have room then."

I look at my watch. It's barely noon. I didn't think the street trade got roaring until dark.

"You're that busy?"

"Not with hookers. Murder damn good for business. People want to be in the room that the poor bugger was in."

"Which was?"

"Come back in an hour, and I tell you then. You hooker?"

What the fuck, if I can fool the god squad maybe I can fool the motel man.

"Yeah. Just need a room for a quickie."

He thumbs through a book.

"Twenty dollar. One hour."

"I was thinking more like four hours."

"You said quickie."

I shrug my shoulders.

"What can I say? I'm a perfectionist. Four hours is a quickie for me."

"You no hooker."

"Am too. Now you got anything for four hours or what?"

"Fifty dollar."

"Deal."

I hand him the cash. He slides the room key under the slot.

"Room 6. You out by four."

"Deal. Thanks."

He slams the sliding glass window shut, leaving me staring blankly at my reflection and the key. I back away. A Japanese couple, younger looking than me, come up to the window, and Motel Guy gives them the same spiel about no rooms, but he doesn't ask her if she's a hooker. They pull out a bunch of traveler's checks, and he looks in his book, and presto, he finds a room. And what do you know, it's the murder victim's room. The Japanese tourists happily pay. Two hundred dollars. Cheap at half the price for a piece of lustkill.

Leaving the Japanese to their tora-tora-tora glow, I walk up the stairs, and I immediately recognize the steps as the ones my dad followed Nikki up, staring at her cute little ass, thinking of fucking it because my mom wouldn't let him do it up her butt. Man, am I pissed. I'm on fucking fire. Tourists pass me by. A bunch of guys, I think they're German, ask if they can take my picture, and I tell them to fuck off. I'm in no mood to be social. They ask if they can fuck me. I give them the finger, and I quickly duck in Room 6 and slam the chain across the door.

I'm safe.

My sanctuary. It's exactly as I remember it from my shoefucks. I'm sure all the rooms are the same, but this one looks like the one Dad did Nikki in. I never paid any attention to what room they went into, but I will. I'm sure this is the one.

And this time I'm prepared. No twisted ankles for me. Through all that research for Ellen's book I learned how to survive shoesex when I knew my body was in for a beating. I lie on the bed, wrap myself in blankets and slip on Nikki's rhinestone platforms.

Two people, one body. . . .

IT'S LATE AT night. I'm walking down Broadway. I see Nikki's reflection in storefront windows. She preens in the window, carefully adjusting the pink ribbons on my two shoulder length pigtails. Nikki lights a cigarette and breaths deep the penetrating smoke.

I want to cough, my lungs searing. I want to rush through this preliminary stuff and get to the Paradise, but I can't. Shoesex takes its time. No fast forward button here.

Nikki slinks past Cutrero's Shoe Repair.

Even though she just checked herself a few minutes ago, she stops and inspects her appearance in our window. But it's not just vanity. There's more to it.

She hikes her skirt up her thighs so the pink-covered swell of her pussy peeks out from under her hemline. Satisfied with her seductive image, she blows herself a kiss.

Nikki's feeling rebellious. I feel it. It's a rush from thumbing her nose at all the fine, upstanding citizens of Oakland while they sleep soundly in their beds.

She adjusts the Celtic cross around her neck, pulling the clasp. She smirks and walks off.

Ten-year-old me is in that building, upstairs, asleep, completely unaware of Nikki walking the streets below. Hi, Violetta, I want to say. It's me, Violetta, but Nikki's in control. Shoefucks don't allow improvising.

She turns down San Pablo. The cruising zone awaits. A bunch of hookers cluster around an idling silver Porsche. I push my way to the front. The displaced whores do not appreciate Nikki's assertiveness.

I hear the nasty comments. The threats. Nikki just sees dollars. There's bills to pay. Two mouths to feed.

She bends down to lean on the Porsche's window frame. Pulling aside the bodysuit, I display her tits. She looks inside the car and blows the john a kiss. Her cross falls forward and sways.

"I can be your little girl, Mister. You can spank me if you like. Would you like to spank little Nikki?"

"Get in."

His gloved hand reaches across to the handle. He pauses, reaches up and stills the swinging cross, stroking it between his fingers.

Bastard, fucking bastard, but at least you didn't get to keep the cross. Nikki would be happy about that.

His face emerges from the shadows. Young, unmistakable eyes. Blue and evil. Expensive suit. Baby-Face Blond Guy. It's him all right. The prototype Dildo Killer.

It doesn't matter how many times I do this shoefuck, coming face to face with Randy Warren makes me jump. No matter how much I prepare myself, he always scares me. It's those fucking eyes.

A hand grabs my shoulder and spins Nikki around.

"Outta my fucking way, girl. He's mine. I was here first. So help me, I'll kick your skinny white ass if you steal any more of my customers. You little bitch, get the fuck out of here or I'll carve you a new pussy."

I'm pushed backwards by a tall Amazon with teased blond hair. Nikki sprawls unladylike on the ground, hurting my butt.

Let the Amazon have him, Nikki. He'll be back for you in a few days, and you'll go with him, and he'll kill you. I wish I could warn you.

Nikki gets up from the pavement and walks further down San Pablo. A green car slows. She knows that car.

I know that car. Toyota, pre-flattened vintage.

The car's passenger window rolls down.

"Hey, Nikki."

Hi, Dad.

"Hop in."

Nikki does. She sits my butt bouncily down in Mom's seat in the green Toyota. Legs crossed, I tease Dad with glimpses of my pink-wrapped pussy.

Look at him. The dirty bastard steals looks as he drives. He's such a pig. He should be home with Mom and me.

We park and Dad follows my wiggling butt to a second floor room of the Paradise.

"Welcome to my new pad, Tommy."

This time I look closely. She doesn't face the door as she opens it, but I catch the number as she walks in.

A six.

This is the room.

A single lightbulb hangs from the ceiling. Paint peels off the walls.

Yeah, this is the one.

Nikki turns on the television. A bad porno movie plays. Volume up loud. Dad stares, counts out $60, eyes riveted to the X-rated action. I unzip his trousers, push them to the floor. He's stinking hard already. Nikki jerks his cock. I cup his balls.

It's always so weird to feel Dad's balls in Nikki's hands.

"These pretty full. You not been getting any? You should come see little Nikki more often. Don't be a stranger. You know I'm always here for you."

"I got plenty for all, babe."

"Yeah, you do. How long we been seeing each other, Tommy? Nine years?"

"Something like that. I don't remember."

"Well, I do. It's been nine years since you first picked me up and helped me out. You watched me grow up. You been like a daddy to me."

I kiss Dad on the cheek as I slip a condom on his dick, rolling it all the way down his shaft. Wow, I feel the burr of his five-o'clock shadow. I never noticed that before.

"I'll be right back, lover Daddy. Make yourself comfortable. What's it gonna be? The usual?"

"Yeah, babe, you know what I like."

As I get myself ready I look at the picture in my Celtic cross, and I think I'm doing this for you so you can have a better future than me. Then I'm back in the room, and I'm performing for the dollars we need.

"Fuck me up the ass, Daddy."

"Bend over, you little cunt. Daddy gonna do you good."

"Oh yeah, Daddy. Fuck my ass. Fuck me with that big Italian cock."

Dad, Daddy, he's really getting off on little Nikki's porn-talk. Was he thinking of me while he fucked Nikki?

He slaps my butt cheeks making Nikki's ass wriggle as his hairy belly slams into my buttocks. Alternating his grip, he squeezes my tits, avoiding the swinging cross like the good Catholic he is. Nikki's sphincter clenches. Dad moans and pushes harder. The chair moves. Nikki teeters, her heel twists over.

Oh fuck that hurt. My ankle. My shoe. I fucking hate him.

Dad roots away, oblivious to my discomfort. He comes. He pulls out. After he's cleaned himself up he notices I'm hurting. He pretends to care. He examines my ankle.

"Ouch."

"It's not broken. The ankle, that is. Sprained I think. You should ice it. The platform heel is cracked. I can fix that. Just bring it by the store on Saturday. I'll do it for free."

"Damn right you will."

"And, Nikki, well, you know, if the kid or wife's there, you don't know me, okay?"

That'll make three of us, lover Daddy.

"Yeah, I don't know you. After years of fucking you, I don't know you, but don't worry, your secret is safe with me, Daddy."

"I'd better be going."

"Yeah, back to the wife who don't know me, who won't let you fuck her up the ass. What's her name? Alice? Alice without the ass—"

Dad backhands me across the mouth. I feel the trickle of blood from my lip. My jaw aches. My ankle aches. My heart aches.

"Oh Jesus, oh Nikki, I'm sorry. You shouldn't have—"

"Leave me alone. You've done enough damage."

"Here's another twenty. Look, I'm sorry."

"Just get the fuck out. GET THE FUCK OUT."

I pick up the broken shoe and throw it at Dad as he exits Paradise.

I COME OUT of the shoefuck all sweaty, but the bed trick worked. My ankle's sore and my jaw aches, but it's not as bad as the first time when I put Nikki's shoes on standing up, and when Dad hit her I went over and hit my head and really twisted my ankle. Wrapping myself in blankets and surrounding myself with pillows worked like a charm. I don't feel that bad, probably because of what I learned. This is the room that Dad and Nikki had butt sex in 1981. Therefore, this is the room she was probably killed in since she told Dad this was going to be her new pad. And since Motel Guy rented it to me rather than to a tourist at a premium I can reasonably assume it isn't the one that Cinderella Victim #2 used. That would have been too creepy.

Now it's time to say hello to the nicer dad. I don't want the memory of him hitting Nikki hanging around, so I slip on Mom's sparkly high heels and relive their anniversary fuck, the first shoesex I ever had. It's weird, to see two sides of my father in such a short time span. Rather than weakening the memory from Nikki's shoefuck, Mom and Dad's anniversary shoefuck strengthens it. It's like I see him for what he was. A man with two lives. He'd been fucking Nikki since she was fifteen. Almost from the time I was born. I'd give everything to ask him why. Was it me? Did having a baby turn Mom off sex, so he went elsewhere? Is this all my fault?

Enough!

I have a job to do, and wallowing in past shoefucks isn't going to catch the Cinderella Killer. I sit in the chair that Nikki bent over while Dad buttfucked her, and I think. There's a connection between all these killings, but it's not obvious, it's not one-to-one. Some things match, but others don't. In 1981 there were a total of six hookers killed in the space of a month. Dad butt-fucked Nikki on the 10th over this chair. The fifth victim, Amazon woman, was killed on the 13th. Nikki was killed on the 17th in this room. She begged for her life and was hung by her stockings from the ceiling fan after Randy Warren sodomized her. I look up and am amazed that the cheap plaster job held, but then again Nikki was a small woman. After Nikki's death the killings stopped. There was no hooker murder on October 12th, but years later there was a DK murder. The third most recent Cinderella Killing on Halloween has no relation to the Prostitute Murders. It is obviously the anniversary of me killing the Dildo Killer. The 12th, 17th and the 31st. What gives?

Wait a minute. Check my mega-ego at the door. The world doesn't know I killed the DK. They think Ellen did it. And Ellen appeared in Oakland on the 12th. The Cinderella Killer has to be some fuck with a thing for Ellen. These killings aren't about me. But what about the 17th? At the same place as Nikki getting offed. What's that got to do with Ellen?

Of fucking course. It's Ellen's book. That's the link. She refers to the DK's rant about previous victims, especially little Nikki and her pathetic pleadings. There's a whole chapter on the Oakland Prostitute murders. This Cinderella fucker is sending Ellen a message. He, or she, the killer could be a woman, maybe somebody pissed off with johns, for some sick reason is using *The Cop That Killed The Dildo Killer* as a blueprint. What an asshole. Doesn't even have the originality to come up with his own significance.

I am fucking brilliant. Sherlock fucking Holmes and Doctor fucking Watson rolled into one ace detective. So when will the next killing occur, Holmes? Elementary, my dear Watson. Today is Saturday, November 2nd. The next event would be on—? Oh come on. Think. The next Dildo Killer/Randy Warren murder was—how could I forget?

November 17th. The DK murdered Bradley Winston, the stockbroker, the first hetero DK murder. It happened the night Marsha and I were going out on the town, ostensibly to have fun, only I was planning to do DK research in the clubs at the same time. We never made it. I'd just completed my stunning outfit with those rhinestone heels I'd found in the wreck of our store, and wham, I'd met little

Nikki and my dad fucked me up the ass and slapped my face, and I'd fallen and twisted my ankle. I was in no mood to go out. Marsha nursed me through the night thinking I'd had an acid flashback to an abusive childhood. I didn't put her straight. I didn't want her to know about my power. I can't help thinking that if I'd been honest then and told her about myself and my quest to kill the Dildo Killer, she'd still be alive today. She'd have been warned and on her guard.

I remember that night so clearly, especially after having just relived the shoefuck again. After I'd recovered from the shock of discovering my Dad's nasty side, I remember feeling so smart that thanks to Nikki's rhinestone platforms I'd figured out the DK was also the Oakland Prostitute Killer. Then the next day the news came out about Bradley Winston's murder, and I realized the DK had outsmarted me again. If I'd gone out with Marsha instead of nursing my ankle and my feelings I might have caught him because Bradley was picked up at one of the clubs we'd planned on going to. The DK was always one step ahead of me, teasing me, loading me up with spine-melting guilt. A year later, when he took Marsha, it was the final insult. I ended his killing reign, but there isn't a day when I don't think I should have gotten him earlier. So many people would still be alive.

Including my best friend.

And here I am in Oakland touring the sites of murders past so I can prevent another one from happening. Am I going to make the same mistakes?

No, I'm smarter now.

More experienced.

I have killed.

I'll do it again.

I have a little over two weeks, and this time there will be no surprises to slow me down. I have time to involve Ellen. We can do this right. We can stop this killer. This trip down memory lane wasn't such a bad idea after all. We'll need a base of operations for the next month so we can be close to the action. We're not going to catch this nutcase from Stinson. I'll rent Room 6 for a month. Ellen can meet me over here tonight. She can bring me some clothes and we can watch a dirty movie and have sex and lay Nikki's bad memories to rest with some good ones of our own.

And figure out how to kill the Cinderella Killer.

I WIPE MYSELF clean and pack up my shoes just in case Motel Guy won't let me have the room, but I plan on being persuasive. This room is my room. There's too much history for me to give it up. It's fated. All these things are interconnected, and I'll be damned if some money-grubbing Motel Guy is going to get in the way.

I march down to the registration alcove. I wait patiently for Motel Guy to look up from whatever lame-ass television program he's watching. When he sees me I dangle the room key in my fingers. The fob swings back and forth. Motel Guy slams open the window. I pull the key back into my palm.

"How much for a month?"

"You said you just wanted room for a quickie."

"Let's just say we've hit it off and are considering a long-term relationship."

"A thousand. Up front. No credit."

"Deal."

I count out the cash. Motel Guy looks flabbergasted and then disappointed, as though he expects me to haggle. I go back to my Bug, catching another tirade of harlot abuse from the god squad man.

I spin by the last murder site. This one is still yellow taped as the forensic people do their thing. I join the crush of the morbidly curious staring at news reporters recording updates for the evening news. I watch detectives being interviewed, and I want to tell them to stop wasting their time,

I know what's going to happen and when, but of course I don't say anything. I learned my lesson in San Francisco. The cops don't know how to deal with me and my power. I'll never make that mistake again, especially now Ellen and me are tight. I couldn't stand it if something happened to her. Maybe this Cinderella psycho is after Ellen, you know, a celebrity stalker type of thing. Well, come and get us, she's an ex-cop, and we can take care of this Cinderella Killer ourselves. Maybe we'll make another fortune from *The Ex-Cop That Killed The Cinderella Killer*. Now there's a sequel.

Yeah, right, we're going to have to think carefully about how we take the bastard out. Ellen won't have the protection or excuse of a badge this time. We've got to be smart. There's no way we'll hand the creep over to the cops. We'll have to kill him and find a way to make it look like a suicide. "Dear Cruel World—I couldn't take all this killing any more, so I committed one more murder—my own."

But we've got to find him first.

The answer will be in the shoes. It always is. I'm not sure which shoes will hold the key, but a pair will show us the way. Maybe it'll be the victim's. Maybe not. From what the paper said all of the johns had just had sex prior to being murdered. Shoesex wouldn't help me with this one other than to record the quick pre-murder fuck. It's doubtful that all three would stop to have sex again after having just come, so they were probably jumped. If so, my only hope of a lead would be from the killer's shoes, assuming of course that he or she dug some sexual gratification out of this. Come on, Violetta, the murderer dresses the victims up in drag and stuffs their feet into hooker pumps. The Cinderella Killer gets off all right.

As I push my way through the murder groupie crowd back to my Bug I realize how different my situation is now, as opposed to when I went after the Dildo Killer. Despite my earlier Holmesian bravado, I am not a detective. I don't know how to find a suspect. With the DK I had Shoe Leather, and I let the killer come to me. I have no such place anymore.

I am so not ready for this.

Two weeks suddenly seem like such a short time, and my own shortcomings loom gigantinormous. I wish Ellen was here. She should be home about now. I use a pay phone to call her to tell her my plan and get her to come over to our adult motel love nest. The phone rings. The message machine picks up, but it won't let me leave a message. It must be full.

Oh shit. Ellen must be crazy with worry. Maybe I should go back to Stinson and meet her, and we can come back to Room 6 at the Paradise together later.

From MacArthur I turn right onto Broadway and head towards the bay side of the freeway. I can turn on to the 580 and take it straight to the 80 and back home across the Richmond-San Rafael bridge. But I head right under the 580 towards downtown Oakland.

Fuck, I've come this far.

A quick drive-by sighting of what used to be Cutrero's Shoe Repair couldn't hurt, could it?

TEN

HE'S HIGHWAY PATROL, and he knows who I am.

"In a rush to kill another psycho, Miss Stewart? Where are you heading?"

At least he didn't call me Ma'am and ask me to step outside of the car, but calling me Miss, it's so—so—dismissive. I hate being called Miss as much as I detest being referred to as Ma'am. One conveys an image of a silly young girl and the other suggests I've got blue hair and grandkids. The Misses and the Ma'ams are put-downs, and it pisses me off.

Can this trip home get any more insulting and delayed? I'm frustrated. I'm ranting. What's worse is that I know it, and I can't stop. Whenever the Universe conspires against me like this I rail at any little thing. Take this traffic stop for example. For the first time in my adult life, I know what the non-cop average citizen feels like when pulled over—powerless and forced to be polite, no matter how big of a dick the cop wants to be. I hate it, but I fight my natural control freak instincts and grovel. I just want to get home to Violetta, so whatever it takes, I'll do it. Which cheek, officer? Right or left? Oh, in the middle? No problem.

"No, I'm not chasing another killer. Nothing so dramatic, officer. That's your job now. I'm retired. I was in a hurry for a meeting in Daly City that I'm late for thanks to fog in LA. I shouldn't have been speeding. I should know better. I'm sorry. How bad was I?"

When on the receiving end of a speeding ticket never, never, never tell a Highway Patrol cop the actual destination, unless of course it's a hospital and there's a valid excuse like a woman about to give birth in the backseat. If the CHPer knows where the speeder's heading in such a hurry he'll radio ahead and tell his fat-assed buddies to be on the lookout for such and such car zooming way above the speed limit. Most people in a rush figure that law enforcement lightning never strikes twice. Once the cop's out of sight, the right foot plunges. The CHP is famous for picking up easy tickets that way, even waiting for speeding cars at off ramps. No way in hell am I going to tell him I'm racing to Stinson across the Golden Gate Bridge.

"You were doing eighty-five, and I'm being kind."

"Ouch."

"You haven't been drinking have you? A few cocktails on the plane maybe?"

"No, not at all."

"That's fine and dandy then, Miss Stewart. I just had to ask. I'll be right back with your ticket."

Miss. Miss. Miss. How would he feel if I called him Sonny or Junior? I bet he probably wouldn't mind because his name is Sonny or Junior. This ranting is getting me nowhere. What can I do to hurry this along? I know better than to offer the bribe of a signed book. He'd take the autographed copy and still give me a ticket. Back at the station he's going to get a lot of mileage out of ticketing The Cop that Killed the Dildo Killer. For a moment I toy with telling him that I suspect something horrible has happened at my house and could he give me a police escort, but that notion vaporizes as quickly as it flared. I don't need to draw attention to Violetta, and most probably there's a very reasonable explanation for why I haven't been able to reach her.

She's freaked, that's why.

And if she's freaked she doesn't need a bunch of cop cars blaring down our street with me in between them. So I look in the rearview mirror and tap my hands on the steering wheel wondering what takes Officer Junior Sonny Dickhead so long to write up a simple speeding ticket.

Every second he delays, my mind conjures up more horrible fates for Violetta.

She's drowned in the ocean.

She's crashed her car.

She's hung herself.

She's dead.

He's back, and I'm almost frantic and surprise, he's holding a well-thumbed copy of my book. And a ticket. Bastard. I summon up my celebrity game face. Its well-practiced smile is a veil under which I've learned to hide my panicked insides.

It works. He seems oblivious to my true state. He smiles.

"I wrote you up for sixty-five. Watch yourself next time, Miss Stewart."

"Oh, I will, and thank you for being so understanding."

"No problem. After all you've been through we wouldn't want to lose you in a traffic accident."

"That would be stupid."

"Don't bear thinking about, Miss Stewart. Say, may I call you Ellen?"

"Yes, please, I'd prefer it."

"Say, Ellen, after you've signed for the ticket, would you mind signing my copy of your book. 'To Leroy' would be fine."

"It would be a pleasure, Leroy."

"I keep your book in the car with me. It's inspirational. I read it over and over during breaks."

"Why thank you, Leroy. I'm flattered."

"Yep, if you ask me, more of the sick vermin out there ought to be taken care of by us the way you did with that Dildo Killer. They should have promoted you, not forced you to resign. A lot of the guys agree with me. Most of the gals too."

If there's one term I hate more than Miss or Ma'am it's gals. It makes me cringe, but this little delay is so close to being over I swallow my tongue and sign his book. As I do so I can't help thinking that what's worse than Leroy's use of misogynist terminology is his suggestion I've become a cult hero. It's frightening how I'm suddenly the poster child for vigilante justice. My book isn't even about that. Do they really read it and understand my message? I condemn vigilante justice, saying I can't condone what I did, but that doesn't seem to register with the Leroys of the world who want to dispose of the right to a jury trial.

Like Violetta does.

That's different. She's not like Leroy. Her power's pushing her, not some redneck notion of hanging justice.

But is there any difference?

Of course there is. I love Violetta. Leroy? Well sorry, Leroy, but even if I were straight there's no future for us. He'd call me his gal, and I'd cheat on him with his sister. My future's with Violetta, and to make sure we have one I have to reach Stinson in a hurry to prevent Violetta from doing the very thing Leroy admires. I pity the next poor bastard who tangles with Leroy. I bet he's just itching for a routine traffic stop to turn ugly, but that's not my problem. I sign the book "To Leroy, who wisely slowed my speeding foot. Best Wishes, Ellen."

He reads it several times and nods. He salutes me and says "Take care, Chief Detective Stewart," before he spins on his heel and walks back to his cruiser. Believe it or not, I'm all choked up. I haven't heard my old title spoken with such respect in ages.

Leroy, he wasn't so bad.

I pull away slowly and merge with traffic in the slow lane. Leroy stays behind me a couple of car lengths, forcing me to be true to my Daly City story, so I turn onto the 380. Leroy goes straight, but I stick to the speed limit and pick up the 280 heading north. Another CHP car passes me. I bet Leroy was true to form, radioing every CHPer for miles to be on the lookout for the speeding Jeep carrying the Cop That Killed the Dildo Killer. Probably one of his buddies wants a book signed. He'll just have to come to the next in-store and wait in line.

The 280 ends and the 19th Avenue crawl begins. It's a bitch, solid bumper-to-bumper thirty m.p.h. Saturday night traffic, holding me back from breaking too many limits. Thankfully the bridge is clear and the rest of the drive to Stinson is just me and the winding road and my nightmarish thoughts. The closer I get, the faster I drive, as if that extra twenty seconds I'll save will make a difference.

It might, and that motivation makes me go even faster. I screech the Jeep into our driveway. The tires slide on blown sand. Our house is dark. I sprint to the porch, stumbling on the step, breaking my fall against the front door. It opens. It's not even locked. I tumble in, steady myself and flick on the lights. My eyes blink at the emptiness.

No Violetta sitting on the couch, scared and waiting for me to return to protect her.

No signs of a struggle. Everything's in its place. Including the morning newspaper, folded open, the front section missing. Next to it a half-drunk cup of cold coffee.

So she does know.

"Violetta, I'm home."

Please, please, please let me hear her voice saying "Hi Ellen, I'm in here."

Silence.

First I spin through the kitchen.

No carving knives missing from the stand.

Next I check the bedroom.

Nothing.

Then the bathroom.

Nothing. Thankfully she's not sprawled upon the floor.

I go back to the kitchen and check the notepad that we keep next to the phone. No "Dear Ellen, gone shopping, be back soon, Love and clitty kisses, Violetta" message. I could check the garage for Violetta's car, but I know it will not be there.

She's gone.

The little red message waiting light on the answering machine blinks so fast it's almost solid. I think that means there's no recording room left. I press play. The tape takes forever to rewind.

"Hi, Ellen, it's Damian—"

What does my agent want? Where's the fast forward button? I should learn how to use this machine.

"—I know you were in LA yesterday. I'm not sure where you are today. You're supposed to be home. We need to talk ASAP. The publisher is getting deluged with press questions about this Cinderella Killer, and our—your—responsibility. The lawyers have crafted a press release I want to run by you and make sure you're cool with it. I'm afraid you'll have to toe the party line on this subject next time you talk to the media. The publisher is very afraid of victims' relatives suing, claiming your book inspired the killings. If you ask me they're overreacting, but that's what publishers do and we jump. So call me as soon as you get this message. Hope the LA meeting went well. How was Onna Nomad? Call me. Bye."

Beep.

"Hello, Ms. Stewart, it's Fentimen Hardcastle, with Hardcastle, Redwick and Bristeaux. It's Saturday at, let's see, nine in the morning, West Coast time. We represent your publisher and would like to discuss the current situation vis-à-vis limiting all of our respective exposures. I think it wise if we present a united Teflon front. Do call at your earliest convenience. My office number is 212—"

Beep.

"Hi, Ellen, it's Damian again. Just checking. Call me. The shit is hitting the fan as we speak."

Beep.

"Ms. Stewart. Chief Detective Harrison, Oakland P.D. I'd appreciate a call. We're looking into the connection between your book and the recent killings here. You can reach me anytime at 415—"

Beep.

"Ellen, where are you? It's Damian. Call me. Please. I'm worried. Call me. I'm going to fax you a copy of the press release. Look it over. If I don't hear from you I'll assume it's okay, but call me anyway just to let me know you received my messages. Even if you don't call me, you should read the fax and be prepared to spout it if asked by the press about the Cinderella Killer. Does that make sense? Oh shit, I'm going crazy. I'm talking to a machine as if it's a person and understands me. I hope to talk to a real you soon. Very soon. I promise I won't use up any more of your message tape. Bye. Please call."

Beep.

"Hi, Violetta—"

My first message.

Beep.

My second message.

Beep.

My third message.

Beep.

"Hey, Ellen, how are—"

I fumble with buttons replaying Violetta's message again and again, as if one more time will change what she said, but it's no use—Oakland. No, no, oh God no. Of all the silly things to do.

Oakland.

How could she go chasing the Cinderella Killer? I feel like I've been punched in the stomach. I sit down, trying not to hyperventilate. Violetta promised she wouldn't go off hunting serial killers without me, and yet the first chance that comes along she's out there playing Nancy Drew with an attitude.

And Oakland of all places.

She practically tore my head off a couple of weeks ago when I suggested she should come with me to the signing.

Oakland.

Damn. I was almost there as I came back from the airport. If I hadn't gotten that stupid ticket and made up that lame Daly City story I'd have gone straight up the 101, and maybe, just maybe when I saw the signs to Oakland some association would have triggered me into going straight across the Bay Bridge.

Why didn't I tell Leroy that my meeting was in Oakland?

I should have guessed Violetta would go to the scene of the crimes, but Oakland? How could I have known? I should have known. If I'd learned to use the answering machine I could have retrieved her messages remotely, and then I'd have known before landing where she'd run off to. I didn't think I needed to learn to use the damn machine because Violetta would always be there, and I'm useless with devices that have more than an on/off switch. Oh screw the answering machine. We should have splurged and got each other cellphones. They may be big and clunky and expensive but we could keep them in our cars and always be in touch in case of an emergency.

Just like this. As soon as I'd left the airport I'd have called Violetta and she'd have told me she was in Oakland and if I'd gone by way of the Bay Bridge I could have been there by now making sure she's safe. As it is I'm at least a hour and a half away from the East Bay. I was going to keep her safe from all this serial killer crap. Some protector I turned out to be. Too busy being a star.

Beep.

Another of my LA messages, my concerned voice reminding me that I've let Violetta down. It's torture to hear my words, but I play the tape through to the end hoping for another message from Violetta. There's nothing, just my calls and a bunch from Damian and the publisher's lawyer and a few enterprising media types who sniffed out my home phone number. They can all wait. I'm going to Oakland.

Wait. Think. Violetta said she'd be back tonight. What if we pass each other on the road and she arrives home, and I'm not here? She'll panic. Fuck, we should have bought cellphones. What am I supposed to do? Stay here and worry. I can't just sit tight and wait for Violetta to come home. What if she's in trouble? Goddamn it, if I'd never made her learn to drive she'd probably still be here.

Enough. That's it. I don't do patience well. I'm going to Oakland, like I should have done in the first place, but first I'm going to leave Violetta a note telling her I went looking for her. I tell her that if I miss her she's to stay put at the beach and wait for me to come home. I'll call in as soon as I get to Oakland, and she can tell me what a silly fool I've been. Love Ellen. P.S. Sorry I wasn't here for you.

I rifle through the drawer under the phone until I find the answering machine instructions. I flip through them until I find the "How To Retrieve Your Messages Remotely" section. I try to read it, but I can't concentrate on this crap. I'm too on edge for memorizing mundane details, so I tear out the page and stuff it in my purse. Hopefully I'll find Violetta, and there will be no need for answering machine science.

I'm half way out of our driveway when I realize worrying about the goddamn answering machine made me forget something important. I'm without my cop's best friend. Old habits die hard. Who knows what trouble I'll face in Oakland. It's better to be armed than dead. I park the Jeep and run into the house to retrieve my gun from the safe. One of the perqs of being an ex-cop, particularly a famous one with a possible need to defend herself, is that it's easy to secure a permit to carry a concealed weapon. I grab enough ammunition to make Dirty Harry proud and head for the door.

The phone rings.

"Violetta?"

"No, Ellen, it's Damian. Where have you been? No, don't tell me. I don't want to know. Did you get my messages?"

"Yes, Damian, I did, but I don't have time to talk right now. I'm in a hurry."

"Did you read the fax of the press release?"

"No, not yet. I'm sure it's fine."

"Well, don't just say that without looking it over. Read it before you talk to any media so we're all on the same above-it-all page, but between you and me, this is manna from heaven. There's no such thing as bad publicity. Just as the first big push was winding down, bang, here comes a few dead johns and everyone's talking about the book again. I don't mean to suggest you were old hat. They were talking about you already, but the hype had died down a teeny bit. Only natural. Now *The Cop That Killed The Dildo Killer* is on the news again, they're talking even more, in all media formats and markets. This Cinderella Killer will be great for sales, and if somebody sues, we'll laugh all the way to the bank. I think we're talking fourth printing here, and don't worry, there's no way they could prove you and the book were responsible for another sicko."

All I can think of is Violetta.

"Actually, Damian, I feel responsible."

"Don't say that. Listen to me. Repeat after me. 'I am not to blame.' Say it. I can't hear you."

"Okay. I am not to blame. Now can I go?"

"Sure, but aren't you glad you got it out of your system? Don't you feel better? You've confessed your doubts to Father Damian, and I absolve you of all blame. As far as you're concerned you can't be responsible for all the crazy sons of bitches out there. You'd better read that fax and memorize it."

"I will. I promise. Thanks. I have to go."

"Do you think we should hold a press conference? The publisher likes the idea."

"Why bring attention to ourselves?"

"Hello? Ellen? Where have you been? Just about every news program has been running what-if stories. What if you hadn't written the book? What if you hadn't been so graphic? What if vigilante justice spurs more killers than it takes care of? What if lynch mobs start prowling the streets? Don't laugh. I think it was on *Hard Copy*. They interviewed a bunch of Oakland pimps who are organizing to patrol the streets looking for the killer. I guess business is hurting because of the murders. One of the dudes said you'd set the example of how to deal with sex criminals. The press conference could diffuse some of that bad association vibe and score a few more minutes of attention. You could appeal for calm."

Pimps on the warpath and Violetta's on the streets over there. Oh no. I can't hang around any longer.

"Okay, set it up. Let me know where and when. I've got to run. Honest. I'm leaving. Right now. I'm hanging up."

"Is everything all right?"

"I'm just tired. It's been a long day."

"Yes, do tell, how was Onna Nomad?"

"Great. Wonderful. Look, Damian, I've really gotta go. Can we do this tomorrow? Or Monday. I promise I won't talk to any press until then."

"It's a deal. I'll ring you tomorrow with all the details on the press conference. Goodnight, Ellen. Chin up. You're finding out that being a celebrity isn't all fun and games, but you can laugh all the way to the bank. Remember that."

I couldn't care less about being a celebrity. It was just a means to an end, a way to assure Violetta and me the wherewithal to live happily ever after. I'd trade all that fame and money to have her here with me right now. As long as we have each other we'll be just fine.

It sounds like a Sonny and Cher cliché, but it's true. What good will this idyllic setting be if Violetta's not here to enjoy it with me? How many famous people have had to come to terms with the realization that without even noticing it, their pursuit of money changes everything.

Well, I may have started this profitable charade, and it may have gained a life of its own, but I can end it too.

GO-GO BOOTS

ELEVEN

I WAIT AT a red light a couple of blocks up Broadway from the place where I discovered I wasn't like every other ten-year-old. I'm in the right lane so I'll have the best view of what was Cutrero's Shoe Repair.

I'm not sure I want to stop. If the city hasn't demolished my earthquake shattered home I'm going to zoom on by. As zoomy as my Bug can zoom. I don't want a crumbling-bricks-and-mortar reminder of where I tried to kill myself. Even if Cutrero's is now a vacant lot I'm not sure I can stop and commune. I'd be able to pick the spot where I stood when the earth made like a trampoline just after I'd said goodbye to Mom and Dad for what turned out to be the last time.

Thinking about that seven-point-one Richter Scale moment brings it all back. I see my parents dressed up like dorky A's fans, waving goodbye as they roll out the door to cheer their team on in the first game of the Battle of the Bay World Series. They'd never been happier. Minutes later they're squashed bits of dead meat. Worst of all, I don't know it for at least a day until old man Grabowski, the neighborhood pervert, comes by to tell me the bad news.

I'd just returned from an uncomfortable night at the Red Cross shelter.

I don't want to believe him. I accuse him of scheming to fuck me because I know what he does to his pretty little store clerks. I fix his shoes so I know his predilection for teenage twat. I tell him so—not how I know, just the dirty details. I scream he's making up lies about Mom and Dad so I'll be vulnerable to his grabby hands. The old bastard stands his ground, albeit as shaky as when the earthquake hit. He's so pale. He blends in with the October sky. I think I've given him a heart attack. He says in a tired voice he knows I'm hurting, that I don't mean the nasty things I say. He and my dad were friends. Were friends. He's talking like Dad's dead!

Reality sinks in, and I cry.

Grabby stays calm. He knows better than to put his arm around me. He says he's not making it up to take advantage of me. He wouldn't do a thing like that to Tommy Cutrero's daughter.

I know he's telling the truth, but I tell him to fuck off. I'd known all along, but I thought I could make it not so if I didn't admit it, at least to a dirty old man like Grabowski and a dirty young woman like myself.

Even now, two years later, the memories are so fucking vivid, too fucking painful. Sitting in my idling car at the stoplight I hear Grabowski's wheezy voice in my ear, his sour breath against my face. "Violetta, your mom and dad aren't coming back."

My lip quivers, tears tumble down my cheeks. I wipe my drippy nose on the sleeve of my leather jacket and the worn smell comforts me, reminds me of shoe leather.

I need a fix.

I reach into the bag on the seat next to me and pull out one of Mom's high heels. It sparkles. I bury my nose deep inside the sequined shoe, as far as I can go, rubbing my nostrils against the delicately worn sole. I inhale.

That's better.

Fuck the normals to my left, the family in the minivan who're laughing at me. I don't act embarrassed, as if I'd been caught picking my nose. I just take another deep breath of shoe, and when I'm finished I face my audience and stick my tongue out at them. They look straight ahead so fast I bet they get whiplash. Serves the fuckers right.

A big-ass truck turns right, and ahead of me I see the Paramount Theatre. It looks like it's being refurbished; there's scaffolding all around it. Then beyond it where my block should be I see the new buildings, strip mall-style. What a relief. Hopefully the real estate mogul who owned the land built a 7-Eleven there or a gas station. I'm so not into hysterical preservation. Something modern and tacky to completely obliterate the painful past is good. I feel better knowing I won't have to gawk at my old home.

I think I can do this. I crane my neck for a better view down the street. A rude honk from behind reminds me that I should be paying attention to the light. I gas the Bug and putter away down memory lane.

It's not a 7-Eleven or a gas station.

It's a shoe store.

I brake to a sudden halt as if someone with really cool shoes had stumbled in front of my Bug. I stare at the glass and neon facade of the store and all the new shoes on display. More rude honks. The guy behind me is getting pissed. He's swearing and gesticulating like an Italian, but I couldn't care less about his angst. I pull away slowly, telling myself I'm not in Oakland anymore. This has to be Oz, or better yet the *Twilight Zone*. A shoe store built on the ruins on Cutrero's—it's too fucking weird.

There's a coffeehouse where Grabowski's Hardware used

to be, so with any luck there's no chance of running into old grabby hands Grabowski unless he traded in nuts and bolts for cappuccinos and espressos. A sandwich place stands where the Souza Bakery was. I circle the block to check out the shoe store again. There's still no parking on Broadway, but at least I catch the store's name before the honks get too annoying: Tony's Discount Designer Shoes For Men And Women.

This I have to see more of. I'm actually smiling. The tears have dried. It's all so improbably fucking silly. I might even bust a gut laughing, but it's not just a joke, it's poetic, like something out of a soppy movie. A shoe store on the site of my dad's shoe repair shop is the perfect way to wipe out the bad memories. It's like what Ellen and I did to Melanie's platforms—having a pleasant fuck in shoes that hold horrible shoesex replaces the violent vibes. Maybe the construction trade is like fucking. They both have erections in common.

Tony's Discount Designer Shoes For Men And Women. It's too fucking much. I laugh like a retard, and all the honks in the world can't bring me down as I stop the Bug to stare. I wonder if Tony's Discount Designer Shoes are any good.

It's no use resisting, I'm a sucker for shoe leather.

What the fuck, I'm going in.

I park my Bug on a side street where there are no meters, and I walk to Tony's. I pretend to window shop. The place has a huge variety. There are some really cool stilettos on display, and a bunch of platforms. This is so neat. I feel like I'm Aladdin standing at the mouth of the cave.

There's a woman and a young guy waiting on people. It's just after five. The sign says the store closes at six. They're not too busy. I'll get Ellen a present. It'll be my way of saying sorry for rushing off without leaving her a note. So what if we bought a bunch of shoes just a few weeks ago. There's no such thing as too many shoes. I might even buy myself a pair or two. Tony's has some cool styles. I'm hooked.

The woman sales assistant is the first to pounce. I tell her I'm just looking as I fumble my way through the sale table. It's the basic name stuff—Via Spiga, Nine West, Gucci, Ferragamo. Nothing too special, but the prices are reasonable. The back of the store catches my attention—a wall display—thigh high lace-up paratrooper-style platform boots. They look like they're made out of black rubber with bright, silver eyelets for the laces. Not exactly Ellen's speed, but on me they'd be killer. They'd go great with the jacket and miniskirt I'm wearing.

"Would you like to try them on?"

It's the young guy.

"Sure. You have a six?"

"I bet we do. Have a seat. I'll be right back."

I don't sit down. I keep looking. I find a pair of white patent leather go-go boots that Ellen will drip for. Fuck, I'll drip for her when she wears 'em. She'll look awesome. I'll make her strip and dance around wearing nothing but the boots, and I'll toss wadded-up dollar bills at her naked butt yelling crude things like, "Shake that tush, woman. Stir your honey pot for me but good." Her legs will tense to perfection in these glossy babies. Then we'll fuck, and afterwards I'll wear the boots to see how slutty we were, and I'll come again being Ellen doing me. I can't wait. Oh be still my beating clit.

"Do you have these in an eight?" I ask the guy when he comes back with a truckload of boxes. I'm sure I look flushed from my erotic daydreaming. He looks at me quizzically, and I wonder if he's noticed I'm horny. Then he looks even more quizzically at the boxes he's cradling, and I suss his confusion. "They're for a friend," I say.

"Oh I see. I thought I'd heard you right when you asked for a six in the thigh highs. I'll go see if we have the go-gos in an eight. I'm sure we do. They're cool, aren't they?"

"Way."

He places the boxes at my feet and looks up at me.

"I brought you the equivalent of the five, six and seven in the rubber boots to try on. They're made in England so their sizes are all off by two. You've got three, four and five to work with. They're cut kind of small. These boots are difficult to fit. They're made out of rubber."

"No shit." Catty, but come on, it's obvious. They stink like rubber gloves, but I'm sure I can develop an appreciation. Once I've sweated up a good fuck I'm sure they'll be more to my liking. Oh dear, I'm porndreaming again. Why am I so horny?

"While you're trying those on I'll go check on my stock of go-go boots. I'm pretty sure we have them in lime green or tangerine orange too."

"Bring them all, and I'll see what works best. Maybe I'll get one lime and one tangerine. Or all three pairs."

He laughs. He's cute.

"If you need any help, just yell. I'll be right in the back."

I take off my high tops and stick my foot into the six. It's way too big. Next I try the five. Pretty good. I wrap the upper around my calf and my thigh and it looks like they'll fit. So I start lacing as the guy comes back with more boxes. This place is Aladdin's cave and the guy's the genie granting my every shoe wish.

"Here we are, lime, tangerine, white, and we even have black. Need any help?"

"Sure. Why not?"

I extend my leg. The young guy hands me the boxes of go-go boots. I check out the colors and make sure the go-go's side zipper doesn't catch while keeping an eye on him. He doesn't try to sneak a peek up my skirt. Not that he'd see too much. I'm wearing black tights. All the same, I bet he's tempted. Being a woman's shoe seller has got to be a pervert's dream job.

"I think I'll stick with the white," I say. "I'm not sure

she'd look good in lime or tangerine, and everybody wears black. Can't go wrong with white. Now, if it were me, I'd probably go for tangerine."

"We have them in a six. Would you like a pair?"

"Sure. That'd be really cool."

Matching pairs. Ellen and me, our legs wrapped around each other, the shiny patent leather sticky with our juices. In between fuckings, she'd dance for me. I'd dance for her. Fuckshoe heaven.

I'm getting so juicy. I shift in my seat as the guy finishes the laces.

"Okay. How does that feel? Not too tight?"

I stand up and flex my leg. It feels weird, like I'm encased in another skin. It's not like wearing tights or leggings. It's much more restrictive. They don't slip and give like leather boots. They grip, like Ellen's legs wrapped around me. Oh shit. I'm getting wetter. If I keep this up it won't only be rubber we'll be sniffing.

"Not too tight at all," I say. "It feels cool."

"You'd better try the other one. Right and left legs can be very different."

"I know. Lace me up."

Like a well-trained slave he does as he's told, and I take the opportunity to check him out. He's tall and gangly. He's got the black bang action going, forever wiping his hair out of his eyes. A silver chain disappears inside his black tee-shirt. It's probably a crucifix. I bet he's a good Catholic boy.

He reminds me of Jimmy, and as soon as I think so, I wish I hadn't thought of that image. I don't want to be reminded of Dildo Killer victims. I'm trying on boots. I'm having fun. This guy is nothing fucking like Jimmy, okay? He's alive, with nice hazel eyes. Jimmy's dead with gaping holes where his nice blue eyes were because the DK fucked him blind.

This guy can't be much older than me. He could be

younger. He still has a few pimples around the neck, but he's cute in a boyish kind of way. He has to be gay.

"There, walk around a bit. See how they feel."

I'm amazed. Both boots fit perfectly. And they're so comfortable. The soles must be at least two inches of rubber, and the close, unforgiving fit doesn't bother me at all. The top of them just reaches the hem of my skirt. Perfect tease material.

"They are killer."

"They suit you."

"Yeah, they do, don't they? I'll take them."

"Would you like to wear them?"

"Of course."

"Will there be anything else? I mean, in addition to the go-go boots?"

"Absolutely. You have such great stock. It's hard to find so many cool styles in one place. Do you have any really high-heeled slingbacks? Open-toed preferably and tall. I mean skyscraper tall."

I'm thinking of Ellen. She looked so sexy in Melanie's platforms. And those slingbacks she bought were awesome, but they weren't high enough. I've been dying to do her with both of us wearing ultimate fuck-me pumps.

"We carry the entire Pierre Silber line. KrissKross six-inch. Slide six-inch. Clarissa. Stone. Mini-Peep five-inch and four. And the classic Marilyn."

He shows me display photographs, and I swoon. Pierre Silber's shoes are so perverted. My eyes rest on the classic Marilyn. Marilyn Monroe—my dad's favorite movie star. I remember Mom wanting to dress me up for Halloween as Marilyn Monroe, and I refused. I wanted to be the Bride of Frankenstein. Would I have discovered shoesex if I'd dressed up as Marilyn Monroe?

How strange to be standing in the space where Dad and I spent so much time as he taught me shoe repair while I sneaked as many foot feels as I could. I was desperate to find new pairs of fuckshoes. Years later here I am in the same space, buying shoes to fuck my lover in. I have to get the Marilyns. They'd be perfect for Ellen. I'll try the Mini-Peeps, five inches of course.

I tell the young guy my preferences, and he's off into the storeroom. I'm sure he's stoked. He's probably on commission, and I've just made him more in one day than he usually makes in a month.

I pass the time looking around the store. All the other customers have left. The woman sales assistant is stacking sales receipts. The young guy comes back with more boxes. He looks at the clock. I follow his gaze. Five after six. Whoops. Times flies when you're trying on shoes.

"You can go if you like, Nancy. I'll lock up," says the young guy.

"You sure?"

"Yeah, I'll finish up here. See you Monday."

"Yeah, thanks. Take care, Tony."

Tony! Not as—

"Tony—as in Tony's Discount Designer blah-blah-blah," I say.

"Yeah, that's me."

"So this is your place?"

"Yeah."

"Cool. How old are you?"

"Eighteen."

"Cooler."

"Yeah. I came into some money, and this place was going real cheap. It's weird. It used to be a shoe repair place before the earthquake, so I guess it was destined to be a new shoe store in this life. I scored a Downtown Redevelopment grant. Got a low interest loan for the stock."

I'm tempted to tell him my link to this place, but I hesitate. I don't feel like opening up my past to a stranger, even if he is cute and into shoes. So I make small talk.

"Are you doing well?"

– 193 –

"Been open a month or so. Doing very well, touch shoe leather."

He actually reaches over and strokes the sole of a pair of shoes. I like that touch. He smiles at me.

"And you're going to be my best customer so far."

"You're into shoes, aren't you?"

"Yeah. I really dig 'em."

"Me too."

"I can tell. You know your shoes."

He holds out two boxes emblazoned with Pierre Silber logos.

"Here's the Marilyns and the Mini-Peeps, five inches. If you want to try on the Peeps I can help you unlace your boots."

"Nah. I'm sure they'll be fine, and if they don't fit, I'll bring them back. I don't want to keep you. It's Saturday night."

"I'm in no rush. I don't have any special plans. Once I close up I'm going to get a coffee at the place a couple of doors down. Would you like to join me? We can talk more about shoes."

He flushes. It's a cute reaction.

"Sure. Okay. That'd be nice."

He extends his hand.

"Hi, I'm Tony."

"Violetta."

We shake. His grip tightens. I like a firm handshake, but this is a bit extreme. He's crushing my fingers. He must masturbate a mega-amount. He's reluctant to let go. He stares at me, shaking my hand long after my wrist has gone limp. I pull away. He reddens and looks at the floor as he speaks. I think he's got a crush on me. Literally. He's so cute.

"Pleased to meet you, Violetta."

"Likewise."

"Violetta, that's an unusual name."

"Mom and Dad were Italian opera nuts. It's from *La Traviata*, their favorite."

"Must have been nice to have such caring parents."

I'm about to say yeah, they were cool, we used to own this place when it was a shoe repair store, when it dawns on me that he wouldn't say it was nice to have such caring parents if he had known the pleasure of a nice family. He said he had just come into some money, so maybe his folks died and left him a bunch. And maybe they were rich asshole parents who only gave him money and not love. Either way, I know I hated talking about Mom and Dad's deaths when they were so fresh, so I get back to neutral ground.

"Yeah, I guess so. Can I give you a hand with all those boxes?"

He takes the hint.

"No problem. I'm used to it. I'll just add everything up, and we can get out of here."

"Great. Thanks a bunch for all your help. You have some really cool shoes here."

I smile at him and he glances away. He really is way cute.

What the fuck am I doing flirting with this guy? It's not like I'm into him or anything, although I have been horny as a goat since I walked in here. What's going on? Ellen and I are monogamous.

Yeah, right, but we never talked about men.

Does a bit of dick count as infidelity to a lesbian? Of course not. Dykes can have boy toys. Saves buying a strap-on or a vibrator, which we couldn't do since the DK kind of spoiled dildos for us, so a natural bit of dick is okay. And a hetero fling wouldn't affect how I feel about Ellen one little bit. I love her. I lust Tony.

Maybe I'm bi. That's it. I never really thought of myself as a lesbian. It just happened. I did enjoy my one real hetero fuck, although I don't want to think about Jimmy right now. But it's too late. Here comes that old memory again. Get out of my head, James Purcell, you're dead. It doesn't matter that it was just about where I'm standing now that I learned Jimmy had been killed by the DK. Doesn't matter one little bit. Jimmy, you're history. This guy is now.

Tony's probably gay. Yeah, but gay guys can fuck women. But. Butt. There's lots we could do. I could suck his cock. He could butt fuck me. Oh, man, Violetta Valery, try to control your raging hormones. I could jump his bones right here, right now. It would be poetic to fuck on the site of old Cutrero's. It's hallowed shoe ground.

It must be all the shoes. Yeah, that's the rub. It's nice to meet someone as obsessed with footwear as me. That's the attraction.

Yeah, okay, so I've analyzed my feelings, but, shit, I can't ignore that fluttering in my pussy area. I should rush home to Ellen and satisfy my carnal urges before I do something we would all regret.

Ellen. Oh shit. I should call her and see if she's home yet.

Hey, wait a pussy-dripping minute, here's a dirty idea. Maybe if Ellen comes over to the motel tonight with me we could both enjoy Tony. Then it wouldn't be cheating if we both had a bit of forbidden dick.

I wonder if Ellen'd go for it. I bet she would. She's a major horn-dog once she lets down her ex-public servant guard. I can see it now—Ellen and me with out butts in the air with Tony taking turns plunging into our assholes as Ellen diddles me, and I do likewise. Oh man, we'd re-write the *Kama Sutra*. We'd all wear shoes. Tony too. The shoesex afterwards would be unreal. I'd have to find a way to get inside Tony's footwear to see what he's thinking and feeling as he fucks two-dyke butt. Two-dyke butt—sounds like a dish from the Tu Lán menu. Next time I'm in there I'll order it and see what I get.

I've got to reach Ellen. If she can make it over here I

won't have to drive all the way home with a drippy cunt. Once she has her cow she'll be pleased I found a way to get over Oakland. That's what she wanted, right? So okay, maybe not in the way she'd have thought of, but she'll come around to a little threeway. Sure she will.

I open the Marilyns box. They are gorgeous. The photo doesn't do them justice. Ellen will look spectacular in them. They're all silver and nothing but straps, soles and heels, no body. The heel isn't killer—about three inches. A very classy shoe. The Mini-Peeps are Mega-Slut all the way. They're see-through plastic, open-toed backless slip-ons with five inch heels and one inch platforms. I wonder if my power will work on plastic? It had better. The things I plan to do in these puppies deserve to be recorded.

Tony spies me ogling the Mini-Peeps.

"You're lucky."

"How so?"

"That's the last pair. They're really popular with dancers, strippers, hookers, but that's not the real reason. Ever since those Cinderella Killings I can't keep them in stock. They're what the killer forces the victim's feet into. I guess it's the closest thing to a glass slipper."

I drop the Mini-Peeps in the box and wrap them back up in tissue paper. The Cinderella Killer. I was having so much fun shoe shopping in my old neighborhood I'd forgotten why I was in Oakland. Fuck. Back to Avenging Angel Sex Goddess reality.

"How do you know?"

"The police were in here with a pair from the first victim. The Mini-Peeps were bagged in plastic but you could see all the blood. The cops wanted to know if I sold them and if I had any records."

"Did you?"

"No. Those Mini-Peeps weren't from here. They were size fours. Really tiny. I don't carry anything that small. Five's the lowest I go. I told the cops to contact Pierre Silber directly, although I doubt they'll have any luck tracing them. There's no individual markings to identify the shoes."

"There can't be that many size fours out there."

"You'd be surprised. Orientals, Pilipinos. I've had them in here asking for them. Little women like them because it makes them look tall and sexy."

I thought of Melanie Courtland and her blue platforms.

"If you get that many inquiries why don't you carry those small sizes?"

"Wow, are you a cop? They asked that too."

"I'm sorry. I was just curious."

"It's okay. It's a reasonable question. I probably will carry the smaller sizes as I can afford to carry more stock, but for now I offer to special order them, but no one's taken me up on it. They just go elsewhere. Pierre Silber is in San Jose, and there are many stores in San Francisco that carry them."

"I didn't read anything in the papers about the shoes being Mini-Peeps. All the reports just said high heels or stilettos. How come everyone but me knows about them?"

"The police told me not to say anything to the press, but you know how it is. I tell a customer like you, and you tell somebody and word of mouth spreads. People are really into sick crimes, and if I can sell a few more shoes out of it, why not? I feel sorry for the victims, but my selling a few shoes isn't going to bring them back or hurt them any more. So why not make a buck?"

I thought of Motel Guy and his rent-the-room-the-dead-john-was-in racket. Tony has a point. Life goes on. I put the lid back on the Mini-Peeps' box and place it on the counter. Tony looks at the box and speaks with concern.

"Do you still want them? Now that you know? I didn't mean to gross you out."

"Of course I want them. I'm as much of a rubbernecker as the next person. And no, you didn't gross me out."

He hits the total button and grimaces.

"It's kind of a lot—"

"How bad?"

"With tax, $565.48. Would you like to pay it all at once?"

"Sure. No problem. Like you say, I'm your best customer."

I count out the cash. This trip has mutated into an expensive jaunt. I'm almost broke. Just enough for coffee. I should call Ellen again and ask her to bring some cash when she comes over. She should be home by now. I'll invite her over to meet us for coffee, and we'll see what happens from there. At some point I'm going to have to tell Tony who my main squeeze is, but not yet. Ellen's such a celebrity. I want to make sure he's interested in me first and the Cop That Killed the Dildo Killer second.

"Could I use your phone? Marin County. Is that okay?"

"Sure. I'll put the cash in the safe, then we can get going. Take your time."

I ring our number. The message tape plays. One long-ass beep follows. Then it hangs up. Fuck me. The tape must be full. That means Ellen isn't home yet. Oh well, the meeting with Onna Nomad must have dragged on. Ellen should be home any moment. I'll ring her again after coffee. I can't wait to tell her about all the cool shoes I bought her, and what my dirty mind has planned.

Tony appears from the back of the store. He picks up my purchases, his lanky upper torso obscured by a stack of shoe and boot boxes. I did go overboard.

We walk to the Bug. He places the boxes carefully under the hood, making sure they won't get crushed while I grab my bag. I figure if we're going to talk shoes, I may as well show him my coolest pairs that I just happen to have with me. As we walk back to the coffee shop I notice how weird it feels walking with a guy like we're out on a date. I haven't done this since Jimmy. Doh! I wasn't going to think of him again. Can I please stop resurrecting Dildo Killer victims who I fucked? It has nothing to do with right now.

I'm having fun. I want to keep it that way.

At the coffee bar I order a mocha java. Tony has a cappo. As we're stirring in sugars the feeling-out process begins.

"So, do you live around here?" he asks me all nonchalant.

"Stinson Beach. That's where I was calling. I live there with my—"

I'm not sure what to call Ellen. Lover, friend, partner, significant other, dyke. Tony is way ahead of me.

"Ah, I see. The size eight go-go boots."

"Yeah, you got it. She's older than me. Her name's Ellen. We're really good friends. The best. She's seen me through some very bad times. How about you?"

"No, Ellen's not seen me through my bad times."

I slug Tony's shoulder. That's exactly the kind of smart-ass comment I'd make.

"I meant—"

"I know what you meant. I live alone. Not too far from here. I walk to work. I don't have anyone in my life right now. I saw myself through my bad times."

Yeah, but are you gay? That's what I want to know. Should I say he'll, she'll or take the gender neutral approach with my next question? I chicken out.

"Well, don't worry, it'll come along when you least expect it."

"Oh I'm not bothered. I'm in no rush to find love. So what brings you to Oakland?"

Here comes the Cinderella Killer responsibility again. Well, there's nothing I can do now to catch the CK, so no need to spoil a good time. If my theory's right I've got a couple of weeks until the next murder. I take a big gulp of coffee and tell the other side of the truth.

"I grew up here."

"No way."

"Yeah, you're gonna die when I tell you where."

"Where?"

"In your store, before it was your store."

The look on Tony's face is priceless. He doesn't know whether to laugh, cry or wait for the hidden camera to be revealed.

"No way."

"Yeah. Big way. This is so weird. The shoe repair shop you mentioned was Cutrero's Shoe Repair. My dad was Tommy Cutrero. He taught me the shoe repair business there."

Tony nods. A smile illuminates his face.

"That explains everything. I knew you were into shoes, the way you held them, the way you inspected them. I had no idea though. That's amazing."

"Isn't it? When the earthquake happened Mom and Dad were killed. I left Oakland. I thought it was about time I buried the past, so I came back. I had no idea a shoe store had been built there. It made me feel so happy. It was like it was meant to be."

"Fate."

"Yeah. I guess. How about you? Where did you grow up?"

"All around the Bay Area. My mom and dad died when I was young, so I bounced from foster home to foster home."

"That's too bad. I'm sorry. What brought you to Oakland?"

"I got into some trouble in San Jose when I was sixteen. The nuns couldn't handle me. I ended up at a runaway home run by bad-ass priests down on 14th Street. Been there ever since. I turned eighteen in June and left. I came into a little cash and was able to open the shoe shop."

"Why shoes?"

"The priests got me a Saturday job at Leeds in the Bayview Mall. I started out stocking boxes and learned all I could. I became a sales assistant, but I mostly ran the store cause the real manager was a flake. They'd have made me manager, but I wanted my own place. The priests turned me on to the Redevelopment Agency, and here I am."

"It's so cool. I started work in Dad's shop when I was sixteen, then I opened my own place in San Francisco when I was eighteen from the money I'd come in to. I called my store Violetta's Shoe Leather."

"Do you still have it?"

"Nah. Sold out. I needed to get out of the City. I wasn't very happy. Let's hope the parallels between you and me end there."

"Hey, don't knock it. If I can get a few more customers like you I'll hit the big time and sell out too. I'll buy Leeds and have a chain of Tony's. I'll live a life of luxury."

We clink coffee cups and drain the dregs. "To Tony's."

"Another?"

"No, I'm wired. Would you mind if I make a call?"

"No. Not at all. The phone's over there in the corner."

I feel Tony's eyes on me as I dial. I'm not so sure he's gay, but he knows I live with a woman. What does he think of me? In the window reflection I see he's looking at me funny, like he's attracted, but isn't sure what to do next. Maybe he's picking up how horny I am. My tights are soaked. Not just at the crotch, but all over. These damn rubber boots are a sweat factory.

Long-ass beep. Fuck. Ellen's still not home. Now I'm pissed. I'm getting so fed up of listening to that frigging message and trying to leave a frigging message at the sound of the frigging beep, but it frigging won't let me. What the frigging hell is going on? Maybe I should stow my hormones and go back home and wait for Ellen. Fuck.

I stomp back to the table, my feet making tiny little squelching noises inside the boots.

"A problem?"

"No, nothing really. Damn answering machine is full so

I can't leave a message. I ought to be going."

He swallows and looks at me with lust in his eyes. He's made up his mind. I can tell he doesn't want me to leave. He looks like he'd like to bone me right here, right now in the coffee bar. Old Grabowski would be so happy.

"Would you like to get something to eat? We could walk down to Jack London Square. Enrico's By The Bay is really cool."

Mom and Dad always took me to Enrico's for my birthday. Going there would be a perfect end to a day of burying old ghosts, but I play it coy.

"I am hungry. I haven't eaten since this morning."

"Well let's go."

Fuck coy.

"Okay. That'd be nice. My parents always used to take me there for my birthday."

"Then Enrico's it has to be."

"Only—"

"Yes?"

"This is so embarrassing. I don't have any more money. I spent it all on shoes, and Enrico's isn't cheap."

"Don't worry. It'll be my treat. It's the least I can do after you bought all those shoes."

"Cool. That'd be nice. Thanks. I can pay you back."

"Never. I owe you so much."

"It was just a bunch of shoes."

"You of all people should know that it's not just a bunch of shoes."

The walk to Enrico's is filled with talk of the significance of shoes—his favorites, my favorites. I tell him about the really cool shoes in my bag. He wants to see them, so I hand them to him. He's impressed. He wants to know all about them. I tell him the ones with the sparkly bows were my mom's, and the glittery platforms were never picked up from the store. So I kept them. I don't let on that I know their history or who they belonged to because I don't want

– 203 –

to tell him about my power. Nikki is mentioned in Ellen's book, and just about everybody has read it, so I don't want to be dropping too many clues. I just don't want to think about murders right now, okay?

Even so, as we saunter down Broadway holding Nikki's shoes, I can't help flashing on the memories contained in her sparkly platforms. We're retracing Nikki's steps, only instead of turning up San Pablo we go straight towards Jack London Square. We're walking away from her death and my dad butt fucking her and slapping her. I'm squeezing the genie back in the bottle. Kind of an appropriate image considering Tony's place reminded me of Aladdin's cave.

It's funny, someone who's not into shoes would wonder why I carried these old shoes around with me, but Tony never asks. He's more interested in the style, the workmanship. He takes it for granted that I'd have them with me. He really is into shoes.

ENRICO'S IS WAY cool. It's so expensive they don't bother to card us, so we buy bottles of Chianti, the kind my dad always ordered on my birthday and let me have a glass. Dinner is fabulous and we split a tiramisu, Dad's favorite dessert. I'm so happy and drunk.

I'm feeling bold.

"Would you excuse me? I have to go to the bathroom and take off my tights."

Tony snickers.

"The rubber boots, huh?"

"Yeah. I'm soaked."

"I was going to warn you in the store, but I thought you'd slap me if I told you to take off your pantyhose."

"I might have. I'll be right back."

"If you need any help unlacing those things, I'll be right here."

I wag my finger at him in mock disapproval. He smiles.

Rakish. He's so totally cute. We're going to fuck. I know it. He knows it.

Ellen doesn't.

But I'm going to correct that. I have a plan. On my way back from the bathroom, feeling oh so refreshed now my skanky tights are off my legs, I ring the beach house again. This time there are four rings, so she must have come home and cleaned off all the messages.

Beep.

"Ellen, pick up the phone. I know you're home. Hello, it's me. I'm in Oakland having dinner at Enrico's in Jack London Square. You're never going to guess what I found out. It's amazing. Amazing good. It's not about the murders. It's just so cool. I've got you a present. Lots of presents. Pick up, pick up why don't you? Look, I've made us some plans that I hope you're cool with. Fuck, where are you? Maybe you popped out for something. The fridge was kind of bare. Look, when you get back, if you're not too tired, come to Oakland. I've had too much to drink to drive. I have a room at The Paradise Motel on MacArthur Boulevard. Room 6. I'll be waiting with a big surprise for you."

When I get back to the table, Tony's paid the bill.

"Feel better?"

"Mega. Only the rubber's still a little clammy. I wish I'd brought the Mini-Peeps with me."

"Why don't you wear the shoes you have in your bag?"

I don't need a shoesex episode right now. I smile politely, determined not to give anything away.

"They're kind of special. I don't want to ruin them. I'll be okay."

"If you'd like to change I don't live too far from here. A block at most. I have several samples of some new lines you might want to try."

"Is that like come up and see my etchings?"

"I—"

I put my finger to his lips.

"Hey, it's cool. I'd like to come up and see your etchings. I mean samples."

We laugh ourselves out of the restaurant. I hold on to Tony's arm. I feel like I should be honest. He's been mega-nice.

"Look, Tony, I need to tell you something."

"That sounds serious. Don't tell me. You're an ax murderer."

"I'm in a serious relationship with a woman."

"It's okay. I guessed from your earlier comments and the number of times you've tried to ring her. Ellen, right?"

"Yeah."

"That's cool. I'm not hitting on you. It's just neat to find someone so into shoes."

He is gay. I'm drunk and horny, and I'd like to think very appealing to a totally cute young male. The Chianti makes me bold.

"Don't you want to sleep with me?"

"No, I'd like to fuck you."

Maybe not gay after all.

"How would you feel about fucking two women?"

"As long as one of them is you, and Ellen's not a dog."

Definitely not gay.

"Oh no, she's gorgeous. I just don't want to cheat on her."

"I understand."

"She's really cool. She'll be so blown away by this."

"How will she find us?"

"I've thought of everything. I have a room at a sleazy motel. I told her to meet us there."

"Where's that?"

"The Paradise on MacArthur. Room 6."

He stops walking, turns and stares at me. He pulls his hand away. The look on his face is one of alarm, turning to shock and finally disgust.

"What's wrong?" I say.

"That's where one of those guys was killed."

"Yeah, so, it'll be kinda kinky. What's the matter, scared?"

"No, no, it's just kind of—"

"Sick?"

"Yeah."

"Are you're cool with that?"

"I don't know."

"Because, Tony, you ought to know, I'm a sick kind of girl. I'm not like any other woman on the planet. I'm weird."

"I can tell."

"You have no idea."

"Oh I think I do. I'm in. As long as I don't end up dead in an alley, in drag with my feet chopped and stuffed into a tiny pair of Mini-Peeps that weren't bought from my store."

"Don't worry, you won't. I'll protect you from the Cinderella Killer, but I may make you wear my Mini-Peeps while you do me and my lover."

"You are sick."

"Told you."

We wrap arms again and head off up Broadway. I rest my head on his arm, my eyes turned downward watching his shoes. Black zip-up boots with a Cuban heel. Very cool. My stare works its way up his legs to his crotch. As he walks his erection bulges through his tight black jeans.

Tony will look oh so good in high heels and nothing else.

TWELVE

I'M HALF WAY to Oakland before it dawns on me—I don't know where to find Violetta.

I thump the steering wheel and let fly a stream of obscenities. My complete lack of preparation pisses me off. It's just not like me to go off half-cocked, but when it comes to Violetta my commonsense takes a vacation. I'm so busy worrying about losing her that I have no room left in my brain for other thoughts.

Back to basics. Why did she run off on her own?

Doesn't she trust me? Of course she does. So many times over the last year we'd agreed we were in this together—a serial killer extermination team. Was she only humoring me? What is she thinking, running off without so much as a note? That cryptic phone call was useless. How can I protect her if she doesn't let me know the plan and her whereabouts? If she were a junior detective under my wing I'd send her back to the academy for more basic training. Rule number one of being a good cop—partners stick together and look out for each other. They don't go solo.

And they don't cover up murders and take the blame for someone they love.

Okay, so who am I to talk about being a good cop, but I can't help thinking like one and treating Violetta like my rookie. Does she have any idea how crazy her missing-in-action stunt makes me?

I feel useless.

I could scream.

I do, and I pound the steering wheel some more, and the outburst calms me a little so I can focus on what to do once I get to Oakland.

Where would that little punk go?

She'd probably head to her old neighborhood. I know from her stories she'd grown up on Broadway, near the Paramount Theater, but I'm not sure of the exact location. Even if I knew where to go what good would it do me? Cutrero's Shoe Repair was wrecked by the earthquake. It's probably a vacant lot. There's little chance of finding Violetta there.

Although, if she's freaked she might camp out in the ruins, so I figure that's the best place to start. Then I'll go by the murder sites. She's bound to snoop around those, although what she'd hope to discover that the police haven't already found I do not know.

The Cinderella Killer, that's who. Violetta may say she's simply looking around, but that's a rationalization to make me feel better. She wants to kill the killer, and if I don't get there and help her she might get herself killed. She was lucky when she executed the Dildo Killer, catching him by surprise while he was exhausted from his last kill. Despite all her tough talk she doesn't know what she's doing. She has no training in unarmed combat, how best to wield a knife, or even better, how to use a gun.

Thanks to her shoesex power she thinks she's this specially ordained assassin of serial killers. She's convinced

Good is on her side and will protect her against Evil. In my fifteen years of being a cop, the only thing that protected me against the Evil bastards I ran up against was my gun, and even then I saw many instances where Evil prevailed and a Good person ended up dead.

I'm so afraid the same fate awaits Violetta. She thinks her power makes her invincible, and such notions lead to carelessness. Careless people end up dead. I know being able to experience the sex people have in shoes is super-human, but it's gone to her head. She may be invincible in the bedroom, but on the street, no way. The silly little fool is going to get herself killed.

Calm down, Ellen.

I remind myself she's only twenty. After what's she's been through it's only natural she thinks she can do anything. She says she is an Avenging Angel Sex Goddess, but I know she's just a punk with a special power no one should be asked to carry.

A punk who I love, who I'll do anything for.

Have done everything for.

Just a few more miles, and I'll be there. For comfort, I reach into my purse and stroke my gun. It's a ritual I developed back in my early days in the SFPD. On the way to arrest a crook I always stroked my gun. It calmed me, made me feel bigger than I was. It worked. I never took a bullet, and I never hesitated to fire one or six off when the situation demanded immediate action.

I'm ready for whatever goes down tonight. I can find Violetta, I can protect her. I'm going to make her come home, but if she's dead set on finding the Cinderella Killer, I'll be able to cover her back and her front and let the bodies fall where they may. No sick fuck is going to hurt my Violetta, but first I have to find her. Sitting next to my gun is my wallet. In it I have a picture of Violetta.

Maybe someone will have seen her.

Her car. There can't be that many pink Bugs puttering

around the East Bay. Someone must have seen her car, hopefully heading out of Oakland towards the Richmond-Rafael bridge.

As soon as I arrive downtown maybe I should call the police, talk to Harrison. I'll pretend I'm there to answer his questions about my book and the Cinderella Killer, and oh, by the way, in the last few hours have there been any reports regarding a young punk girl with an attitude causing mayhem and hopefully not murder.

I'll talk to Harrison but no way will I mention Violetta. I'll keep her off Oakland PD's radar screens. She and the police don't get along. The last thing I need is for her to be pulled over and lose it because I alerted the cops. She's bound to be an emotional wreck. The littlest thing could set her off, and I know what she's capable of with that mouth of hers.

I'll find Violetta on my own. I have to. We're connected. Soul mates. Sole mates, she often says. We've come too far to let our love affair slip away because I was out of town when she needed me.

I will find her. Oakland might be a big place, but as far as Violetta is concerned it's a small town, and I'm heading straight for the heart of her childhood universe. The freeway bypass of the 880 collapse takes me to Oakland by way of the 580. The exit drops me on MacArthur Boulevard and I loop back towards Broadway. Hookers stand on all four street corners. Cars stop. Red brake lights glow appropriately. Hookers bend on platformed legs and talk into rolled down windows. Business doesn't seem damaged by the killings. Maybe the pimp patrols have forced the Cinderella Killer underground. And maybe Santa Claus will bring me back my youth for Christmas. The Cinderella Killer is operating to an agenda. There's something special about the dates. When the next one comes around no army of pimps or irate hookers will save the next victim. Serial killers always find a way.

Or they get caught.

Or they run into Violetta and me.

I pull around the sex-for-sale drive-thru and head downtown. I pass the bookstore where I did my in-store on October 12th. Was the Cinderella Killer there? Did I sign a book for him? Or her? Was my signing the event that triggered the murders? It couldn't have been a spur of the moment killing. Too much planning went into the ritual of the cross-dressing and the shoes. The Dildo Killer took months to plan his killing spree. Had the Cinderella Killer been planning these murders for an equally long time? Was my signing just a coincidence?

Or is there a deeper association?

What's special about the fairy tale connection?

And why the 12th, 17th and 31st? Is the Cinderella Killer paralleling the Dildo Killer murders? If so we're safe until November 17th. That's when the DK killed Bradley Winston. That was the murder that lead to me being put in charge of the task force. I was so excited. When I took the podium to face the press I had no idea where my assignment would lead. I just wanted to catch a killer and advance up the SFPD chain of command. It all seems like another lifetime, another me. All I want now is Violetta.

I've traded one obsession for another.

The 12th, 17th and 31st—they're also significant dates in Violetta's life. She was morbidly convinced of the link between her and Randy Warren. I blew her off. Is there a link with another killer, and is it my fault? Is there something to this destiny fantasy that Violetta's obsessed with? She was dead set against coming to Oakland on her birthday. I should have listened to her. Bad things happen there, she said. I should have told the publicist to cancel the event, but I was too caught up being the star. I lost sight of why I went down that yellow brick road in the first place. By earning enough money I thought I could keep the bad things away from Violetta. It's hard to do long distance.

I can fix this situation. There will be no more trips, no publicity, no movie consultancy. We'll make do with what we've got. I'm going to find Violetta and take her back to Stinson, and we'll never again be apart. Tonight I quit being a celebrity. Goodbye yellow brick road.

Humming the old Elton John song I cross Grand Avenue, and on the right I see the Paramount Theater. Violetta never said what side of the street she lived on. It had to be the same side. When she described her experience in Nikki's shoes she said she walked down Broadway, passed the Paramount and stopped in front of Cutrero's and then on to San Pablo. She didn't say anything about crossing Broadway. But maybe she missed that detail because I'm already passed the Paramount and I don't see any ruined buildings. It's all new strip mall shops. What was Cutrero's is probably a parking lot.

I bet that made Violetta feel horrible. Poor kid.

I decide to make one more circuit before exploring on foot. I turn to the right and backtrack several blocks and from the darkness a flash of pink catches my attention. I swerve my Jeep down a small street, and there is Violetta's Bug.

She's not in it.

Elation turns to worry. I use my spare key and check inside. There's no sign of a struggle. I look under the hood trunk and there's several boxes of shoes and boots. What a relief. If she's been shoe shopping then things can't be that bad. There's a bag with her high tops in it. Tony's Designer Discount Shoes For Men And Women, 1830 Broadway. So she bought some new shoes and is wearing them. I feel much better. She probably got carried away shoe shopping and lost track of time. That's so like her. She's probably having something to eat.

I'll case Tony's Shoes, and if I find nothing I'll wait at Violetta's Bug for her to return. While I'm checking out the neighborhood we might miss each other so I'd better leave her a note telling her I'm in Oakland, and that I'm worried, and she must go home right away, and I'll meet her there.

I crumple up that directive and write her another, less dictatorial, note. It says I love her, and I came to Oakland to be with her. I want to help her through the Cinderella Killer ordeal. Please leave me a message on our home phone telling me where to meet her and when. I have the answering machine instructions with me. I'll figure out how to retrieve her words. Love you so much. And I'm not mad at her. Love Ellen.

I'm not mad at her. I'm not mad at her. I'm not. Really.

Eighteen-thirty Broadway is a couple of blocks down from the Paramount. There's the shoe shop, a coffee bar and a sandwich place. It's almost ten. The only place open is the coffee bar, so I park the Jeep on the street and enter. The place is full of people having intense conversations. Classical music plays. I approach the counter. A guy with a pierced nose and a scraggly beard asks what I want.

"Coffee. Black."

"Just coffee?"

"Just coffee."

"We have several blends."

"You choose. Something with caffeine."

Nose Ring pours me a mug and I pay. As he hands me my change I ask him what he knows about the neighborhood.

"Before the earthquake did this place used to be a shoe repair shop? Cutrero's?"

"I have no idea. I'm from Berkeley. There's a shoe shop on the corner."

"Tony's."

"Yeah, Tony's. He comes in here a bunch. He's from around here. He might know. He was in earlier."

"Have you seen this young woman?"

I show him Violetta's picture. It's us sitting in the back

– 214 –

of the limousine on the night of her birthday.

"Are you a cop?"

"No."

"You look like a cop. Are you her mother?"

"No. I'm her lover. Not that it's any of your goddamn business. I was supposed to meet her in Oakland on Broadway near the Paramount where a shoe repair store used to be. Have you seen her?"

"Yeah. She was in earlier with Tony."

I try to hide my shock. Violetta should be with me, not some stranger.

"When?"

"I don't remember exactly. Right after he closed, I guess. Six-thirty maybe. They left together. She had a mocha and he had a cappo."

"When did they leave?"

"I'm not sure. Eight. Something like that."

"Did they say where they were going?"

"Nah. You sure you're not her mother?"

"Does this look like a mother-daughter thing?"

In the photograph I'm planting a big wet one on Violetta's cheek and my arms are wrapped around her waist. One hand's squeezing her boob.

"I guess not. Only—"

"What?"

"Well, it's none of my goddamn business, but your lover friend and Tony looked kind of well, you know. . . ."

"No, I don't."

"You know, friendly."

"Friendly?"

"Yeah. Friendly."

"Well that's her. She's a very friendly girl."

I spin around and march towards the door. I know I'm being irrational, that having coffee with someone isn't a crime, but I feel like one of those sorry women who just found out that her husband of twenty years has been cheating for twenty-one with young boys.

I try to calm myself. There's an innocent explanation for this. I've had lunch with Michael Donovan. We're friendly. Someone casually watching us laugh and joke and squeeze hands could conclude we were 'friendly.' But he's a friend who I've known for years. So this little tête-à-tête is nothing like Michael and me. Who the hell is Tony and why does he rate the Michael kind of treatment?

"Hey, your coffee."

As I turn back to tell Nose Ring what to do with his coffee I notice a pay phone. So I grab the mug and head to the phone and pull out the answering machine instructions. If Violetta is okay and having fun on the town maybe she left me a Not To Worry message. It takes several attempts of punching various number combinations, but I finally get the damned thing to work. There's one message. It's from Violetta.

Dinner at Enrico's. The Paradise Motel. MacArthur Boulevard. Why is that address familiar? Jesus Christ. That's where Nikki and Violetta's father had their tryst. That's where Nikki was murdered. What is Violetta up to? She sounded so happy in her message.

She was drunk.

This Tony had better not take advantage of her.

My blood boils.

I'll kill him.

Okay, take it easy. It's probably just the shoes. Violetta loves to talk about shoes and Tony has a shoe store.

The Cinderella Killer forced the victims' feet into stiletto shoes.

Tony has a shoe store.

There were stiletto heels on display. I saw them as I walked by. Violetta must have seen them too.

My coffee mug slips out of my hand and shatters. Coffee splatters and oozes like fresh blood. The intense conversations falter. Everyone looks up at me. Nose Ring comes running with a towel. "Are you okay?" he says when he sees my face.

I don't answer. I run out of there. I'm on my way to the Paradise Motel.

Tony is the Cinderella Killer, and he has Violetta.

THIRTEEN

A MOUNTAIN OF shoe boxes and their scattered contents litter Tony's small living room. I feel like the Queen of Shoes as he slips each brand-new pair on my feet. We ooh and ahh at how gorgeous the shoes and boots look on my bird-like legs. Each successive unboxing eclipses the last. I am mega-fucking-impressed with his collection. He boasts some truly awesome styles. This is shoe heaven. The only explanation for such a bounty of footwear is that I was right earlier when I suspected Tony was the genie. His shoe store wasn't the cave, though. His apartment is, and I've found the treasure.

Thanks to all the shoes the cave reeks of shoe leather and it makes me high. And hornier than the horny I was and have been ever since I set foot inside Tony's shoe store.

As I admire a pair of intense purple platform wedges with coiled springs embedded in the four inch soles he pulls out yet another box. I'm about to say enough, let's fuck, when he displays the contents to me.

I wolf-whistle and follow my expression of adulation with an "Outstanding."

"Aren't they?"

They are ballet shoes. Not normal ballet shoes that a ballerina would dance in but lace-up rigid shoes formed into the shape of a dancer's feet when she's standing *en pointe*. The shoes are impossible to walk in. The heels are as tall as the sole is long. They're a bondage shoe. These are exquisitely made. The black patent leather glistens like a mirror. The stitching is precise. The laces are as soft as velvet. They are the ultimate fuck-me pumps, the Crown Jewels of his treasure. I have to have them.

"Want to try them on?"

"No way can you stop me."

I rip off the spring platforms, and Tony does the ballet shoe honors. As he ties the laces on the first shoe and looks at me with an expression close to a leer I realize that we will have sex before we get to the motel. How can I refuse in these beauties? Ellen will have to pass the time getting good and juicy watching a porn flick until we get there and star in our own.

I point my foot for the second shoe. Tony loosens the laces and holds open the throat. I slide my foot in and he pulls the laces tight.

My sole makes contact with shoe leather. My soul makes contact with another.

Two people, one body.

They're fuckshoes.

They're fucking fuckshoes.

I should have known that my power would sneak in somewhere, but I didn't expect it with new shoes. Idiot Violetta.

They can't be new shoes. Somebody has fucked in these.

Oh fuck, what a genius I am. This is going to look really weird to Tony. How am I going to explain this spaz episode to him? He'll think I'm a nutcase having a fit. He'll run a mile. I've got to get my feet out of these things.

I try to wrench my foot away from Tony's grip, but he holds my ankles with that same vice-like grip with which he shook my hand. He looks up at me and sees the panicked look on my face.

He's not leering at me. He's sneering at me.

Two people, one body.

He's fucking me. I'm tied to the bed. Only it's not me. I'm Teresa. Sister Teresa. I'm a fucking nun.

"Tell me how bad I am, Anthony."

"You're a slut, Sister Teresa."

"Call me that word."

"You're a cunt."

"And you're punishing me for being a—"

"Cunt. You're a dirty cunt who makes young boys fuck her."

"Yes, that's right, I'm so awful."

As I say these words I struggle against my bonds.

"No, no, you must stop, Anthony. I don't want this. Let me go," I say in my best defenseless voice.

"There's nothing you can do, Sister Teresa of the Horny Cunt Church. I tied you to the bed like you told me to. And you're wearing the punishment shoes."

"And now you're raping me because I'm a—"

"Say it."

"I cannot. It's filthy."

"Then you're filthy, because you're a—say it."

Tony takes his hand from mauling my breasts through my disheveled habit and grips my chin and cheeks between his thumb and fingers. He squeezes my mouth open.

"Say it."

"Cunt."

"I didn't hear you."

He takes his hand away and thrusts it up my habit, rubbing my sex as his thing batters my—my—.

"Cunt. I'm a filthy cunt. Sister Teresa is a filthy cunt."

"That's better. That's what you want isn't it?"

"Yes, yes, I'm a filthy cunt who wants Anthony to—"

"Fuck her."

The wetter he makes me the easier the dirty words flow.

"Yes, fuck me, Anthony. Fuck me hard. Punish me for thinking impure thoughts about you and all the other boys here in my care."

He sings his response like a proud schoolboy.

"I'm fucking Sister Teresa. I'm fucking Sister Teresa."

"And you're going to come on my habit."

"And you're going to come too. I'm going to make you come, just like you showed me."

His fingers play with my clitoris. He fumbles, not knowing exactly where to touch, but remembering the vague area I showed him the first time I seduced him. Anthony's so young, so inexperienced, but so eager. He learns well. Oh, dear Lord, that feels so wonderful. Thank you God for punishing me in this way. You do work in mysterious ways.

I see Anthony Anderson's face grimace above me. His body arches. His young cock stiffens. His teenage balls bounce against my bottom as he pounds into me. I feel his shaft pulse.

"Pull out, Anthony, pull out."

He does as commanded, and I feel the warm jets of his release splatter on my thighs and drip down onto my habit. My orgasm rises. He slows. It slows. I snap at him and he responds. He knows who's boss.

"Don't stop you lazy boy. Now that you're free of temptation for another week, Anthony, play with me. Play with my cunt and set me free from impure thoughts."

He slides his finger in me and rubs my clitoris with his thumb, smearing his heated come over my sex. I melt onto his hand and begin to cry. Holy Father forgive me for I do know what I'm doing.

I'm coming. I'm coming. Jesus Christ forgive me.

But he doesn't. He punishes me for being a slutty cunt. "You're a slutty cunt, Violetta Cutrero," he says. "A slutty cunt."

Tony's on top of me pounding into me like I'm his well-lubed fist with his super-tight grip. I'm tied to his bed in a weird reconstruction of his kinky scene with Sister Teresa. Maybe tying up a girl like his nun from Catholic school is the only way he can get off. The ballet shoes are still on my feet. My leather jacket's hanging on the bedpost. My tee shirt is pushed up to my neck so my tits are exposed. He's biting them as he slobbers his insults. He thrusts hard into me, and I like the urgency because I'm so horny from the shoesex with Sister Teresa.

Tony probably thought that when I went into my shoesex episode I was just trying to seduce him like that nun did, so he tied me up. He doesn't know I'm aware of his dirty deal with a bride of Christ. He said he had trouble with nuns in San Jose. Some trouble. And now he's fucking me and the ballet shoes are recording it, wiping out the old memories that he doesn't know are there. I just hope he takes the shoes off me when we're done, or this could go on all night. It's just like the time I lost my virginity with Jimmy Purcell. He thought he was the world's greatest lover because I came so much, even when he stopped for a breather. But it was my power. If he hadn't eventually taken off my Granny boots I'd have worn off his dick.

And he might still be alive.

Oh fuck that. Why does Jimmy Purcell keep coming into my brain. My pussy. No, it's not Jimmy. It's Tony. He must think I'm a real crazy nympho, but it doesn't seem to stop him from enjoying himself. He bites my nipple and his hand clutches my cunt. He's rough with my pussy, pressing my clit against his grinding body. Sister Teresa taught him well. He's good.

"Oh, Anthony—Tony, that feels so good."

He looks up at me with that dirty sneer.

"You're a cunt, Violetta Valery Cutrero."

"Correction. I'm a horny cunt."

"You're a horny cunt with a big mouth."

He pulls out. He straddles my tits. The cold heat of his sweaty thighs presses down upon me. His balls slide up my cleavage as he pulls my head to his cock.

"Suck it, you horny cunt, suck my cock."

Not a problem. I open my lips and swallow his dick. I remember back to when I discovered my power for the second time. By accident I'd slipped on cheerleader Tracy Stevens' Nikes and found myself sucking off the Oakland High's star running back Nelson Dawkins. I may not have ever done oral for real, but I've sucked off a lot of shoesex cock, so I know what to do.

Tony's an adventurous dude. With his cock in my mouth he rotates his body around mine and falls between my legs. He licks at my pussy as I gnaw at his cock. I feel the cool metal of the cross around his neck pressed against my stomach. It doesn't feel like a crucifix. The chain tangles with my pubic hair as he works his face into me. The room fills with slurping noises. It sounds like a lollipop tasting convention. I laugh at the thought, and my spasming throat does all the right things to Tony's cock. It steels and his balls contract. He bites my clitoris, just like he did my nipples. I scream, my tongue battering the pulsing head of his dick.

He stops biting. He pulls out. My scream subsides. He spins around and plunges his cock into me and before the tip hits my pussy walls he's orgasming. His mound smashes into my clitoris, and I come as my body arches off the bed, pulling tight against the ropes until they burn into my wrists and ankles. Tony collapses onto me, and his cross burns into my cleavage, but I don't relax against the rigor mortis of coming. He kisses me and I taste my cunt on his face.

"Tell me how bad I am, Anthony."

"You're a slut, Sister Teresa."

"Call me that word."

"You're a cunt."

Oh fuck, I'm Sister Teresa again. Our sex and the previous episode are blurring together and repeating. Tony's on top of me, mauling my breasts through my habit. The hem is pushed up to my waist and he's slapping his skinny-boy body into my pale thighs.

"Oh, Anthony—Tony, that feels so good."

I struggle against my bonds.

"No, no, you must stop. I don't want this. Let me go," I say in my best defenseless voice.

"There's nothing you can do. I tied you to the bed like you told me to. And you're wearing the punishment shoes."

"Correction. I'm a horny cunt."

TONY'S SITTING AT the edge of the bed, a ballet shoe in his hand.

I look down at my feet. One is bare. At least the shoe-fuck's over. My body feels the aftereffects. My pussy is soaked, tender. My arms and legs ache. My throat is sore, dry, painted with stale Chianti.

"Tony," I croak.

He doesn't answer. He stands, turns and stares at me with that trademark sneer. He hurls the shoe to the bed. It lands on the pillow next to me and slams into my head.

"That wasn't very fucking nice. Game's over. Untie me. I'm thirsty. We'd better get to the hotel. Ellen will be waiting."

He ignores me. He pulls on his jeans and zips them up.

"Untie me or I'll scream the fucking place down."

"Go ahead, Violetta Valery Cutrero. No one will hear

you. These lofts are deserted. No one wants to live here since the earthquake."

"Okay, Tony, enough's enough. We had killer sex. Now untie me and we can have more fun over at the hotel. With my partner."

He pulls on a pair of Doc Martens. He tucks his cross into his tee shirt as he turns to speaks to me. I was right. It's not a crucifix. It's much larger. It looks familiar. I have one like that.

"No can do, Violetta Valery Cutrero. I have to go out."

Why does he sound so disgusted? What gives? Wasn't the sex good? Thanks to the shoefuck he probably thinks I'm a nympho-slut-psycho. Maybe he's scared by the zombie way I acted.

"Tony, I know things look weird, but untie me. I can explain."

I'll make something up. Acid flashbacks worked with Marsha. She felt sorry for me. I need Tony's sympathy to get out of this wack palace.

"There's nothing to explain."

"Then let me go. You can't leave me here tied up."

"Oh yes, I can. I have a date with Ellen at the Paradise."

"She'll kick your ass."

"Oh no she won't, because you're going to help me."

I'm about to tell him Ellen's the Cop That Killed the Dildo Killer when he walks over to the bed, and I think he's been kidding all along. He's going to let me go. He picks up my panties from the side of the bed and rubs them on my soaked pussy.

"Thanks, you bast—" I say, thinking he's playing with me, but he stuffs my panties into my mouth, and I retch against the sodden cloth. I try to spit the wad out, but he ties my tights around my head, holding the gag firm in the back of my throat. Oh fuck, this is what the DK did to Melanie. It's how he gagged her. Oh no. It can't be.

"Drink on this, slutty cunt, Violetta Valery Cutrero. I

don't want to take the chance of you screaming when the occasional police car swings by."

I shake my head from side to side, but I can't free the gag. Neither could Melanie.

"Don't worry, I'll be soon back with Ellen and we can all have a party. To make it easy on her I want you to write a note to your lover telling her the following."

He holds a pad of paper to my bound hand and puts a pen between my fingers. He tells me what he wants me to write. I shake my head.

He squeezes my neck with his free hand. His eyes glare at me.

"If you want to see Ellen again, please do as I say."

I've been concentrating on the wrong story. I should have stayed focused on *Grimm's Fairy Tales* and not got lost in all the *Thousand and One Nights* imagery. My trip to Oakland was successful after all. Tony is the Cinderella Killer. He has to be. Rather than panic me, my discovery calms me. What the hell, I'll write the note. Ellen will kick his ass. He has no idea who he's dealing with, and I'm not going to warn him, so I take down his dictation. She'll never in a million years fall for it. Tony's in big trouble. She's saved me once. She'll do it again.

He rifles through my purse and takes my car keys and the motel key. He throws on his leather jacket and picks up a large shoulder bag from the side of the bed. He unzips it and pulls out a long-bladed knife. He slips it in a sheath and slides it inside his jacket. In the short space of time he holds the bag open I see a collection of Mini-Peeps, clothes, wigs, makeup. He sneers at me. He wants me to see the contents. He wants me to know that he's outsmarted me. I don't give him the satisfaction of looking surprised.

He walks to the door, pauses and comes back to the bed.

"How inconsiderate of me. I shouldn't leave you alone while I'm out having fun with your lover."

He picks up the ballet shoes and slides one on my foot.

As much as I wiggle from side to side I can't stop him. As he slides the second shoe onto my foot he says, "I knew you had the power."

Did he just say what I thought he said? And then as I feel the familiarity of two people, one body, the last thing I hear is Tony's voice saying, "So long, sis."

FOURTEEN

I SCREECH MY Jeep into the Paradise parking lot, reminding myself to play it cool. No need to attract attention.
So as nonchalantly as it is possible to walk through a poorly
lit parking lot in a bad part of town, I stroll through the
assembled groups of villains to the building. I ignore the
"Hey, Fine Mama" come-ons comfortable in the knowledge
that Smith and Wesson are by my side.

I follow a trail of garish arrows up a urine smelling flight
of stairs. Room 6 is midway in a block of ten rooms. I pause
outside. Its door, like every other one on this floor, is
painted a dull enamel red. It looks like the color of dried
blood. Not a good omen, but I do my best to ignore the
symbolism and focus on the practicalities of gaining entry.
The lights are off. The drab curtains are shut. I listen for
noises, but with all the racket from MacArthur Boulevard
it's impossible to tell if there's anyone in the room. No way
am I going to knock, and I couldn't kick in the door. I'd
probably break my leg. A key from the hotel manager will

do just fine. I'll open the door, surprise Tony and free Violetta. I'm sure he's not expecting company. Violetta won't have told him about me.

As I weave my way through the parade of ragtag hookers and their pimps to the motel's night window I concoct a convincing story to weasel a key out of the front desk.

"Yes please. You want room? You lost?" asks the Indian guy behind the counter. He looks at me as though he can't believe I would want a room at the Paradise. I don't know whether to be flattered or insulted. I answer him in my sexiest voice.

"I'm meeting a very special friend here. Room 6. Violetta Cutrero."

"Round back. Up stairs. Turn right."

My sexiest voice didn't cut it, so I try irate.

"I know where it is. She isn't here. She left a key for me at the front desk."

I'm betting that the Paradise doesn't have room phones so he can't call Room 6 to check on my story. He rummages through a ghetto of cubbyholes.

"No key here. You come back later."

"No, you don't get it. I'm supposed to wait in the room. You know—"

He looks at me blankly.

"You know—all ready for her."

More blank looks and worse, a shoulder shrug. I pull out the picture of Violetta and me in the limo. I appeal to his romantic nature.

"See, we're lovers. This is a special night for us. It would really spoil things if I wasn't in the room lying on the bed dressed all sexy when she gets back."

He smiles. Bingo.

"Twenty dollar."

As far as money-grubbing entrepreneurship goes, his attitude doesn't bother me, but I don't want to appear too eager in case he gets suspicious.

"She's already paid for the room."

"Extra key twenty dollar, yes please."

He sticks out his hand through the night slot.

"Oh, I see. No problem."

I fork over the money and he hands me a key. As I turn towards the hallway leading back to the rooms I notice he palms the twenty into his pocket. I should have waved the money under his nose in the first place and saved all the haggling.

The Paradise is a strange place. It sports the expected by-the-hour denizens of the sex industry, but it's also crawling with tourists—not the solitary skulking kind who catch a blow job or a bit of pink in between tour bus stops, but camera-toting groups acting as if the Paradise was the next stop after Jack London Square. Before I reach the stairs two groups ask me to take pictures of them with the motel's glowing neon sign in the background. They must figure I'm one of the few people around who won't run off with their expensive cameras.

Why is the Paradise so popular? Surely it can't be because of my book. The motel and several others featured prominently in the first section of *The Cop That Killed The Dildo Killer* when I described Randall Warren's role in the prostitute murders. Maybe some enterprising tour operator is taking macabre-minded tourists on a journey through Oakland's murderous past. Oh Christ, I hope they don't recognize me. I don't need the hassle of an impromptu signing while Violetta might be in danger.

The tourist groups—one Japanese, the other German—argue about room numbers. Maybe it is my book that's caused this flurry of out-of-town interest. I'm not about to tell them that it was Room 6 where Nicola Anderson was killed by Randy Warren. I don't want an audience for my rescue mission.

As I slip away a hooker intervenes in the debate and deflates my self-importance by telling them they're all wrong, the dude that was offed by the fairy princess killer was in Room 28. And further, it's the tourists' lucky day, the hooker has it rented. For fifty bucks a pop she'll give them a short tour and let them take pictures. She'll even pose on the bed for them—nothing dirty—that costs extra.

Money is no object for the rubbernecking tourists. The requisite cash is rapidly exchanged. The tourists scamper up the stairs, and the hooker smiles at me and follows them. I can guess what she's so smug about. She's made more in ten minutes than she would with the usual thirty minute trick and she didn't even have to get fucked. Murder always benefits some people, and I should know.

Murder. *The dude that was offed by the fairy princess killer*. The hooker obviously means that one of the Cinderella Killer victims had his last meal here, so to speak. That's why the Paradise is suddenly so popular, and that's the connection to my book. The Paradise is one of Tony's killing grounds, and I bet he chose this location out of *The Cop That Killed The Dildo Killer*. Tony is paralleling Randall Warren, but he doesn't realize how well he's doing. He's in for a pointed surprise if Violetta has her knife with her. He may end up paralleling the DK all the way to sliced and diced hell, and this time how will I cover for Violetta?

I'm suffering from analysis paralysis with all this thinking. I need to act, be more like the old damn the torpedoes Ellen, so I sprint up the stairs. Between the two floors above and the other rooms on this level there's a constant flow of people, but eye contact is mostly avoided. No one pays me any particular attention, and if I time my interloping correctly the clip-clop of platform heels and other assorted shoes will mask the noise of me inserting the key into the lock.

I grip the knob tightly to prevent it from rattling as I slide in the key. The teeth bite. I turn the knob slowly, feeling the lock retract. Once it's free and the door is ready to swing I drop to a crouch. I pull my gun out of my purse and ease off the safety. I hope there isn't a chain lock on the door, but just in case I crack the door open slowly until it passes the point where a chain would anchor it. I scramble into the side of the doorway so I'm not backlit by the streetlamps. I tense into a ready-to-fire position with both hands on my gun. I hope my white knuckles don't make me a target.

The room is still. All I hear is my own breathing, reminding me I'm alive. I survived. It's been ages since I did a blind entry, but the old heart-pounding relief of not coming face-to-face with a sawn-off shotgun or a rabid pit bull hasn't diminished.

Through the sights of my gun I scan the room. It seems empty. The bathroom door is open. Somebody could be hiding in there, so I turn on the room lights and shut the front door. There's definitely been someone here. The bed clothes are all messed up. I check out the bathroom, behind the door, in the shower. Nothing.

Room 6 is empty.

And I've got to pee.

I put my gun on the sink, unbuckle the studded metal belt that was a gift from Violetta, unzip my jeans and work them down to my knees. Do I ever have to go. It must be nerves because I sure didn't drink that much at the coffee bar. I pee like a racehorse. I wipe away the last few drops and stand. With a clatter from the metal belt my jeans fall to my ankles. I'm about to flush when I hear a noise.

It's the front door opening.

Fuck.

At least my gun is in easy reach. I pick it up and hold it at arms length, ready to fire. I can't risk making any noise so my jeans will have to stay down. I freeze. I listen.

Doesn't sound like two people.

Maybe it's Violetta.

Maybe it's Tony.

There's only one way to find out. I've got to confront

the intruder. I hope it's Violetta, and once she gets over the shock of my dramatic gun-toting entrance she'll see me in my state of semi-undress, burst into laughter and we'll have the wettest and fondest of reunions.

In one kangaroo hop of a jump I launch myself out of the bathroom and into the room. I hit the opposing wall, brace myself and point my weapon into the room.

"Freeze, motherfucker." Old habits die hard.

It's a young black guy. He's on the other side of the bed, near the bedside table and the lamp. He looks at me, disbelief in his wide eyes. He smiles. It turns to laughter. I can understand why. I'm naked from the waist down, pointing a gun at him, my jeans around my ankles. He looks from my face to my gun to my pussy to my jeans in a rapid cycle of amazement as he figures out what to do.

I know what I must do. I have to enforce my dominance, or this situation could rapidly get out of my control.

"I mean it, asshole, this isn't a peep show. Put your hands in the air, slowly, or I'll blow your brains out by way of your cock."

He does as I command. His laughter turns to a wolf whistle.

"Cool it lady. I don't want to hurt you. I don't want no trouble. I ain't no pervert. I ain't looking for a piece of ass, although I must say you sure do look mighty fine and have a mouth like a mad dog ho. Under better circumstances I could dig you."

"Tony?"

"Say what?"

"Are you Tony?"

"No."

"Where's Violetta?"

"V-O who?"

"What are you doing here?"

"I work for Fat Andy, the pimp. I'm helping him keep the streets safe from the fairy killer dude so all his working ladies can do their things. I'm just delivering this."

He waves a bag in his hand.

"Some dude gave me twenty bucks to drop this off. I get another twenty when the job's done. I'm just the poor messenger boy. I ain't trying to rob or rape you so put the gun down. Please."

"Fuck you. What dude? Where is he?"

"Out there—"

He moves to turn to point to the parking lot. His hand slides across his chest possibly reaching inside his windbreaker.

"Careful."

His hand drops to his side and then immediately back above his head when I indicate to do so with an upwards twitch of the barrel of my gun.

"Out there in the parking lot."

"And you just did what he asked?"

"Shit, yeah. He was just a normal skinny white dude. He said it was for his girlfriend. What kind of kinky shit are you two playing? You into that S and M sex? Whips and chains? It's cool."

I'm tempted to tell him that the dude he was doing a favor for was probably the Cinderella Killer. That'd please Fat Andy immensely. But I can't risk a mob scene with Violetta's safety in question. I have to take care of Tony myself.

"He's not my boyfriend, and what I'm into is no concern of yours. What's in the bag?"

"It's a note and a scarf. The dude said to leave 'em on the bed. Look, lady, I'm just going to put them down right here and get the fuck outta here, and you two can play your psycho games without me. I got a job to do. Fat Andy will be mighty upset if some shit goes down while I'm here jawing with you. You don't want to get Fat Andy mad now, do you?"

He places the note and the scarf on the bedside table. I motion to him to move away from the bed.

"Look out the window. Is the guy who gave them to you still out there?"

As he looks through the ratty curtains I crouch down and pull up my belt, jeans and panties with one hand while holding my gun on him with the other. It isn't easy, but with a bit of hip wriggling, which my intruder seems to appreciate, I manage to pull them up to my waist. I can fasten them later.

"I don't see him, but that don't mean he ain't out there. He owes me twenty."

"What's your name."

"Dexter."

"Dexter what?"

"Dexter Porter."

"You got any ID?"

"Driver's License."

"Where is it?"

"Wallet. Back pocket."

"Turn around, spread your legs and put your hands on the wall."

"You a cop?"

"I have the gun. The way this works is I ask the questions. You answer them and do as you're told. Got it?"

"Sure. You the man."

I retrieve his wallet. Dexter Porter. Okay, so he's not Tony. He's probably telling the truth. Tony wasn't taking any chances coming in here blind like I did.

"Turn around."

I hand him his wallet.

"Can I go now, lady?"

"No, Dexter, you're going to help me. Wait there."

I examine the note and the scarf. The note is from Violetta. I recognize her scrawl.

Ellen, put on this blindfold and lie naked on the bed and wait for my big surprise. Love, Violetta.

So Tony was trying to trap me. I'm sure he made Violetta write that note. If that bastard's hurt her then what I do to him will make what Violetta did to the DK look like mild acupuncture.

"Dexter, you're going to go out there and tell this guy you've done your job. I'll be following you. Once you get your twenty get the fuck out of the way. I'll give you another twenty once I get what I want."

"Shit, lady, don't you think your guy's guessed there's a fuck-up underway? I been in here a while jawing with you. He's gonna know this little operation didn't go down smooth."

"Maybe you're watching a porno. Maybe you're taking a piss. Maybe you're seeing what you can steal. Maybe you got no choice."

I point my gun at his head. He winces.

"Okay, okay, but if he ain't around don't shoot me."

"Move."

Dexter opens the door. I let him take a few steps onto the landing. I follow in a crouch, keeping my body below the railing. Dexter shuts the door. I motion him on. When we get to the stairwell I straighten and follow him down, my gun in my hand covered by my purse. We pass hookers and clients and a couple of camera jockeys who don't follow the no eye contact rule. Dexter scowls at them and they quickly move on. This tourist craze has got to be a huge boom to the muggers. There's more Sonys, Nikons and Canons up for grabs here than in a looted electronics store.

I wait at the bottom of the stairs in the shadow of the Coke machine. Dexter strolls off across the parking lot. He slaps hands with two friends. They look over in my direction and Dexter's friends slink off. Dexter turns and steps towards me. I motion for him to stay. He slowly turns around. A figure approaches.

This must be Tony. He's tall and skinny and obviously white. I can't see his face too well, but everything about him is out of place. He doesn't belong here even though he's wearing the requisite hooded sweatshirt. The guy asks a question and Dexter nods in answer. I assume he's saying that he delivered the scarf and the note. Tony pulls something out of his pocket. Must be the twenty. The scene looks like a typical drug deal, only I know better.

I pull my gun out of my purse, but before I can make a forward move I hear breathing behind me.

Too close.

I spin around and lurking in the shadows waiting to pounce are Dexter's associates. They have baseball bats.

"Don't even think of it, assholes. Back off. I mean it. Drop the weapons, or I'll blow off your kneecaps."

They stop inching towards me and look at each other for mutual support. The bats go down. I turn. Tony's running away. Dexter's running towards me.

His friends pick up the bats and advance.

I don't hang around.

I take off after Tony.

Dexter tries to intercept me, but all the running on the beach with Violetta pays off. I easily dodge his bulk. He stumbles to the ground in a lame attempt to tackle me. I put the gun to his head. I look at his buddies.

"You two take one step closer and Dexter gets a thirty-eight caliber lobotomy."

Dexter knows I mean it.

"Do as she says. She's wacked."

Dexter's baseball bat boys stop, but they don't put down their sluggers.

"You told him, Dexter. Why?"

"I didn't. He heard you shouting like a crazy bitch. He got scared."

"You're a fucking liar. You sent your goons after me."

"Shit, you were acting demented. I thought you might

be the killer. Fat Andy thinks it's a psycho bitch who don't like johns. You sure do fit the bill. We were gonna hold you until the cops got here."

"Stupid fucks."

I slam his head down to the asphalt and run to my Jeep. Police sirens punch the night. No time to hang around and answer questions, so I floor it and take off down the alley after Tony.

Dexter yells, "What about my twenty, bitch."

I give him the finger and in the process of steering with one hand I wipe out a garbage can. Trash splatters on the hood and windscreen. I overcorrect and the Jeep skids sideways. I brake to a halt inches from slamming into a wall. I use the wipers to scatter the mess so I can see ahead of me. I maneuver out of the tight spot, pushing the garbage can noisily out of the way. I turn off the side street and put distance between me and the Paradise.

Where would Tony go?

He's probably heading downtown towards his store, so I swing across MacArthur towards San Pablo, careful to avoid the police presence at the Paradise. I snake through blocks of dilapidated buildings and greasy restaurants, catching possible sightings. I slow and stare, but all I achieve is suspicious glances back in return.

I hit a dead end so I U-turn and head back towards MacArthur, figuring if nothing else I'll take Broadway. I'm half way to the main street when I pass a narrow alley. It's only wide enough for a dumpster, so I can't turn the Jeep down there but I'm sure I see a hooded figure moving in and out of the lamplight. The scene reminds me of an old, faded black and white movie; it's strobe-like, hypnotic, like something Hitchcock would film. Ignoring the obvious fact that there are probably hooded figures in every narrow alley in Oakland I stop the Jeep and run after the figure. I have my gun in my hand, but I don't want to use it unless I have to. I need to find Violetta without attracting more cops with reports of shots fired, and a wounded or dead Tony won't be much help.

The figure hears my footsteps and turns. He sees me and runs. I yell after him.

"Tony, stop, I have to talk to you."

He turns his head in startled recognition that I know his name. He runs even faster. He stumbles, hits the ground hard. He picks himself up, and is away, but I'm almost on him.

"Tony, where's Violetta?"

He leaps for the top of a wall and scrambles to the top. I slip my gun in my pocket and leap for his dangling foot. I slam into the wall but manage to grab his leg. He swings me to and fro, trying to dislodge my grip, but I hold fast. He kicks at me with his free foot and his boot cracks into my knuckles. I scream, but there's no way I'm going to let go. If he wants to play rough, so be it. If I could reach my gun I'd shoot him, but if I let go with one hand I'll never hold on, so I push up his trousers and sink my teeth into his leg.

He bellows but whatever satisfaction I feel is short-lived. He aims his free foot at my head and stomps down. My head slams against the wall and I'm stunned. I fall to the ground, getting a second whammy when my head hits the pavement.

My vision blurs and I know I'm blacking out, but I pull my gun out and aim at the indistinct shape crouching on top of the wall. Our eyes meet in that last moment of clarity before blackness swallows me. He's staring. A smile of recognition spreads across his face. His lips move.

"Ellen—Ellen Stewart. Now it all makes sense."

I know those eyes.

I pull the trigger.

FIFTEEN

"FUCKING CUNT, WHY didn't you tell me Ellen wa
Ellen Stewart?"

Oh man, I'm so disoriented. What the fuck am I doing
here being yelled at?

I don't even know where here is.

I'm mega-exhausted.

I feel like I've been gang-banged by the same person.

Now it's coming back, and ouch, I'm not sure I want to.
to. I know what's been going down in this smelly cramped
room, on this creaky old bed. For the last forever I've been
caught in an endless shoesex loop of the twisted Sister Te
resa and me tied to the bed being done by Tony. My pussy
feels like a steaming swamp through which John Wayne and
the whole fucking cavalry went for a ride. This can't be
happening to me. It must still be shoesex and all that nasty
stuff didn't really happen.

Yeah, that's it. I'll feel much better once Tony takes those
damn ballet shoes off my feet. Almost at the same time tha

my hopes rise from this wishful thinking I see my bare feet pale and cold with sweat.

No, I'm out of it.

There's no excuse for this ugly little scene. This is reality. Tony's standing at the edge of the bed, between my legs, ballet shoes in hand, staring at my gaping cunt, screaming his questions about Ellen.

"*The Cop That Killed The Dildo Killer*. Why didn't you tell me? You stuck-up cunt, were you deliberately trying to make a fool out of me? Wasn't it enough that you got everything?"

What is he talking about?

Didn't he go out?

How long have I been under?

How much does Tony know? And how?

Why is he raving like a mental patient? Was it the way I acted when I was under the shoefuck? It probably really weirded him—

Oh shit. Now I remember. Tony's the Cinderella Killer. I have so many questions, and yet it's me that's being interrogated, and I couldn't answer if I wanted to because the stupid fuck still has me gagged with my panties and pantyhose.

"Why didn't you tell me she was Ellen Stewart? This has ruined everything."

He hurls the ballet shoes across the room and the heels take a good sized chunk of plaster out of the wall. Never mind the wall, the shoes will need fixing. A polishing at least. I think of shoe repairing. How I would bring the ballet shoes back to good as new. In desperate times I cling to the familiar. Those were the days when all I had to worry about were soles and heels. Now it's all souls and heals, and if Tony's who I think he is then I'm going to have to kill him. In my present fucked-out state I'm not sure I'm up to slaying.

Tony's raving brings me back to the painful present. It's

not a good sight to see first thing out of a marathonly per
verted shoefuck. I'm full of self-pity and doubt and my bod
feels like it's been through a meat grinder, so I basically los
it. I thrash against the ropes and gurgle the most hideou
noises thanks to being gagged. Tony climbs on to the bed
grabs my shoulders and presses me down with his skinny
ass weight to stop my skinny-ass moshing. He pulls the un
derwear gag out of my mouth. His knuckles are scuffed rav
and he's bleeding. As he tugs the gag over my nose h
smears blood over my face.

I cough and sputter all over him in return. He isn't faze
in the slightest. He keeps ranting about Ellen. The dude i
obsessed.

"Ellen is Ellen Stewart."

Tony's temper tantrum doesn't make much sense to me
Everything is so hazy.

"Of course Ellen is Ellen Stewart. So fucking what? Ge
over it."

He slaps my face as though it's me that's hysterical an
delirious. I taste blood. I know it's not from his knuckles
because I feel the pain knife through my skin. He stand
and paces the room, talking to the floor as though it's me
I suck the blood off my split lip.

"You don't get it do you? I thought you were smart
Violetta Valery Cutrero, but you're really stupid."

Now I'm pissed. He's got no fucking right to say I'n
stupid or mock my parents for the name they gave me. It'
a great fucking name. He's going to regret taking that ga
out of my mouth. I hawk a big wad of blood and spit a
his feet.

"Excuse me, Ein-fucking-stein. Forgive me if I'm a littl
slow but for the last however many hours I've been in a
endless shoefuck—"

I stop myself, but the words are already out. Ope
mouth, insert foot, that's me. Tony looks at me with a sneer

"Exactly. A shoefuck. Shoesex. I know about you, an

here's the burn, Violetta Valery Cutrero. I have the power too."

Silence from me.

Silence from him.

"No fucking way."

"Did you think you were the only one?"

"I—"

Everything comes back to me in gory flashback as though I were living it again in a horrible shoefuck. How Tony tricked me into putting on the fuckshoes and then fucked me so that the sensations overlapped. How he made me write that note to Ellen. The knife. The bag of shoes and Cinderella Killer crap. How he put the shoes back on me. How I've been here ever since. When he left he said he knew I had the power. How? Duh, he had to have the power. Takes one to know one.

"I—"

Words fail me. Tony has no such problem. What is it about killers and speeches? The DK went on forever. Why don't they just join the Toastmasters?

"It's understandable you'd be shocked. Of course you thought you were the only one, the chosen, the special goddess of shoesex. It's such a drug, isn't it? The ultimate high, reserved solely for you. And why not? No one else ever mentioned shoe sex did they? You kept your secret well, pretending you were so into shoes for fashion reasons, and no one else was as into shoes as much as you, as Tommy fucking Cutrero's only daughter, Violetta Valery."

Now my power has pulled the most devious trick ever. It's destroyed the notion I'm special. If there's another person with the power there can be hundreds. This is just about as big of a shock as discovering shoesex in the first place. I thought I was the only one. I thought I was special. Now I'm just like all the others.

My voice shrinks out of me in wimpy surrender. Tony's right. I am stupid.

"You were so into shoes. I should have known."

"Oh, Violetta Valery, we have a lot more in common than a keen interest in footwear."

I look at Tony, my chin quivering. I know what he's going to say. He wasn't referring to Sister Teresa earlier when he said "So long, sis." I am special after all. And so is he. The connection isn't an interest in shoes.

"Tommy Cutrero was my father too," Tony says in grand soap opera dramatic style. I almost hear the crash of the canned music.

In one of my bolder moments of childish precocity I once asked Mom and Dad why if they were Catholic and didn't use contraception how come I was an only child. I knew from my power they sure had sex more than once, and Dad wasn't a whisper-outer, so I figured Mom was on the pill or some other un-Catholic device. I was looking for a basic flaw in their Be A Good Catholic Kid manifesto. I got a teary story instead. With Mom crying up a snotty storm Dad told me that after I was born they tried to have another kid but something went wrong and Mom couldn't have any more babies. Maybe what really happened was that they gave the baby up for adoption. My parents were dirt poor in those early days. Maybe Tony is my long lost brother.

"You're my brother," I say with a fondness I actually mean. And just when I think my world can't be rocked any further, rumbling out of Tony's mouth come words as devastating to me as the Loma Prieta quake.

"Half right. Nicola Anderson was my mother."

That I didn't expect. I should have. Sister Teresa mentioned Anthony Anderson when Tony was coming. My power was trying to warn me, and I was too busy shoe-fucking to notice. And there were so many other signs. The cross around his neck. I knew it was familiar. It's identical to the Celtic cross worn by Nikki, the one I retrieved from the DK's souvenir collection. The DK even mentioned it to Melanie Courtland when he told her not to beg. Two different shoefucks and I still didn't see it. And how about the way Nikki called Tommy "Daddy" with such sarcasm. I should have known. My feet, Nikki's shoes, Melanie's platforms, they had all the answers. I remember how Nikki thought of Dad. Disgust, pity, fondness, jealousy of my mom. It was more than just a hooker-client business transaction. He was the father of her child. The child she mentioned when she begged Randy Warren for her life. Everything fits together. Oh motherfucking Christ, Dad, Dad, Dad, how could you do this to me and Mom?

Oh, man, I don't feel so good at all.

Maybe it's the shock of finding out that my father not only fucked Nikki up the ass and beat her up, but he also made a bastard with her when she was nothing more than a kid herself.

Maybe it's all the Chianti percolating with the manicotti in my stomach.

Maybe it's all the thrashing I'd done on the bed.

Maybe it's the blood from my split lip souring my throat.

Maybe it's the hours of shoesex and the endless orgasms.

Maybe I'm just a wimp.

Whatever.

I pale as Tony finishes speaking his revelation. His smugness evaporates as I throw up. Tied to the bed, lying on my back, I make like a Technicolor fountain hooked up to a busted sewer line. It's fucking gross. The vomit splatters down on my face and drips through my hair onto the bed. Linda Blair's got nothing on me. All join in with the devil and say, "It's not your mother that sucks cocks in hell, Violetta. It's your father."

I do the fat rock star bit and start choking on my chunks. Tony takes half-brotherly pity on me and unties my wrists and sits me up. A couple of good slaps on the back followed by a some hefty heaves, and I'm breathing again.

"Thanks."

"I couldn't let my half-sister die like that."

I don't like the way Tony added 'like that,' as though there were some ways he would let me die, but I'm not in the feistiest of moods, so I let it drop. I'm not so sure I'm glad to be alive anyway.

"I'll get you some towels," he says in a tone of voice I don't recognize, and then I suss it's kindness. Gone is the derisive use of Violetta Valery Cutrero. He's a different person. The hate's gone. Weird. It's as if by saying what had been bottled up inside him for all this time he now feels sympathy for me. Fuck, I have a brother. He has a sister, and despite what he thought of me, he's found out I'm not so bad. Maybe blood's thicker than vomit.

Either that or he's a schizo. I remember the shrink's article in the *Tribune*. Brother or not, I'd better humor him just in case the evil Tony returns. I don't want him to take this Cinderella connection too far and kill his cute sister now that he's done the ugly ones.

While Tony's rummaging in his bathroom I take the opportunity to undo the rope around my ankles. If I can get free then I'll at least stand a fighting chance. It's hard going. My stomach doesn't want to be compressed as I bend to reach my feet.

"Let me help you."

I'm exhausted. I flop back down on the bed into a pool of vomit while Tony unties my legs. As soon as they're free I swing my feet to the ground and try to stand, but my legs are too wonky, I keel over. Tony steadies me, and before I can say I'm fine he picks me up and carries me to his shower. He dumps me inside. The water's already running at a nice temperature, which I can't help but notice and appreciate. Tony is definitely trying to be nice to me.

"Thanks."

"No problem." He sits down on the toilet and pulls the shower curtain across to prevent the bathroom from flooding. I sit in the corner letting the water wash over me. The only thing I have on is my tee shirt. It's mega-skanky, but I don't have the energy to pull it over my head.

"This feels good," I say, not really knowing what else to utter. There's so much we have to talk about but right now more than a shower curtain separates Tony and me. I don't know where to start.

Tony does.

"You know I'm the Cinderella Killer."

Well, that's a nice matter-of-fact way to begin the getting to know each other process. What do I say in response? No, really? You don't say. Well I never would have thought that. What a shock.

I respond with my own revelation.

"Yeah, I do, and I killed the Dildo Killer."

"No, I'm serious. I killed those three men. I did it to avenge my mother's murder."

The closed shower curtain is not conducive to an open kimono conversation, so I pull it back far enough to see Tony's face.

"I know. And I'm telling you I killed the Dildo Killer because that's what I do. It wasn't Ellen. She took the blame and the fame so I wouldn't go to jail. We're in this together, but I did the dirty work and Ellen cleaned up my mess."

The penny drops. Tony's eyes light up in recognition. I see that familiar sparkle. It's like looking in a mirror. He has my eyes.

"When I read her book I wondered how she knew so much about the Dildo Killer and the victims. When I found out tonight that your Ellen was Ellen Stewart it all made sense. You used your power to get her that information, but I had no idea you were the killer."

"Yeah, I used my power to make the book more realistic, but that was a freebie. I use my power to catch and kill serial killers. I figured it out. That's why I have it. That's what I do. Trying on all those victims' shoes and the DK's footwear was preparation for the next one."

"Are you going to kill me?"

"That's why I came back to this fucking town—to kill the Cinderella Killer. I figured there was unfinished business. I knew it was all connected somehow to the Dildo Killer. I had no idea how connected it was."

"You didn't answer my question."

"It depends."

"On what."

"Did you hurt Ellen?"

"Sort of."

"What the fuck do you mean?"

"We hurt each other. She chased me down an alley and I fell. That's how I skinned my knuckles. She tried to drag me off a wall I was climbing to get away from her. She hung onto my legs and bit me. I kicked her away and she hit her head, but she tried to shoot me. I'm pretty sure she's okay, but I didn't hang around. I limped to your car and drove here. Look what she did."

Tony rolls up his trousers. His leg looks like a pit bull mistook his calf for a slab of rare meat.

"Jesus, she kicked your ass. I told you she would. You'd better clean that up. Stick it in here. And your hands."

Tony pulls off his shoes and tentatively slides his leg and his hands in the shower. I dab at his wounds. He winces. And then I think, wow, he's my brother, and I'm caring for him. I suddenly feel all warm and friendly inside. The same thing must have happened to him when I threw up and he helped me. There was no evil Tony, just a very scared, frightened and hurt kid who'd lost his Mom to a sick killer.

Man, caring, what an amazing sensation. Makes you think soppy thoughts.

We were ready to kill each other a few minutes ago, and now, now we're like brother and sister. Are brother and sister. Fuck, I have a family again, and so does Tony.

It's as if he reads my mind.

"I had so much hate for you, but then I realized we're both victims. We're both in this together. It dawned on me when you were getting sick. You're my only family. I couldn't lose you."

Oh shit, I'm going to cry.

Luckily, the shower water hides my drippy eyes. I don't want my half-brother to think I'm a full-wussy sister.

"You'd better put some first aid cream or something on the leg and the knuckles and bandage them up. You don't want to get an infection."

"Guess that means you're not going to kill me."

"Guess so, but you'd better explain something."

"Shoot."

He pulls his soaked leg and hands from my attentions and dabs them dry with a towel. I feel mega-better. Playing Florence Nightingale did me the world of good. I stand up and pull the tee shirt off my head and let it splat on the shower floor. I soap my naked body. Tony watches me. It feels kind of funny. I'm showering in front of my brother, and I bet he's getting a boner. This is a way sexy scene. But he's my brother. Half brother. Yeah, but we were full-on fucking a few hours ago. Man, I'm getting hot and wet, and as trashy novelesque as it sounds, it's not just from the shower water. I'd better ask my question now before we do a showerfuck scene.

"What was with the ranting about Ellen being Ellen? Why did it spoil everything?"

"You don't want to know. It was a stupid idea. You'll have a cow."

"Look, I promise I won't freak."

"Sure?"

"Sure. If I do tie me up on the bed again. Just change the sheets first, okay. I'm just starting to feel human again now that all the barf's been washed down the drain."

"Okay. You're funny."

"Yeah, well, what was the big plan that Ellen spoiled?"

"When you came in the shop I had no idea who you were. When you said your name I knew. All my dreams had come true. You see, I opened my shoe store on the ruins of our dad's shop in the hope that one day you'd come back to the old neighborhood and be attracted by a shoe store."

"How sweet."

"No it wasn't. You don't get it. I wanted you to come back so I could get my revenge. I was so full of hate for you. You had everything while I got shuffled from foster homes to nuns to priests."

"Wasn't my fault. I didn't know."

"I know. It wasn't rational. You just represented everything I hated about Tommy Cutrero. The sins of the father and all that religious guilt crap."

"How did you find out he was your dad?"

"When I turned eighteen the priests gave me the stuff that the police had taken from our apartment and from Mom."

I reach over and pull the cross out of his shirt.

"She had one just like this."

"Yeah, how did you know?"

"I'll tell you once you've finished your story."

"Most of her belongings followed me around from home to home to be given to me when I was old enough to understand. I had no idea she was a prostitute. She told me she was an actress. What did I know? To me she was this neat woman who dressed up every night and read me fairy tales before she went out. She was like a princess."

"Is that why you chose the Cinderella theme?"

"Yeah. Among her stuff was an old copy of *Grimm's Fairy Tales*. I had no idea how gruesome it was. I was only nine when she was killed. I guess she edited out the nasty parts when she read me bedtime stories, but when I read it and learned everything else, it was kind of like I was meant to act it out in revenge. It was like she'd given me the tools to avenge her death. Stuffing a page in the dead dude's mouth was my way of letting Mom know I'd come through for her."

"You must have been very angry."

"That's an understatement. When I was a kid I remember the Social Services people telling me she'd had a bad accident. It didn't much matter to me then. I didn't care how she died. Back then I just knew she wasn't coming back, and there was no one to look after me but a bunch of fucking retards with name tags who shipped me out to a supposedly loving home as soon as they could."

"No wonder you hated me."

"That's not the half of it. She left me a letter explaining that my father hadn't died. She had lied that he was a fighter pilot killed in Vietnam so I wouldn't get teased at school. In her letter she said she didn't want to make trouble for my real father. He'd been kind to her. He didn't even know the baby was his. She had me when she was sixteen and raised me on her own. She'd been on the streets since she was fourteen. I guess our dad took pity on her and gave her money and—"

"Fucked her. Man, she was just a kid."

"Yeah, well, I don't think Mom was ever a kid. She was tough and looked older than she was, but she could look really young too. I have some photos of her with me, and she looks pretty hot. You want to see?"

"Later, when I get out of the shower. So I guess she told you who your dad was and you went looking and found out he was dead."

"Exactly. So I did background research on the Cutreros and found out they had a daughter. I traced you to San Francisco and Shoe Leather, but you'd sold it and moved on. You covered your tracks pretty well. So I opened the shoe store figuring one day you'd show up. I figured we'd be fated to meet."

"So what started the killings? Where does Ellen fit into all this? Will you soap my back?"

I hand the bar of soap to Tony, and he rolls up his sleeves and goes to work. It feels damn fucking good. He has soft hands.

"I didn't know how Mom died until I read Ellen's book. Finding out she begged for her life because of her concern for me, and he laughed at her, it was the last straw. It pulled everything together, and all my hate boiled over. I was convinced it was my destiny to kill, especially when Ellen came to town to sign her book on the day that I planned to start. I waited for hours to get my copy signed. It was like she was giving me her approval. I know it sounds crazy, but you have no idea how insane it made me to find out what that guy did to Mom."

I turned my head to face him.

"Tony, I fucking do so. I lost two good friends to that motherfucking monster bastard cocksucker. I know how crazy it made me. That's why I sliced him into pieces. I went berserk. Ellen would never have done that. She's too cop."

"If she—you—hadn't killed that Warren guy I would have gone after him, but since he was dead I went after the kind of men that used my mother."

"Like Tommy Cutrero."

"Yeah, I guess so. I figured they're as much to blame as the guy that killed her. And since our Dad was dead, when you showed up I figured why not go after his daughter? When I heard you had a friend and you had a room at the Paradise I figured it'd be a perfect way to set the both of you up as the Cinderella Killer, especially with you being a shoe repairer. But then when I found out Ellen was Ellen Stewart I couldn't do it. She was such a hero to me. She killed the guy that killed my mom, but now I find out it's you. Oh man, this is fucked."

I turn around and put my hands on my hips. Tony drops the soap.

"You were going to kill Ellen and me and make it look like a suicide. Come on. Get real."

I don't tell him that I'd spent a lot of time figuring out how to kill the Cinderella Killer and get away with it in the same way. He looks so helpless as he speaks to his feet rather than looking at my gorgeously appealing naked body.

"Okay. I'm not exactly an expert at this. I'm not a sick fuck like that Dildo Killer dude. When it got right down to it, I couldn't even stay mad at you. You looked so helpless, puking and choking, and I felt so bad for what I'd done to you. I guess I'm not a very good killer."

It must be the Catholic in me, but all this confession has got me horny. I pull Tony into the shower.

"No, but you're pretty killer at this."

I unzip his jeans and slide them down to his ankles. He's stinking hard before they hit the wet floor. I push him back against the shower wall and wrap my hands around his neck and my legs around his waist and I climb onto his cock and fuck him with my lips locked to his so we don't have to talk anymore.

Neither one of us is wearing shoes, and we don't fucking care.

Sixteen

"HOW MANY FINGERS am I holding up?"

"Three."

I know how many fingers I'd like to hold up. I'd love to tell these morons to fuck off, but I've got to play their game if I'm to get out of here in a hurry and get back to saving Violetta. I almost had Tony. He knows I know about him, so Violetta is in even more danger. Every minute I play patient is one more opportunity for Tony to do something desperate, so it's hard to keep my temper in check.

"How many fingers now?"

"Two."

"That's good."

"How about now?"

"One."

"Excellent. Now follow my finger."

"No, I don't know where it's been."

I burst out laughing. I know it's childish, but it's the kind of thing I do since hanging around Violetta. I've picked up her warped sense of humor.

The paramedic laughs.

"Okay, you'll live. You don't seem concussed, but you have a couple of nasty lumps. If you have any residual pain or blurring of vision get yourself to a doctor immediately. How does the hand feel?"

I flex my fingers where Tony kicked me. They're sore, but I'll be able to squeeze a trigger well enough. Which I did. I wonder if I hit him?

"It's okay."

"It's probably adrenaline. You're really going to hurt as soon as you calm down. I'll leave you a few painkillers."

"Thanks."

"Don't mention it. You were lucky we were cruising by and saw your Jeep. I wouldn't give you much chance of survival lying unconscious in this area for very long. The rats, human or rodent variety, would have had you."

"Thanks. I mean it."

"No problem." He turns to the burly Oakland PD detective who has been pacing up and down outside the ambulance. "She's all yours."

Unfortunately, I am, and I know it. I tell myself to be polite and cooperative because it's my only chance to get this over with quickly. I don't want to go down to the department to be grilled. I get up from the back of the ambulance and step out into the alley. He pounces right away.

"Ellen Stewart, Chief Detective Harrison. Mind if I ask you a few questions?"

"Not at all. Call me Ellen."

I wait for him to offer his first name. He doesn't. He lights a cigarette. He doesn't offer me one, so I don't have a chance to protest. Instead I cough. He ignores me, blows a cloud of blue-gray smoke around us and steers me down the alley into the foul smelling gloom. At least the cigarette smoke masks the stench of rotting garbage and stale urine.

"Let's walk. Harrison's fine."

"I see. Kind of like Sting."

He looks at me blankly. I continue, hoping to strike a responsive chord. Now I know what Violetta feels like when she tries to explain the latest band sensation to me.

"Or Madonna. Just the one name—Harrison."

He shrugs his shoulders, collapses his lips and shakes his head as a sign of not having a clue what I'm talking about. Oh well. It was worth a try. I'd hoped my attempt at witty banter might have distracted him enough so I could ske-daddle after just a few questions. To quote Violetta, It ain't gonna happen. No fucking way. Harrison is old school. He knows I'm up to no good, and he's going to make me squirm until I tell him everything. At least that's what he thinks. He shouldn't underestimate me. I know all of his tactics. I was trained by the old school.

"What are you doing in Oakland?"

"Actually, I was looking for you. You left a message on my machine."

"Well, you found me. It would have been easier on your head to have made an appointment. We have these amazing devices. They're called telephones. You call. People talk. Arrangements are made. People meet."

This interview isn't going well. He's toying with me like a cat playing with a trapped mouse. He's using sarcasm. Whenever a detective uses sarcasm it's a sure sign the cop thinks the subject is boxed in a corner. I did it all the time to the bad guys. Oh well, if he wants to play sarcastic cop it's time to cut the comradely crap. I had enough of Harrison's kind at the SFPD.

"Very funny. I didn't realize you were an amateur comedian. You're pretty good. Keep working at it, but don't give up your day job. Look, Harrison, I was going to call you, but I got into town kind of late. I've been in LA. I'm here doing research for my next book. Detective Donovan of the SFPD suggested I talk to you because you thought there might be a link between *The Cop That Killed The Dildo Killer* and the Cinderella Killer. My publisher thinks that my take on these killings will make a great sequel. That's why I'm here. Do you have any comments for me?"

"Fuck you."

"Was that on the record or off?"

"On—on all the way. Now stop playing big shot games and tell me what were you doing in this alley."

"Meeting someone, but I got set up. The guy tried to steal my purse. He didn't know I had a gun. He thought I was a reporter, an easy mark. Are you seeing an increase in muggings what with all the reporters and tourists crawling around the murder sites?"

"Where did you meet this contact?"

I figure they know I'd been at the Paradise, so what have I got to lose by using honesty? Through all the interrogations I've conducted I learned a little bit of truth goes a long way when lies are expected.

"At the Paradise."

"Dexter Porter?"

"No. He's useless."

"He said you tried to kill him."

"Oh come on, you can do better than that. He's a cheap two-bit hood, and you know it. He broke into my room with a lame story about protecting hookers from the Cinderella Killer. He tried to shake me down for protection, and I showed him where to get off. I hurt his macho pride, that's all. Men can be so fragile, don't you think? I'm surprised you fell for his whining, or was it too much of a male bonding experience for you?"

"Who's Violetta Cutrero?"

Shit. Shit. Shit. They must have checked the room registration. Time to fall back and punt the cunt.

"She's my assistant. She does advance work for me. I use her name as an alias so people don't see my name. Being a celebrity can be a pain. Just you wait and see, Harrison. Once you solve the Cinderella case you'll be having to deal with fame and all of its demands. I know an excellent agent. I'd be happy to put in a good word for you."

"I don't plan on killing anyone and making a fortune out of it by writing a book that encourages other sickos to do the same."

"And if you won the lottery you'd still come to work every day, right?"

"I play by the rules."

"Do you read also? I don't encourage vigilante justice in my book. I don't believe in it."

"Is that why you waved your gun around and chased a guy out of the Paradise parking lot? Who was he?"

"I don't know. Ask Dexter. He said the guy could give me good information. I gave the creep some money, and he took off running. I might have made a fortune from my book but I hate seeing a hundred bucks go to waste, so I took off after him. I lost him in that rat's maze of alleys. So I asked around and was sent here. I wanted to get the word on the street about the Cinderella Killer. I wanted to find out all the stuff you guys aren't saying or hearing."

"And you got mugged. Swift."

"Well, yeah, it'll make a good story for the book."

"When you were here on October 12th was anyone hanging around you more than normal?"

"No. Detective Donovan said you asked for the security tapes. I'd be glad to look through them."

"Already erased."

"Too bad."

"You don't remember anything?"

"No, sorry. I've done hundreds of appearances. There's always some starstruck types who can't get enough, but nothing sticks out. No one came up to me and said 'Sign this to the Cinderella Killer please.' Do you really think there's a connection?"

"Don't be cute. You know there is. That's why you rented out the room at the Paradise for thirty days. You want to be here on the 17th for the next killing."

Jesus Christ, Violetta rented out that flea pit for a month. I try not to act surprised, so I throw up a wall of bullshit.

"If there is a connection I might be able to help you, but I need a sense of the environment. Total immersion. It'll make for a better book, and I just might find the killer for you."

He stops walking and faces me. He grinds his cigarette under his size fourteens. Why do I think he's imagining it's me and not some smoldering cigarette butt under his foot?

"I'm only going to say this once, Ms. Stewart. I don't want you anywhere near this case. You're bad news. I know people think you're some kind of hero, but what you did in San Francisco was against everything I stand for. You're a bad cop. Now get the fuck out of Oakland and don't come back, at least on my watch. Go gold digging somewhere else."

"Excuse me, did I miss something? When was martial law declared? Who made you Der Fuhrer?"

"We can play this anyway you like. If you want to be difficult I can get Dexter or some other asshole to press assault charges. You can spend a lot of your blood money on attorneys, or you can fuck off and let me and my men do our jobs. We don't need your interference. We don't need your kind of help."

My turn for sarcasm.

"I see. So you're saying I'm not welcome in Oakland."

"Well now, that bump didn't damage your brain after all."

"Oh no, I can see things perfectly well. I know where I stand. Can I have my gun back, please?"

He empties it of bullets and hands it back to me.

"We also took the stash you had in your purse."

"Budget cuts that deep that you've got to steal ammunition? Wow, things must be bad in Oakland."

"Just go."

"Can I get gas first? I'm almost out."

"There's plenty of stations right on Broadway by the freeway on-ramp."

"How convenient. Any news on my attacker? Was there any blood in the alleyway?"

He laughs as he lights another cigarette.

"We found nothing, so I don't think you hit him. There are about two hundred guys that match the description in the area, and I'm not going to waste valuable resources on a routine mugging. It was a routine mugging, right?"

"Wasn't routine to me, but I know what you mean."

"Goodbye, Ms. Stewart. I don't want to see your ass in this town again."

I put my hands in the waistband of my jeans and put on my best redneck accent.

"Wow, sheriff, are you saying this town ain't big enough for the both of us?"

"You might think it's funny, Stewart, but I'm not joking. Keep it up and you'll be laughing out your ass in a jail cell."

"Okay, peace. Good night, Harrison. Good luck with the case."

The fat bastard ignores me and walks back to his car. The joke's on him because I've already solved the case. Man, is he going to be pissed when Violetta and I turn in Tony the shoe-selling Cinderella Killer.

I retrieve my purse from the black and white cruiser that responded to the Paramedic's call. One of the beat cops pulls out my book from the glove box.

"Would you mind?"

"Not a bit. Just don't let the fat bastard know you're a fan."

"He's not so bad. He and the rest of the old guard are threatened by you. Secretly, they're all envious."

I sign her book and hop into my Jeep, feeling like I can conquer the world. As I crank the ignition I check under the passenger seat. The other box of bullets are still there, wedged into the springs. Well done, Oakland PD. I'll reload as I fill up, and I'm not getting on the freeway.

Not until I find Violetta.

SEVENTEEN

TWO EMPTY BEER bottles mark the passage of time. I've just finished regaling Tony with the story of how I discovered my shoesex power.

"Anyway, that's the short version. I actually wrote every little detail down in chronological order. Ellen and I put it in a safe place cause it tells the real story of how the DK died. Maybe one day I'll let you read it."

"I had no idea things had been so rough for you. I always assumed you had it easy."

"Yeah, well, don't you judge anybody until you've fucked a mile in their shoes."

"Ha ha."

"When you found out about the power did it fuck you up?"

"Not really. I was older than you, and I'm a guy."

"What the hell is that supposed to mean?"

"I was a thirteen-year-old boy. Anything that gave me a hard-on was cool."

"Everything gives a thirteen-year-old boy a boner."

"Exactly. I didn't really understand it, I just enjoyed it. It was a way to have a wet dream on demand. Another beer?"

"Sure. How did you find out you had the power?"

Tony stands from the chair at his rickety kitchen table and retrieves two more Anchor Steams from the fridge. His hair's still wet from the shower. His fresh white Depeche Mode tee shirt shows little wet spots where he didn't dry himself too well. Or I'm making him sweat, the idea of which turns me on. His black jeans are tight, very tight. Even barefoot his legs look skinny and long, and he's making my clit throb. He could fart and I'd swoon. I feel like the female equivalent of a thirteen-year-old boy.

We clink bottles and gulp down a couple of mouthfuls. True confessions is thirsty business. I switch positions, conscious that I'm sticking to the vinyl chair through the extra large Morrissey tee shirt Tony loaned me. I'm sure it doesn't help my state that the only thing I'm wearing is the tee shirt. Okay, on me it's a mid-length dress, but I'm naked underneath, and the entire scene of us exchanging shoesex war stories is just too damn titillating. I take another swig of beer, stifle a burp and Tony continues telling his tale.

"Being shuffled from foster homes meant I was always given hand-me-downs. I was at—don't laugh—the Jerkowitzs'—"

"No fucking way."

"I kid you not. They had two children—Amy, she was seventeen and Eric, he was fourteen."

"Amy was boning Eric?"

"No. You're hung up on incest aren't you?"

"Nothing wrong with incest."

I smile. It's infectious. Tony grins from ear to guilty ear. We clink bottles.

"To incest."

"To incest."

"Well, I guess it's only half incest."

"Does that mean if I get pregnant the baby will be only half retarded?"

"Oh shit."

"Don't worry. I may be Catholic, but I take precautions."

I don't, but I don't want to worry Tony. I've been fucking a woman for the last year so I haven't had to worry about birth control, but if one of Tony's sperm gets through I'll have an abortion. He looks relieved, so I continue.

"I was just making a stupid comment. The longer you're around me you'll find I do such things and learn to ignore me."

"That I could never do."

"We'll see. Get on with your story. I'm dying to hear what Eric and Amy did if they weren't boning each other."

"He was spying on her."

"That's good. Voyeurism is good."

"There was a crawl space under the house. The Jerkowitzs' was one of those old places with hardwood floors with lots of cracks for spying on cracks."

"That's bad. Not the spying—your attempt at humor. Leave the wise cracks to me."

I flash open my legs and give Tony a view of my vertical smile. He picks up two of the empty beer bottles and holds them like binoculars aimed at my pussy. I snap my legs shut and hold my head high in feigned modesty.

"Pervert. Continue."

Tony puts the beer binoculars down, and I resume my normal slouch.

"Eric didn't always have the best view, but his imagination made up for what he couldn't see. The tiniest fleeting glimpse of a boob or an upper thigh or a bush was enough to send him off, and if she sat on the bed at just the right angle, Eric got a full beaver shot. Well, at that age, you can imagine."

"Squirt city."

"You got it. There must have been a swamp of spunk under the house. Eric's sneakers were full of peeping tom sex. He once saw Amy and a girlfriend comparing body parts as they dressed to go out. He—I—came three times in a few minutes."

"So how were you supposed to wear Eric's shoes if putting them on made you come? Hi, I'm Tony the tripod, pleased to meet you. That's not my hand you're shaking, by the way."

"Now it's you who're stretching for a laugh."

"So what did you do, Mr. Critic?"

"It was simple. I made up a story that the sneakers gave me blisters."

"Oh that's rich. You didn't tell the Jerkoffs where they gave you blisters."

"Of course not, but I got a cool new pair out of it, and I retrieved Eric's sneakers out of the trash."

"And you experimented and learned."

"Yeah. I didn't really appreciate my power until I ended up at Saint Aldopho's and was around a bunch of repressed nuns who spent a lot of time doing nasty things in their shoes. For a laugh I volunteered to be on shoe polishing duty. Man, the things I saw. Nuns are the biggest whores, and Sister Teresa was the biggest ho of the lot. She was hot all the time. I was being extra nice to her, putting her shoes away in her closet, and I found the ballet shoes. She caught me admiring her footwear and things grew from there. We were eventually discovered, and the Mother Superior kicked me up to the priests at Saint Bart's and sent Sister Teresa off to some mission in Central America caring for old crones. Before they sent her away I broke into her room and stole the ballet shoes. I figured she wouldn't complain."

"The church must have been scared shitless you'd sell your story to the tabloids."

"They were bricking it. That's where I got the money to

open my shoe store. The church gave me twenty grand to keep my mouth shut."

"Wow. Not bad."

"Yeah, well, I figured somehow it was payback for losing my mom. She'd been taken from me, and I'd been given this amazing power in return. And once I knew how to use it there was no stopping me. I checked out the priests' shoes and found one dude in a dog collar who was doggy-styling some of the younger kids. I scored another ten grand for that tidbit. The priests were really happy to see the back of me. I think they figured I was an angel of God sent to correct their evil ways."

"It's kind of weird. I ended up believing I was given the power to kill serial killers. You blackmailed perverts."

"Hey, you play the hand—"

"Foot."

"—the foot that's dealt you. You got all the insurance money. I had to fend for myself. You'd have done the same if you didn't have any cash and all that power."

"Look, Tony, it's cool. I didn't mean anything by it. I just thought it was interesting that in different ways we both used our power to bring retribution to people, and speaking of payback, I'll give you half of the insurance money."

"You don't have to do that."

"But I do. I'm sure our philandering dad would have wanted it if he'd known about you."

"Okay, but you don't have to."

"I insist."

"Since you insist, how much is half?"

"About a hundred grand, give or take a few tens. I don't exactly remember. I put what I had left towards getting the beach house with Ellen."

"How then are you going to give me half?"

"Ellen and I have a deal. We split everything from the book. It's a joint effort. Trust me, we have enough to give you half of Mom and Dad's insurance."

"What if I want half the book money in exchange for keeping quiet?"

I slam my beer down, sending a gob of it splattering on the floor.

"If you can still use blackmail, I can still kill a serial killer."

"Hey, cool it. I was only joking."

"Yeah, well, I guess we've got a long way to go before we understand each other's little ways. Sorry."

"No problem."

"So."

"So."

"What now?"

"Another beer?"

"Okay."

This time I do the honors. We clink bottles, take big swigs and belch up a storm, laughing at our burpy duet. We're Cutreros all right. Dad would be so proud. The Anchor Steam and the laughter calms me. I can tell Tony is anxious to put the nastiness behind us too.

"Want to see those pictures of Mom and me?"

"Yeah, sure. I'd love that."

He retrieves an envelope from a bedside table. He thumbs through it and pulls out a few snaps and hands them to me. He's right. Nikki was hot. And Tony was a cute kid. I'd only ever seen Nikki's reflection in our shop window when I was in her shoes. She and Tony look so happy. From what I know of Nikki's appearance the photograph must have been taken just before she was killed. She's wearing the Celtic cross. He is too. Tony notices it immediately. He pulls his out of his shirt and holds it up.

"Mom got these for us just before she died. They have pictures in them."

He presses a clasp and his has a little picture of Nikki. I remember the picture in the cross I took back from the

DK. All that time ago I was looking at a picture of my brother and I didn't know.

"Hers had a picture of me in it."

"I know."

"How did you know Mom had one too and that it had a picture of me in it?"

"I have it. Randy Warren took it from her. When I killed him I took back some of the things I knew he'd taken from people. I'll give it to you."

"How did you know the cross was Mom's?"

I think of saying it was a lucky guess, but I owe him the truth. He has so little of hers.

"You know those glittery platforms that I showed you earlier?"

"That were left in your store?" He pauses, and I realize I should have lied. "No way," he says, his eyes wide as the bottom of the beer bottle hovering halfway between his lips and his hand.

"Yeah. They were Nikki's."

Before I finish speaking he's out of his chair and to my bag. He grabs the shoes and I'm after him. I snatch at his hand, but he pushes me away and runs into the bathroom. He slams the door and locks it.

"Tony, you don't want to do that. It's not pleasant."

"I never knew my real mom. Those pictures, my book, this cross and her letter are my only memories. I wanted so bad a pair of her shoes, but all her belongings, except for her papers, were trashed by the Social Services Nazis."

"You don't understand."

"No, you don't understand. It doesn't matter how bad it is. At least I get to see her, be with her again."

I do understand. How many times have I slipped on Mom's sparkly high heels just so I can see Mom and Dad again, even though I always run into the Dildo Killer trying to pick up on Mom? It never stops me. I do understand.

"Tony, listen to me. I do understand. Just put them on

sitting down. Don't do it standing up or you'll hurt your ankle. I'll be right here."

There's no reply.

I sit on the floor and wait.

And think.

What if experiencing our father's abuse of his mother drives Tony way over the edge? If reading about Nikki's death made him kill three johns in ceremonial fashion, what the fuck is being in Nikki's platforms going to do? Could I stop him from a killing rampage? Yeah, I could. Would I is another matter.

Fuck, it occurs to me, am I here to kill Tony? Is this some kind of test of my serial killer resolve? Fate gives me a brother who's a killer and then sees if I have the balls to take him away from myself. How fucking biblical. It would be so easy to off him when he's under the shoesex influence.

My knife's in my inside jacket pocket.

That bathroom door wouldn't survive a good kick.

I could kill Tony and zoom out of here, and one more nasty crime wave would be over. It would be poetic justice. He was going to set up Ellen and me. I could return the favor with little effort. There's probably enough evidence in his apartment to link him to the crimes. I could make it look like suicide. Slit his wrists, and he'd bleed to death while wearing Nikki's shoes. The cops would find him in hooker platforms and figure one more cross-dresser couldn't take being a woman trapped in a man's body. Then they'd find the size four Mini-Peeps, and the Oakland Police would take credit for case closed.

I wish Ellen was here. She'd know what to do. She's probably worried sick about me. Since she was at the Paradise she must have got my message. She knows about Tony and has no doubt figured out he's the killer. If she thinks he's got me then she's not going to take any prisoners getting to me. No wonder she tried to shoot him. I'd better

call the beach house and leave her a message to let he
know I'm okay.

I go to use the phone, and just before I pick it up I hea
Ellen's voice telling me to be smart.

Think.

If you want to make a clean getaway that can't be trace
you don't want to call our number. It's routine murder
suicide investigation procedure to check phone records t
see who was called. We don't want a call from Tony to ou
house linking us to his death. And another thing. You'd ge
your prints all over the phone, and you'd forget to wip
them off. The cops would know someone else had bee
there, so if you're going to off him, Violetta, start actin,
smart. You've got to clean up any evidence linking you t
Tony's apartment.

Okay.

I put on my new rubber boots. It takes a long while t
lace them up. I need the time to think, and maybe if I dela
long enough Tony will come out of the shoefuck and th
opportunity to do my duty will have passed.

Okay.

I'd better take the puke-stained sheets, and make sur
there's no stray Violetta vomit lurking around. Beer bottle:
I'd better take the empties. I wonder if there's any of m
pubes in the bathtub?

Okay.

Boots are on. With air-cushioned platform soles I shoul
be able to kung fu through the door in no time. My sho
leather trimming knife is ready and willing to take a secon
killer on an all expense paid one way trip to Hell.

Think.

If I want to make it look like Tony killed himself the
the knife needs to be left at the scene. No way am I goin
to give up my trusty blade, so I put it back in my pocket.

Okay.

I search through the kitchen and fuck me, Tony isn't we

equipped in that department. There's a butter knife and a fork, but nothing for carving or slitting wrists. What did he use for slicing up his victims?

Think.

He'd use the knife he killed people with to kill himself. That's a no-brainer, but where's the knife? It must be in his shoulder bag. I look all over the apartment, and it isn't here. He had it with him when he went out. It must be in my car. He said he drove the Bug here after Ellen bit him.

Okay.

I'm not going out there to find my car. Someone might see me. I might get locked out of the building. I bet he has a razor in the bathroom. I'll either slit his wrists or electrocute him.

Okay.

I'm going in. After three. One. Two. Three.

The rotten jamb splits and the door flies open. Tony's lying there on the floor, quivering, twitching. He's helpless, and I know I can't kill him. I realize I never really thought I could. I was only going through the motions just to give me a big fat excuse to break down the door. I want to save him, not kill him.

If this is a test then I fail. Give me an F with a big fucking F, and I'll fuck fate, my power and its responsibilities. I'm running this show. The hell with destiny. Tony's my brother and that's all that matters.

I squeeze between Tony and the toilet, and I hold him tight and rock him and prevent his body movements from crashing into something and hurting him. I could pull the shoes off him and stop the shoefuck, but I wouldn't want that, and being related to me, he won't either.

We both know the feet can't be denied.

Tony's ankle bends over, and I know that Dad's just come in his ass. After a few moments Tony's head whips, and I know he just felt Dad's backhand across his face.

– 271 –

Blood trickles from his lip. He comes too and sees me holding him. Our eyes meet.

"I'm sorry," I say.

Tony bursts into tears. I hold his head against my chest, and I try to rock away the pain and the tears the way Marsha did for me after I'd worn those glittery platforms for the first time.

"So THIS IS what we're going to do."

Tony pours two tumblers of Jack Daniels. He turns as I speak.

"Yeah?"

"I've thought a lot about this. You can't stay here. Can that chick, your assistant—"

"Nancy."

"Nancy. Can she run your store for awhile?"

"I guess so. Sure. She has keys."

"Good. You're coming with me to the beach house. We're going to sit down with Ellen and figure out what to do to get you out of this mess."

"But she tried to kill me."

"And she arrested me, but that was before she knew she loved me. Once she knows you're my brother all will be forgiven. Don't worry. She might be pissed at first, but Ellen's cool. We're in love. She'll do anything for me. She saved me from the cops once. I'm sure she'll do the same for you, and then we can figure out where we go from there."

"You think so?"

"I know so. The three of us will make an awesome team. Let's get packing."

We clink tumblers and down the whiskey in one gulp.

"Wow, that burns," I say through a cough.

"You're a lightweight, Violetta Valery Cutrero."

And this time he says my full name with fondness, and I feel so fucking good. In a whirlwind we gather up as much crap as we can that would link Tony to the murders. I put my leather jacket over the tee shirt dress. I stash Nikki's platforms and the ballet shoes in my bag with Mom's shoes. As we're leaving we take one more look around. I feel bad, but I've got to ask it.

"Tony, like, you don't have any body parts in the freezer do you?"

"No way. What do you take me for, a sicko? Come on."

"Well, serial killers sometimes keep souvenirs. What did you do with the toes and bits of feet you chopped off?"

"God, it was so gross. I almost puked. I tossed them into the dumpster behind Ming's Chinese. I figured no one would notice among all the bits of chicken and duck and dog."

This anecdote strikes me as so funny. Tony is no serial killer. I burst out laughing, as much from relief as the humorous nature of his story. I made the right decision not to kill him. I passed the test.

"Come on, let's get out of here," Tony says.

He puts his arm around me and closes the door to his apartment. I'm still laughing as we walk down the metal fire-escape stairs to my car. They're slick with moisture from the Bay, and I slip. Tony catches me, stopping me from tumbling down the stairs, but I twist my ankle.

"Ouch, fucking ouch."

"Are you okay?"

"Yeah. The rubber boots probably saved me from breaking my ankle, but I think it's sprained."

He helps me down the stairs, and I rest against the Bug while he picks up all the crap we spilled when I fell. I can't put much weight on my foot.

"Would you mind driving? My ankle hurts."

"No problem."

"You sure? You had a rough time in your Mom's shoes. And there's Ellen's bite. You're limping yourself."

"Trust me. No problem. I'm a guy. The Jack Daniels fortified me. I'll be fine."

"Tony, just a friendly hint. Cut the 'I'm a guy' crap around Ellen. At least until she gets to know you."

"Okay."

"And let's stop at a pay phone. I want to let her know where we're going so she knows not to hang around here."

"Anything else?"

"Yeah."

"What?"

"Home, Anthony," I say in the haughtiest English accent I can muster.

He starts the Bug, and I put on BAD II, and we bop our way onto Broadway and head towards the freeway and home.

Once we find a phone.

EIGHTEEN

PARANOID HARRISON ORDERS the black and white to escort me to a gas station on Broadway and see me out of town. I refrain from making a snide comment about Oakland PD being too busy to investigate my mugging but not too busy to chase me out of town. Something about discretion and valor and living to fight another day comes to mind, so I comply, and to tell the truth, I don't have the energy to be witty. The paramedic was right. As the adrenaline goes away, the pain grows. My head throbs.

I go by way of the alley where Violetta's Bug was parked. Her car's not there.

Maybe I chose the wrong street. With my police shadow I don't have any latitude for wandering, so I pause before turning onto Broadway, ostensibly being a good driver and looking both ways before pulling into the intersection. Yes, it's the right location because I'm just a few blocks up from Tony's shoe store in exactly the same place as I circled earlier. I might be a little hazy from the bumps on the head but I'm sure of the street. Maybe Violetta escaped. I don't want to consider the alternatives. I feel woozy enough without nasty thoughts churning my guts.

I make a left turn onto Broadway and head north. I turn into a Chevron station and say to the cops as they pull alongside me, "Fill her up." They laugh and I continue, "You mean this isn't the full service get out of town isle?" I amaze myself with my ability to make stupid chat while my heart's racing, my stomach's lurching and my mind's contemplating endings that even Jack the Ripper wouldn't dare do.

The black and white's radio crackles and the cops say they've got to respond to another call, so please don't get them in trouble with Harrison. The freeway on-ramp is just half a mile further on Broadway. Do everybody a favor and go home. I assure them that I'll get on the freeway, and they take off with a wave and another thanks for the autograph.

I give the clerk behind the bulletproof glass my credit card and start pumping the gas. Once it's flowing I leave the pump to do its business, and I sit in the Jeep. Making sure no one is close enough to see in, I hold my gun below my knees and load it. Then I stash it in my purse along with enough extra bullets to end a small war. Walking back to the clerk to sign my bill I feel considerably safer now that I'm accompanied by a fully loaded Mr. Smith and Mr. Wesson.

I visit the bathroom, and pee standing up to avoid sitting in urine puddles. I realize how every muscle in my body aches. The adrenaline has reached empty and the pain's rushed in to fill the vacuum. I could do with the Jacuzzi at the beach house in a bad way. Hot bubbles, cool, salty fog, warm, soft Violetta, the two of us sipping wine, naked, kissing each other. It would be heavenly.

Soon, I tell myself. Soon.

It's something to look forward to, but first, now that my

immediate needs are taken care of, I must plan. Yet as soon as I start to deliberate what to do next my head pounds like it's the woofer or the tweeter or whatever it is that makes that booming noise in Violetta's stereo. Maybe my head's been throbbing all along, and I'm only just noticing. Or it grew worse. It's blinding. I close my eyes and breath deeply, trying to stop my body from shaking. It's a bitch of a dull pounding centered where Tony's boot made contact and it spreads out from there to meet up with the other dull throb where my head kissed the wall and the pavement. I'll take some painkillers, but there's no way I'll drink water out of that sink, so I make my way back to the clerk and buy a bottled water.

Sitting in my Jeep I swallow three of the pills and wipe the sweat from my brow. The cold water makes me feel better, so I drink the whole bottle. The shakes stop and at least now I can think without setting off a marching army in my head. I figure I'd better lie low until Harrison cools down, and I feel better. The Paradise isn't that far from here. I'll get on the freeway so I don't get the beat cops in trouble, and then I'll loop back through Berkeley and spend the night in that flea pit. I'm in no condition to drive the ninety minutes to Stinson, most of it on poorly lit, very windy roads.

At least that's my excuse if I get caught.

Maybe Violetta will be at the Paradise waiting for me. That would be so very perfect. She can give me a massage. Massage—message. I'd better leave her a message on our machine in case she checks in. Maybe she's already left a message for me telling me she's okay. I could retrieve it now that I know how. There's a phone by the side of the gas station, so I swing the Jeep next to the booth and make the call.

The machine picks up after two rings which means there's a message. That much about the damn machine I know, but it confuses me, and I don't remember the blasted sequence to retrieve messages so it beeps at me, and before I know it it's recording me, and I'm fumbling in my purse for instructions. I feel so inept. It must be the bumps on my head. I'm just not thinking too clearly.

"Oh shit, hi, Violetta, it's me. This machine will drive me crazy. I'm still in Oakland. I'm okay. A bit of a head-ache, but I'm going to the Paradise, so if you get this, meet me there. It's about—let's see—oh God, is it that late? It's about two a.m. There's another message on the machine, so I'm going to call back and get it. It has to be from you. I love you. I hope you're okay. I almost had Tony, so I hope you got away. I love you. I need you. Bye."

I hang up and fumble through my purse for the answering machine operating instructions, and I find them right at the top next to my gun. Damn that goddamn headache.

To retrieve messages remotely dial the number and when the beep sounds press the # key followed by the number nine key.

Now why couldn't I remember that. I dial our number again and on the beep I do as instructed and wait to hear the message.

The tape rewinds. It takes forever. Reading those damn fine print instructions in this light was a killer on my eyes. Oh God my head hurts. I massage my forehead and as my hand pulls away from my eyes I see a pink car sputtering along Broadway. I snap my head from the phone and confirm I wasn't hallucinating.

It's Violetta's Bug.

She's in the passenger seat. I can't see who's driving, but I'll bet it's Tony.

I drop the phone, and as I'm jumping into my Jeep I hear the beep at the beginning of the message, but I don't have time to go back and listen now. Violetta's life depends on me.

I screech out of the gas station, steering with one hand

while I remove my gun from my purse with the other.

Christ, my head hurts, but at least this action should pump the numbing adrenaline through my veins again.

The pain will stop soon.

NINETEEN

WHILE TONY FILLS the Bug with gas at a Shell station near Jack London Square, I call the beach house and leave Ellen a message saying that Tony and I are headed to Stinson and not to worry. Everything is way cool, and I have the most excellent news. I don't want to tell her I have a brother in a phone message. It's going to be a shock to her. She needs to hear it from me personally. There are no other messages on the machine, which kind of worries me. I'd have thought she'd have called to let me know she was okay, so now I'm not just kind of worried. I am mega-worried.

I hope she wasn't hurt in that fall. Tony will feel really bad if he's hurt her.

Or maybe she's headed back to Stinson?

Or maybe she's gone back to the Paradise?

That would be the most logical thing to do, and Ellen is nothing if not logical. It's all those years of being a cop.

"Everything okay?" Tony says as I hobble back to the Bug.

"Not really."

He walks around to my side of the car and throws his arms around me, and I tell him how worried I am. He says it's no problem to swing by the Paradise to see if Ellen is there, as long as I stand in front of him if she is. He doesn't want to be shot by a pissed-off Ellen before I have time to explain that we're all now good friends and relatives.

"You're scared of her, aren't you?"

"She's the kind of woman who shoots first and asks questions later. I know."

"You're scared of her."

"So what if I am?"

I kiss his cheek.

"It's so cute that you can admit it. Ellen's going to love you, don't worry."

As we pull out of the gas station I remember a question I've been meaning to ask all night.

"When did you first know I had the power?"

"When you told me your name I suspected as much because when I found out that my father was like this master shoe repairer I figured that was why I'd been given the power. Since you were his daughter I guessed you had it too."

"But he didn't have the power. I'd have known. The only shoesex he enjoyed was the direct kind."

"I didn't know that. As far as I knew he'd passed on the torch to you, but now that you say he didn't know about the power maybe shoesex is like some ancient Italian curse. Maybe it's because I grew up around nuns and priests that I think like this, but maybe this fantastic power is passed through generations of shoe repairers to their kids, but they don't have it because it would be too weird to have a family of fuckshoe addicts. They're like carriers. You know, how parents can pass on genetic defects that are dormant in them."

"Charming. I've always wanted to be thought of as a mutant disease."

"It could be true. We'll never know, because he's dead, but I knew for sure you had the power when we were walking back from dinner along Broadway, and I suggested you put on the shoes in your bag, and you gave me that lame-ass excuse about not wanting to damage them. It was as transparent as my tennis shoe blister story."

"And you kept quiet through all that trying on of shoes. You must have been going crazy."

"I was. I thought for sure you were going to guess what I was up to."

"I didn't suspect a thing."

"Well, it all turned out for the best. I had to get all that bottled-up nastiness out of me."

"Hey, no problem. Feel free to use me as a punching bag anytime you got to vent off some angst."

"I'm sorry."

"I mean it. I'll do the same to you, and we'll all get along just fine."

"Okay. It's a deal."

"You know, Tony, I've been thinking. If what you say is true about Dad, maybe we should do some research. We could still find answers. He had relatives on the East Coast. Maybe you, me and Ellen should go to New York and talk to old Cutreros. Or better, let's go to Italy and do like family tree research. I bet we'll find some dusty legends of kids with weird powers in their feet."

"That'd be so cool."

"Wouldn't it? It would help you get to know Tommy Cutrero beyond what you saw in your mom's shoes. When we get to the beach and things have settled down I'll let you put on Mom's sparkly shoes, and you'll see a different side of Dad. He wasn't all that bad."

We don't say much else as we putter up Broadway. I'm thinking of Dad, and I'm sure Tony is too. Despite all the nasty things Tommy Cutrero did, it's kind of wonderful that because of him, Tony and me are together, and now nothing's going to tear us apart. Ellen, me and Tony. We're going to be one big happy family. We can go to Italy and go underground until all this Cinderella shit blows over. They'll never be able to connect Tony to the killings. Ellen will be so proud of the way we went through his apartment making sure there was nothing to link him to the murders—

Oh fuck.

The knife. Where's the killing knife? The bag Tony took with him when he left the apartment to go after Ellen is in the back seat, so I twist around and unzip it, and there's stilettos, wigs, clothes, but no fucking knife.

"What are you doing?"

"The knife! Where's the fucking knife?"

"What knife?"

"Don't be stupid. You fucking well know what knife. It's not hidden in the apartment is it? If it is we'd better go back and get it."

"Oh that knife. It's not at the apartment. I forgot to tell you. When I was busy escaping Ellen I hid it in case I got pulled over because there were cops all over the place."

"Where did you hide it?"

He slides his hand under the driver's seat and in this super fast move pulls a long stiletto blade out. He holds it aloft as though he's going to knife me. He pulls a hideous face and yells, "Here's Tony" as he makes stabbing motions.

Now I know what the Dildo Killer felt like when I pulled back the shower curtain and came at him like a crazed Benihana chef. I scream and back away into the passenger door. I reach for my knife in my inside jacket pocket, but before I can unleash it Tony bursts our laughing.

"Got you. You should have seen the look on your face."

"You bastard." I slug his shoulder.

"I guess I deserved that. Don't worry, you'll soon get used to my warped humor. Here, you'd better put this away."

He leans over to hand the knife to me, and part of me wonders as the six-inch blade nears my body, will I ever be able to trust my schizo half brother, the Cinderella Killer?

TWENTY

I SWERVE THROUGH traffic to catch up to Violetta's Bug. Luckily, her car is no speed demon, and I'm up to the driver's side rear bumper in the space of half a block.

And not a moment too soon.

The sonofabitch has a knife poised to strike at Violetta and she's backing away. She looks like she's screaming.

My cop instinct takes over.

There's no time to think. I angle my wheels at the Bug and accelerate.

Don't ram the car. The impact could plunge the knife into Violetta. So I brake, straighten out and accelerate until I'm level with the driver.

He's lowered the knife, so I hesitate. She's fighting him off. That's my Violetta.

Jesus, my head hurts.

He lunges towards her, and I know I shouldn't have waited. I'm getting soft.

I lean over, aim the gun with my bruised and shaking hand and fire off several rounds at damn near point-blank range.

TWENTY-ONE

MY WORLD EXPLODES in a blur of flying glass and blood. One minute Tony's laughing, and I'm trying to do the same, and the next it's like the Bug blew up.

The knife is on the floor at my feet.

There's blood all over me. I think I've been stabbed, but as I look up from my stomach I see Tony, or what's left of Tony, slumped over the wheel.

I'm alive. He's not. He can't be. Half of his face is missing. I can't look. I stare ahead, and the view's not much better. The Bug is accelerating under Tony's dead left foot towards a lamppost. I reach over to the steering wheel, and Tony's bloody stump of a head slips from the wheel onto my hand, his lifeless eyes staring at me, accusing me. Through the gash in his face where his jaw should be I swear I hear his voice screaming at me that the fucking Cutreros brought him nothing but bad luck.

I wrench my hand free, and as I do so I tear away his Celtic cross, and I clutch it tight. I panic, trying to get as far away from that horror as I can. I hold the cross up as though Tony's a vampire and I can ward him off. I push back with my legs against the seat, making myself part of the passenger door upholstery, the pain in my ankle a mild irritant compared to the pain and fear in my heart.

In the seconds before the collision I try to make sense of what's happened.

Some bastard shot Tony, that's what.

Why?

Who?

The Bug misses the lamppost, but careens into a fire hydrant, and I'm thrown around by the impact. The seat belt holds me tight, but I wish it hadn't because Tony's head is flopping around and bits of it splatter on me, and all I can think of is getting the fuck out of here before his head drops in my lap. Water from the hydrant splashes down over the car and in through the smashed windshield. It's like a sudden storm's swallowing me, and I let go of whatever was holding me together and instantly I'm crying up as much of a storm as the fire hydrant's gushing water.

I've got to get out of here. I press the door latch down and the door sticks, and then it's wrenched open and someone's pulling me out onto the sidewalk, and I'm holding so tightly onto Tony's cross and my bag of special shoes because right now, they're the only comfort I know.

"Violetta, are you hurt?"

It's Ellen. Ellen, my dear sweet, Ellen. She's okay. She's fine, and she's holding me and we're being drenched in the fountaining water, and it's dead romantic. She's come to save me. I knew she would.

"Ellen. I'm okay. Tony—"

And she pulls me tighter to her, and says, "Don't worry, it's over. He's dead. he can't hurt you."

And I see the gun in her hand.

The gun in her hand.

The gun.

Her hand.

TWENTY-TWO

"HE WAS GOING to stab you."

Violetta sits up, and as she does so she pushes me back. She stares at me with the kind of look I've only ever seen in the eyes of a victim's family when they watch the murderer die. Her eyes are so cold. The eyes. The eyes are so familiar. That's the second time tonight I've seen that look.

"He was my brother. You killed my brother."

The eyes. In the alleyway. Tony. . . .

"Do you understand what you've done? You've killed my brother."

This is too surreal. It's like I've been dropped in a Jimmy Cagney movie—You dirty rat, you killed my brother. My head spins with pain. I can't help it. I laugh. Violetta slaps me and screams.

"He was my brother. It's not funny."

"He was what? This isn't making any sense."

"My brother. Nikki was his mom. My dad got her pregnant."

She holds up a bloody Celtic cross and thrusts it into my face.

"He had a cross just like Nikki's. Her picture's inside. Look."

She pops open the cross. It's Nikki.

"The little boy in the cross I took from the DK was Tony. My brother. We were coming to you for help."

"But he was the Cinderella Killer."

"Yeah. And I'm the Dildo Killer killer, but you love me. He wasn't going to hurt me. It was our goddamn book that pushed him over the edge. When he read how Nikki died he snapped. He wasn't a hardened serial killer. He hated killing."

"But the knife."

"He was joking with me."

"What can I say to you? I only had a split second to react. To me it looked liked—oh, Violetta, I'm sorry."

"Sorry. Sorry fucking sorry. Is that all you can say?"

Now she's standing, but she stumbles. I try to steady her, and she tears her arm away from me.

"Don't touch me."

The Bug's hood has popped open by the impact. Violetta reaches inside and pulls out a pair of white patent leather boots.

"Here."

She thrusts them at me.

"Take them. They're a farewell present."

I don't know what to do. I feel so cold. She throws the boots at my feet.

"They're a present from Tony's store from me. Go-go boots. Wear them and think of me and Tony and walk away from me. I never want to see you again."

She pushes past me and limps out through the curtain of water and into the Oakland night. I follow, holding the boots and my gun and I scream after her, "Violetta."

She turns.

"What are you going to do, shoot me?"

"I was trying to protect you. That's all I ever wanted to do."

"I don't need your kind of protection. I have my power."

"You're upset. I know. I can't say anything to make you feel better, but don't leave me. I love you. We can work this out."

"I love you too, Ellen, but I'll never forgive you. I was so happy to have found a small portion of my family again, and you took that from me, and you know what, Tony knew you would. He was so scared of you, and I told him to trust you."

"I didn't know."

"Fuck, Ellen, how could you have known? How could you have known that Tony and I spent the whole night fucking our brains out, and I thought I could love you and him, and we'd all be happy together, one big extended fucking family. That was my mistake, thinking I could love. The feet cannot be denied."

She points at the go-go boots.

"I'm gone."

She limps away, and I fall to my knees. All I hear is the pounding in my head and the splattering of the water on the sidewalk, and then I realize it's my tears that are making the noise, and they're mixing with the water and are being washed away along with everything I held dear.

"Violetta," I cry into the night, but she's gone.

Police sirens cut the air.

I look at the go-go boots.

She's gone.

I look at my gun.

She's gone.

I cradle the patent leather boots to my face. They feel cool against my pounding head, and the smell is calming. I know what Violetta means about the smell of shoe leather.

I put the gun to my head.

Without Violetta there's no point.

I see my reflection in the wet go-go boots.

The sirens are nearer. They're screaming Violetta's name.

Go-go—

Forthcoming

Captive IV: The Eyes Behind the Mask
by Anonymous

The Captives of Cheluna feel a dread fascination for the boy whose duty it is to chastise. This narrative follows a masked apprentice who obeys his master's orders without pity or restraint. Emma Smith's birching would cause a reform school scandal. Secret additions to the frenzy of nineteen-year-old Karen and Noreen mingle the boy's fierce passion with lascivious punishment. Mature young women like Jenny Woodward pay dearly for defying their master, whose masked servant also prints the marks of slavery on Lesley Hollingsworth, following *Captive II*. The untrained and the self-assured alike learn to shiver, as they lie waiting, under the caress of the eyes behind the mask.

Available now

Captive V: The Soundproof Dream
by Richard Manton

Beauty lies in bondage everywhere in the tropical island of Cheluna. Joanne, a 19-year old rebel, is sent to detention on Krater Island where obedience and discipline occupy the secret hours of night. Like the dark beauty Shirley Wood and blond shopgirl Maggie Turnbull, Jo is subjected to unending punishment. When her Krater Island training is complete, Jo's fate is Metron, the palace home of the strange Colonel Mantrique.

Available now

Images of Ironwood
by Don Winslow

Ironwood. The very name of that unique institution remains strongly evocative, even to this day. In this, the third volume of the famous Ironwood trilogy, the reader is once again invited to share in the Ironwood experience. *Images of Ironwood* presents selected scenes of unrelenting sensuality, of erotic longing, and occasionally, of those bizarre proclivities which touch the outer fringe of human sexuality.

In these pages we renew our acquaintance with James, the lusty entrepreneur who now directs the Ironwood enterprise; with his bevy of young female students being trained in the many ways of love; and with Cora Blasingdale, the cold remote mistress of discipline. The images presented here capture the essence of the Ironwood experience.

———

Available Now

Ironwood
by Don Winslow

The harsh reality of disinheritance and poverty vanish from the world of our young narrator, James, when he discovers he's in line for a choice position at an exclusive and very strict school for girls. Ironwood becomes for him a fantastic dream world where discipline knows few boundaries, and where his role as master affords him free reign with the willing, well-trained and submissive young beauties in his charge. As overseer of Ironwood, Cora Blasingdale is well-equipped to keep her charges in line. Under her guidance the saucy girls are put through their paces and tamed. And for James, it seems, life has just begun.

Order These Selected Blue Moon Titles

Souvenirs From a Boarding School $7.95	Shades of Singapore $7.95
The Captive $7.95	Images of Ironwood $7.95
Ironwood Revisited $7.95	What Love $7.95
Sundancer $7.95	Sabine $7.95
Julia $7.95	An English Education $7.95
The Captive II $7.95	The Encounter $7.95
Shadow Lane $7.95	Tutor's Bride $7.95
Belle Sauvage $7.95	A Brief Education $7.95
Shadow Lane III $7.95	Love Lessons $7.95
My Secret Life $9.95	Shogun's Agent $7.95
Our Scene $7.95	The Sign of the Scorpion $7.95
Chrysanthemum, Rose & the Samurai $7.95	Women of Gion $7.95
Captive V $7.95	Mariska I $7.95
Bombay Bound $7.95	Secret Talents $7.95
Sadopaideia $7.95	Beatrice $7.95
The New Story of O $7.95	S&M: The Last Taboo $8.95
Shadow Lane IV $7.95	"Frank" & I $7.95
Beauty in the Birch $7.95	Lament $7.95
Laura $7.95	The Boudoir $7.95
The Reckoning $7.95	The Bitch Witch $7.95
Ironwood Continued $7.95	Story of O $5.95
In a Mist $7.95	Romance of Lust $9.95
The Prussian Girls $7.95	Ironwood $7.95
Blue Velvet $7.95	Virtue's Rewards $5.95
Shadow Lane V $7.95	The Correct Sadist $7.95
Deep South $7.95	The New Olympia Reader $15.95

Visit our website at www.bluemoonbooks.com

ORDER FORM
Attach a separate sheet for additional titles.

Title   Quantity   Price

_____   _____   _____
_____   _____   _____
_____   _____   _____
_____   _____   _____

Shipping and Handling (see charges below)   _____
Sales tax (in CA and NY)   _____
Total   _____

Name _____

Address _____

City _____ State _____ Zip _____

Daytime telephone number _____

❏ Check   ❏ Money Order   (US dollars only. No COD orders accepted.)

Credit Card # _____ Exp. Date _____

❏ MC   ❏ VISA   ❏ AMEX

Signature _____
(if paying with a credit card you must sign this form.)

Shipping and Handling charges:*
Domestic: $4 for 1st book, $.75 each additional book. International: $5 for 1st book, $1 each additional book
*rates in effect at time of publication. Subject to Change.

Mail order to Publishers Group West, Attention: Order Dept., 1700 Fourth St., Berkeley, CA 94710,
or fax to (510) 528-3444.

PLEASE ALLOW 4-6 WEEKS FOR DELIVERY. ALL ORDERS SHIP VIA 4TH CLASS MAIL.

**Look for Blue Moon Books at your favorite local bookseller
or from your favorite online bookseller.**